THE LOST LEGENDS

Book of Monsters

AR Archgate Press

Published by Archgate Press, Dallas, TX
Cover and print design by R. T. Swindoll

ISBN # 978-1-953820-04-4

ACKNOWLEDGMENTS

This book only exists because incredible people agreed to work with me. Each and every story was a delight to read, and I'm grateful for my role in bringing them to my readers.

I am especially thankful for Renea McKenzie, who painstakingly scrubbed and edited each story until we could see our faces in them. And for Ryan Swindoll, for his design work, inside and out; you'll have to look long and hard for a more attractive anthology series than *The Lost Legends*.

I can't thank them enough. But I'll keep trying.

TABLE OF CONTENTS

Foreword

Author Information

FOREWORD

What is a monster, anyway? I'd hardly be the first person to point out that the word *Monster* shares some meaning with the Latin word for *Demonstrate* (the words even look similar, if you squint) which doesn't paint a very scary picture. But monsters are always demonstrating something to us, and even in the most simple of stories, those inhuman interlopers have something profound to say.

The original Godzilla film, for example, would surprise those of us who grew up with the later, sillier movies, because Godzilla's first appearance is a very dark and grim look at the world's fears over nuclear power. Frankenstein, before he was a green linebacker sporting neck bolts, begged us to explore the nature of the soul. Grey-skinned alien invaders ask us to reflect on our possible insignificance in the universe. This is big stuff.

So an egghead might ask you to carefully read the stories you're holding in your hand and ask yourself at the end of each, "What did this story *reveal?*"

But...please don't do that.

Children don't ask for monster stories around the campfire because they want to consider metaphysical implications of the wolfman. The teensters who once crowded drive-in movie theaters, squeezing tubs of pop-corn between their thighs, didn't park their cars in front of *The Creature from the Black Lagoon* so they could go home after and host an academic discussion.

You see, the word *Monster* also refers to something wondrous, something incredible and marvelous. The pages of this book are here to evoke a sense of discovery and awe, to remember what it was like the first time you saw Dracula rise from his coffin or King Kong tower over a frightened New York.

In the same way, I invite you to settle in and lose yourself in the second entry in *The Lost Legends* anthology series: *Book of Monsters!*

–Adam D. Jones

TYPE A
PERSONALITY

Adam D. Jones

"You'll have to do better than that," said Baron Dirk von Stirling, the world's last vampire. "I can barely feel a thing."

Helen tightened her grip on the wooden shaft and slammed the mallet down as hard as she could. The sharpened stick, so thick her fingers could barely grab it, made a gory mess, piercing through his rib cage.

The Baron's eyes flicked to the wound and then, apologetically, back to Helen. "Sorry." He shook his head. "Nothing."

"I'm calling it. The wooden stakes don't work." She pulled it out and closed her eyes at the unnatural sight of a large, bloodless wound; it chilled her to the bone just like it had the last nine times. She warily opened one eye and saw the wound had already healed.

Dirk thumped his unscathed chest and lamented, "Just like new."

Helen tossed the stake into a corner of the Stirling family crypt where it landed in a pile with nine other wooden stakes of varying diameters.

The Baron sat up in his coffin. "Maybe you should have gone through my sternum. You're always shoving that thing slightly to the side."

"Your heart's not in the exact center of your chest, Baron. It's slightly to the side."

"Really?" Dirk gazed down at his pale chest. "I once ripped a man's heart out and showed it to him before he died, but, you know, in the heat of battle you don't notice a little thing like which side of the chest it came from." The Baron buttoned his silk shirt. "Tasted good. Fresh heart is always better."

Helen flipped to a blank page on her notepad and wrote: *Stake through the heart—unconfirmed.*

She looked over her notes. They had painstakingly stabbed sharp wooden sticks into his chest all morning to no avail. "Time to try something else. Sunlight?"

"I suppose. The stake through the heart thing sounded more..." He clawed at the air. "...climactic!" Torchlight from the concrete sconces lit the ancient, noble features of his pale face. "Hmm. Maybe this way can work too. After living in the shadows for eight centuries, I see the sun in all its beauty...and then—" He snapped his fingers. "Nothing! A pile of ash! Yes, I like it. A *glorious* death!" He hooked a leg over his coffin and climbed out, heading for the doorway. "It's dramatic!"

I think you mean melo-*dramatic,* Helen mentally corrected.

"As you wish." Helen tucked the clipboard under her arm and prepared to follow the Baron up the stairs that led to his mansion, but the Baron had stopped at the first step.

He turned back and stared into the corner at the discarded wooden stakes. He frowned, and, after some thought, arranged them into a neat row. At first the order seemed haphazard, but Helen realized he had placed them alongside one another in order of growing diameter. He grunted something to himself and rearranged them, this time in order of length. Satisfied, he dusted his old hands and returned to the stairwell.

Helen made another note: *Habitual organizing—confirmed.*

That was among the more obscure pieces of vampire lore, not something she expected to confirm during this unbelievable experiment.

She followed the Baron up the stairs and out of his crypt, where she lost herself in the tall rooms. Wooden shafts vaulted high overhead until they were lost in shadow, and their overbearing presence reminded her of the immensity of her task: vampires were real, and the last one of his kind was ready to die.

It had only been a few weeks, but it felt like an eternity since the courier had arrived at her office door with a letter in hand, a letter written on honest-to-goodness vellum with an honest-to-goodness quill pen. The authentic vellum had made her heart stir—it was the real thing and older than some of her manuscripts—but the content was ludicrous. It had to be a joke. Helen was a renowned archivist of medieval manuscripts, and her friends at Kalamazoo were always looking for a new prank.

But…the vellum was *too* perfect. The ink, according to her analysis, had been scribbled with a feather quill, not a pen of any kind. It was remarkably difficult to write skillfully with a quill; no one could do it very well without practice. And no historian she knew would waste genuine vellum on a prank.

So Helen had followed the instructions in the letter; she drove to a quaint city in the countryside and found herself face-to-face with a very real, very depressed, vampire.

The Baron now stood at the double doors that led outside of his mansion, ready to embrace the daylight. He put a hand on each handle. It was mid-day, and the sun would blast him like a furnace. "This is it. Helen, I thank you for your help. I'm the last of my kind, if I haven't mentioned it, and my time is over. It's people like you who will make the world from now on. I'm only a relic, and it's time for me to be put on a shelf."

Helen gave a solemn bow and quietly watched.

With great showmanship, Baron Dirk von Stirling threw open the double doors and embraced the blazing light of noon.

But nothing happened.

The Baron's silhouette stood, unharmed, against the bright sunlight. "Well…this is embarrassing. I really thought that would work."

"Are you kidding me?" Helen wanted to punch him.

"You know, it's actually nice. Vampires get cold. Most people don't know that."

"You've *never* gone outside during the day in eight hundred years? Seriously?"

"Well, Helen, do *you* step in front of trains just to see if it actually kills you? None of the vampires I knew ever went outside until dark. Admittedly it seems sort of silly now..."

"It's just ridiculous. In the books, lots of vampires go outside during the day. Even Dracula!"

Dirk pursed his lips and looked away.

Helen couldn't believe it. "You've never read *Dracula*?"

"I keep waiting for a Latin translation."

"Nothing gets translated *into* Latin, you antique. It's a dead language!"

He turned on her. "Dead? It is immortal! Do they not say *semper fi* where you come from? *Rigor Mortis? Habeas Corpus?*"

"*Status quo.*"

"Exactly! Latin is forever, just like..." He seemed triumphant, but the Baron hanged his head. "I suppose the Latin language is only as immortal as I. Come along, Helen, let us find a glorious death for me and for the Latin language."

She gestured to the doorway. "*Carpe diem?*"

"For the last time." The Baron strolled out of his front door like he owned the town. In his mind, he probably did. She imagined there was a time in the deep past when his title was real, when the people who walked these streets were his subjects. He trod the cobblestones in his soft leather loafers and confidently straightened his buttoned vest as if he wasn't the only person not wearing shorts and sunglasses.

The Baron wasn't in danger of turning to dust, but his eyes didn't like the bright light. He turned from the sun as often as possible while they walked away from the mansion, choosing shaded paths. Helen wondered if the sunlight was just annoying to vampires. A weakness, but not a fatal one.

She noticed they were walking toward a crowd. "Where are we going?"

"There's a market this way." He sniffed the air. "I can sometimes smell their food. Maybe someone there will be helpful."

"Garlic!" Helen scribbled it down. "I bet we can find it raw."

He squinted at the sun. "We're lucky the market's outdoors. I can never go into stores unless they have one of those *OPEN* signs."

"That...is surprising." Helen turned the page and scratched more notes. The old myth about vampires needing permission to enter a building was among the last pieces of lore she had expected to confirm.

"It's probably the most infuriating part of being a vampire. Would you believe I can enter the shopping mall freely but have to ask the proprietors to invite me into each of the little shops inside?"

She finished writing and snapped the notebook shut. "So...garlic."

"Yes, garlic. Not glorious. But...there is some romance in dying amongst my people. The Baron nobody knew... hey, that's not bad. Write that down. The Baron nobody knew. I like it."

"Sure." Helen stepped first into the throng of people crowded around the rickety market stalls. Near the center of the market she spotted a man laying garlic bulbs along his table. "That looks fresh. So you've never had..."

The Baron was gone. Helen's heart skipped a beat. She'd led a vampire into a crowd of people and now he was on the loose! What was she thinking? She retraced her steps, pushing through customers until she glimpsed him...leaning over a wooden crate arranging tomatoes next to a baffled vegetable vendor.

"There." Dirk stood tall to admire his task. Sixteen

tomatoes sat in four flawless rows. "Perfection! Are there more?"

"Come on, Dirk." Helen pulled on his elbow, feeling the coarse, faded fibers of his old coat. "You'll spend the rest of your life here if you try to arrange every little thing."

"I once spent a year arranging the Sun King's paintings. Poor guy died before he could see my work. Shame."

Helen dragged him to the vendor and purchased a large head of garlic. It barely fit in her hand. "Are you sure about this?"

"Sure?" He snatched the garlic. "Of course. I've lived for too long. It's time."

She grabbed his wrist as the garlic head was an inch from his mouth. "But...look around. You could get to know these people. Wasn't there a time before you were like this? Before you were a...you know? Maybe this is your chance to reconnect with the world."

He frowned at her. "Oh, yes, the great Baron Dirk von Stirling, who once led a siege by riding his horse over a pile of corpses that led him over the city wall, will now peruse your wares while discussing the weather. Shall I also join them for arts and crafts time? Maybe I would look good in a pair of those yoga pants I keep hearing about? I think not."

With that, he took a large bite before Helen could warn him about the papery exterior. The pale garlic lobes splintered. He swallowed, waited, and then held up the remains of the garlic with sad admiration. "This is...not very good," he admitted.

The merchant spoke up. "I've never seen anyone do that. Your first time?"

"Yes!" The baron took another bite, then spoke with his mouth full. "Have you any more?"

"Sure!" The merchant began filling a canvas bag.

"Do you actually have any money?" Helen whispered.

"I'm the Baron, Helen. They give me whatever I want

in return for not killing them."

The shopkeeper froze.. "What did he say?"

"We'll pass on the garlic." Helen handed him a few dollars for what the Baron had already eaten.

"No problem." The grocer unloaded the canvas bag. "Anything else I can do for you two?"

Helen shrugged. "Know how to kill a vampire?"

"Everyone knows that." The grocer noticed Helen and the Baron were suddenly leaning in very close. He shrugged. "Holy water."

"Of course!" The Baron clapped. "Holy water! A wonderful idea."

"Yeah..." The grocer placed a CLOSED sign on the stall and backed away.

Helen nudged the Baron away from the market. She'd seen a cathedral on the way, the kind with buttressed walls and rising roofs—exactly where holy water would be found.

She led him by his cold wrist out of the market and along the cobblestone streets toward the rising church. They were nearly to the steps when she realized a potential problem.

"Dirk, can you even go inside of a church? There's probably a million crosses in there." She wondered if she would have to bring the holy water out to him.

"I'm certain I can enter a church. I've visited plenty of them before. Even took mass once."

Helen opened her notepad. "That's...odd. Every story says you can't even look at a crucifix."

"Why? Because I'm *evil?* Most of your politicians go to church."

"Well, then it's not likely the holy water is going to do much. Do you still want to try..."

She realized he'd stopped following her. The Baron stood a few paces behind where he watched a group of children playing with a soccer ball. His eyes centered on a young boy who had fallen. The child sat roughly on the cobblestones, rubbing a skinned knee.

The Baron stared.

"Something wrong?" asked Helen.

"That boy...will he need help?" He took a step toward the child.

"With what? He just fell. Kids do that; it's fine. You haven't been a kid in a very long time."

"True...true...but do you think he will need help?"

"Help?" Helen studied the Baron, who was completely lost in thought. "I don't understand..."

The boy got to his feet and chased after an errant soccer ball. Helen noticed his knees were red. One of them even bled.

"Don't you think he'll need help..." The Baron took another step toward the children. "...cleaning up all of that blood..."

Helen felt her chest seize. She pulled on his elbow, but the Baron didn't budge. It was like tugging on a building. "Baron. The holy water? Remember?"

"Holy water..." He slowly turned to her. "But...that could kill me."

She stepped back. "Isn't that the point?"

"I think you were right, Helen. I *should* be around my people again! The smells. The sounds. It's got me *feeling* things I haven't felt in ages!"

He leveled his gaze at her, narrowing his greedy eyes, and Helen became very aware of her own pulse running through a vein in her neck.

"Let's get the holy water." She nearly stumbled over cobblestones as she walked backward. The church was only a few steps away. "Or maybe a priest can help us."

"Oh, yes." He rubbed his hands together. "Why don't we visit a priest!"

Her heart thumping, Helen turned and ran. She heard the Baron's deep laughter as she jogged up the steps in a clumsy, mad dash, feeling the Baron's presence creeping up on her. She threw the door open, slipped inside, and then pulled it shut with all of her strength. The door closed with a resounding, hollow sound like the toll of a dull bell.

"How will I follow?" she heard him say from the other side of the door. "If only someone would invite me in. Oh, wait, these idiots put down a welcome mat. I love churches!"

Helen dipped her hands into a nearby basin and collected as much water as she could in her palms.

The Baron threw open the door and laughed, letting his hollow baritone fill every corner. "Helen, I am very disappointed. I asked you to kill me and you've only brought me back to life!"

She threw true. The holy water landed in his old face. He blinked.

"Would you be disappointed to discover that was ordinary tap water?" He stepped across the threshold. "Slightly alkaline."

Helen tried to run, but couldn't keep herself from glancing back to keep her eyes on him. She staggered down the aisle like a drunk bride, passing endless rows of empty pews. There wasn't another soul in sight.

"I know!" The Baron stopped chasing her. "Let's do that thing where you run faster than me but I'm still right behind you!"

Only barely aware of his words, Helen ran faster down the aisle. She turned at the altar and rushed past an old piano on one side and a row of confession booths on the other.

"Boo!" The Baron, suddenly behind her, knocked her to the ground. "Isn't that fun? No matter how fast you go, I'm always right there! Isn't that weird?" He towered over her, tapping his chin. "If only we were at your home. I could do that thing where you open the ice-box door and don't see me until you close it. Gets 'em every...what are you doing?"

Helen crawled to the piano and reached up. Her fingers found the keys, as quickly as if her grade school lessons were just yesterday, and after skimming down seven notes in succession she scampered toward a confession booth.

"I've seen humans do strange things when they were about to die, but playing a musical scale?" He slowly walked in her direction. "I can't fathom a reason..." He stopped.

Still on the cold floor, Helen continued to inch toward the confession booth.

"Helen. That wasn't very nice. You only played *most* of the scale."

The Baron roared and turned to the piano. With a flourish, he spread out his cloak and sat on the bench. "You didn't finish! What sort of *monster* only plays the first seven notes? It's unresolved! But not for long." He extended his strong fingers and slammed them down on the resolving note in four separate octaves. "Beautiful, eh? Now, for you—"

The Baron turned to face an empty church.

"Helen, this is silly. I can smell you hiding in that confession booth. I'll be right there."

Helen checked the lock, but she knew it wouldn't matter. The priest's side of the booth was about as secure as a pillow fort. She heard his footsteps and waited, but...there was nothing. Not even a jiggle of the handle.

Instead of barging into her side of the booth, the Baron entered the other side and spoke through the screen. "Would you like to hear a confession?"

"Let me guess. You can't enter my side of the booth without permission?"

"Curse you! Curse all of you! But you can't stay in there forever, Helen. If you come out, I won't eat anyone else for a week. Cross my heart." He performed a cross gesture over his sternum, just to the side. "Or you can stay in there, all night if you wish. It's Saturday. In the morning you'll get to watch me devour the parishioners, one by one. It'll be my own feast day!"

An idea crossed her mind, momentarily canceling out her fear. Helen leaned close to the screen. "You know, Baron, I just thought of something."

"That's adorable, Helen, but stop trying to save your life. *Someone* should try and die with some dignity today."

"You know those hymnals in the back of every seat? I bet there's a lot of dog-eared pages."

He stared coldly through the screen, then flippantly crossed his arms. "I don't care."

"Oh, that's healthy, Baron. Good for you. So you don't mind that someone folded a few dozen pages in each book? That's real nice. Just try not to think about it. All those pages. Folded in the corner."

He sat back in the chair and shook his head. "Doesn't bother me."

"Mmmhmm." Helen stared him down.

She was prepared to face off with him for the entire night, but after only five minutes, he ran from the confessional and started at one of the back corners of the church, flipping through the first hymnal he found. At the sight of a bent page he raved in the air, then set himself to the task of carefully folding it back. "Don't you move, Helen! I'm not done with you." The Baron licked his finger and turned the page. "Another!"

She crept out of the booth. The Baron continued his work, completely consumed.

Whispering a Hail Mary, Helen grabbed a long altar cloth and laid one end of it along a row of lit candles. The tiny flames grabbed the cloth and set the edge aflame. She trailed the other end into the confession booth and tucked it under the old cushion before rushing outside through the church's back door.

She ran around the block and then casually approached the front of the church, hoping she didn't look like an arsonist. A few glints of orange in the windows told her the fire had kicked off exactly like she'd planned. The old wood of the confession booth had looked like it might go up in flames just from being too close to a window on a hot day, and the rest of the church looked just about as flammable.

Bystanders gathered as smoke darkened the stained glass. By the time the fire brigade arrived, the roaring fire was eating everything inside the stone walls, and Helen knew the Baron was still straightening pages.

She had been the only bystander listening closely. As black plumes rose to the sky, a cackling voice cried out, "Yes, *this* is a glorious death! Ah ha! No—it burns!"

"*Mea culpa,*" Helen whispered, and then wrote her final note: *Death by immolation—confirmed.*

TO LAY AND LIE IN THE SUMMERTIME

E. K. Simmons

Maya sat on the stoop of her apartment with a cup of coffee growing cold in one hand and a lit cigarette in the other. The morning sun did not pack the same punch as it did in the afternoon during this month of July, but she could feel the strands of hair that escaped her messy bun start to stick to her neck. She watched a small army of ants overtake a cicada carcass while she took a drag and almost didn't notice the scuffed, brown leather shoes in front of her until they planted themselves on top of the unfolding feast.

"Hello, Maya."

She squinted up at the man in an ill-fitting gray suit, holding a clipboard like an old timey census worker.

"Well hello there, John. I was wondering when I'd see you again. It's been too long."

In truth, John had been avoiding the routine check-in that Maya was due. Of all the Sirens that had decided forcibly drowning and eating men was no longer an appealing occupation, Maya was the only one that still made him uncomfortable. Most of the time, they locked themselves away in their libraries, or constructed large aquariums to take care of, or simply slept away their days. And all of that was dependent on if they took a human form at all. Whatever shape they shifted into, they all could be categorized by their distinct lack of interest in people and all they represented. With the exception of Maya. Maya looked very interested in him, like she could still eat him if she wanted to, and that he was lucky she didn't.

He cleared his throat and brought the clipboard inches away from his eyes. He always looked like it was his first presentation at his first grown-up job. "I'm here on behalf of the Society of Retired Sirens and All Seducers & Consumers of Men to perform your scheduled check-in. Can I ask you a few questions?"

Maya flicked cigarette ash. "Only if you put that silly clipboard down. You memorized all those questions decades ago, and you know the answers are always the same."

He looked over the top of the clipboard. "Your answers are never the same, and you know it. You like to pretend there's a contest for which canvasser can collect the most interesting responses."

"You win every time, don't you?"

John didn't bother responding, except to ask, "Have you, since the last check in, found yourself involved in any incidents of local male drownings?"

"They all died traumatically without my involvement or consumption."

"Have you been using music for the nefarious plot to seduce and consume men?"

"You really need to update the language in these questions."

John let his shoulders slump and lowered his clipboard. They both knew The Society had a problem keeping up with the current evolutions of human behavior. Sirens might have remained the same for eons, but the people being feasted on were far removed from the Good ol' Days when everyone "did what was right in their own eyes."

"The last update was in 1927, and they don't believe enough has changed on the human level to warrant an updated form. It's not exactly Sodom and Gomorrah out here anymore."

"Well that's a fair assumption on Their part. I just have to wear a tank top with no bra on my own stoop, and it's turned every head for the last hour."

John shoved the clipboard to his face again, and Maya reveled in the blush spreading over his cheeks after he couldn't help but glance to see if she was telling the truth.

Maya carried on. "Besides, you and I both know that The Society is just a bunch of stuffy immortals who don't know about humans on the ground level. I bet if one walked into Court, they wouldn't even recognize it."

"Maya we have this discussion every time I see you. Will you just tell me if you've eaten anybody in recent memory?"

At that moment, Maya's door swung open, and a stereotypical tall, dark and handsome figure squinted from behind it, hair mussed up and eyes puffy from the sleep that was just disturbed. John ignored the similarities in features that they shared. That felt like reading too much into the situation.

"Oh...uhh...I thought you left."

Without breaking eye contact with John, Maya smiled. "Just talking with my neighbor. I'll be inside after this cigarette."

The door closed, and John looked more disappointed than she had seen him in a long time. She didn't flick the cigarette fast enough, and ash fell on her bare feet.

"Did he look eaten or drowned to you?"

"Maya, you're playing with fire."

"They follow me around, it's not my fault."

John remained unconvinced.

She continued. "Mostly it's just the insomniacs. They find me calming. Then they fall in love with me and it gets messy, but I have yet to eat any man that pretends he can bury himself in my bones and call them home."

With half of the questionnaire still blank, John turned away. He got halfway across the street, filling in generic responses for the remaining questions, before he yelled back, "That one's gonna make me this month's winner, just so you know." And then he was gone. The ants Maya had been watching earlier continued their seemingly undisturbed feast.

Back at the office, John shuffled the overflowing stacks of papers around on his desk mindlessly. Keeping tabs on all of their retirees was messy, unorganized work, but what formal administrative work wasn't? The department was understaffed, behind on technology, and anyone who did defy the turnover rate had the same disinterested grumpiness that exuded from their ageless being.

John woke up earlier that morning with a dull headache behind his eyes and seeing Maya only exacerbated it. He finished filling in the blank spaces on her report and signed his name. He had filled out her reports often enough that making up responses for her no longer felt like lying. He stuffed it in his outgoing box and reached for the pill bottle that had ended up under February's reports and was already planning how to take it easy for the rest of the day.

He threw back the pills and reached for the water, then froze. Metaphorically. He stared off into the distance like nothing was wrong as a sudden realization ran through his veins like ice water. The bitter taste of the disintegrating medication in his mouth broke him of the spell, and he washed it down with half the bottle of water.

John dug Maya's report out of his outbox. He glanced through the responses again even though he knew everything he'd just written down. He stood up abruptly, gathered his things, and went to find his supervisor to inform them of a sudden and unpredictable migraine that just shot through his head, which he needed to go take care of at home in a dark room.

Then he promptly took a bus across town to the Annex.

The reason the Annex of the Society was across town and not merely adjacent to or below John's office building also had to do with the Society meeting of 1927. Back when everyone was still smoking inside, they had to put out a small fire due to an unattended cigarette, and everyone realized simultaneously that all of the handwritten records that had been kept since Persephone could still be seen walking around on the regular, could go up in flames at any moment. (By some miracle the numerous lanterns and candles that had been lit for centuries never caught so much as a moth on fire, which solidified in everyone's mind the true evilness of Big Tobacco.)

In reality, the reports now stacked up in the office until somebody decided to haul them across town to the inconspicuous, brick building that was only accessible through public transport to prevent trespassers from peeking inside.

The building itself looked like a decrepit home with a brick facade on the edge of a rundown neighborhood slowly being gentrified. The inside kept the home motif with different rooms stuffed with paper, all in various stages of yellowing. John tried to touch as few cobwebs as possible as he made his way to the room with Maya's records. Her's was one of the most cluttered rooms in the place due to how far back her records went. John sifted through the reports he had been signing off on since the Victorian era and thumbed through several centuries of history until he reached what the Society knew to be the start of her retirement around the mid 1600's in the Caribbean. She was one of the few retirees from the area that century. He wandered back and forth from the reference section in the kitchen, to Maya's room for hours, piecing together ancient and faded ink, looking at maps that hadn't been dusted off in centuries, and feeling like he should have brought a red string with him to follow his train of thought.

It was midnight when John next looked at his watch. As he locked the door behind him, he called the overnight supervisor saying he wouldn't be able to come in in the morning.

The buses had stopped running in that area of town this late into the night, but he wasn't far from Maya's apartment and headed there on foot.

He knocked on her door when he arrived. The moment before he knocked a second time, it opened to reveal Maya in a thin bathrobe, a perfect movie-style bun perched at the top of her head.

"Two visits in one day, John. You should be careful, people will start to talk."

"I have a few more questions for you, Maya."

Her surprise was genuine, as was her intrigue. As a response, she held out an open palm as an invitation to proceed.

"In all our conversations, where you delight in making me as uncomfortable as possible, you have never once offered up a reason for your retirement. Never cared to tell me why humans still fascinate you so, when every other of your kind has deemed them below their notice. Never explained why you washed up on shore in Havana during The Golden Age of Piracy and decided, of all the time periods, *that* was when you were done. I've gone through your records. You've been choosing your words carefully for centuries now."

Maya tilted her head and with raised brows, offered him a smirk. Her normal comebacks were silenced as she waited for him to finish piecing together the puzzle she'd been offering for almost four hundred years.

"You don't eat men; you eat women."

She smiled then, and he wasn't sure if it was the shadows, but he swore he saw the rows and rows of spiked teeth he knew she once had. Teeth she wasn't supposed to have anymore.

"I've been telling you, the Society needs to update those forms."

John stood, open-mouthed, at a loss for words.

"You think there were any women worth eating on those ships? They were few and very far between, and after a few decades of barely a decent meal, I gave up. I signed away my old form to the witches at the docks and stepped onto land. I hummed my way past a church on the mainland, and the most beautiful set of green eyes and soft mouth followed after me. They tasted better than anything I had seduced in a century. When your lovely

Society came to ask me questions, I answered them, truthfully, and went on about my business."

John hadn't noticed the background noise of running water until it shut off.

A faint, feminine voice called out. "Maya?"

John's familiar, disappointed face returned as Maya's smile got bigger.

"I'll be right there, lovely," she called over her shoulder. She turned back to him and said, "I've got to go now, John. Do keep me updated if the Society ever starts looking past the bridge of their own nose and changes the language on those ancient forms. I'll be seeing you soon, I'm sure."

And with that, she closed the door in his face.

John stood there for what most would consider an awkward amount of time before he rubbed his face in his hands.

As he turned away, he muttered, "I have so much paperwork to do tomorrow," to nobody but the empty street.

BABY JUNIOR

R. T. Swindoll

On chocolate strawberries night, Mom came into the kitchen to find the staging bowl of whipped chocolate scraped clean and Baby Junior standing behind the island with chocolate-smudged lips and chocolate-streaked cheeks.

Mom put her hands on her hips.

The chubby little two-year-old looked up with a mischievous smile, baring little white teeth.

"What did you do, Baby Junior?"

Mom did not sound angry—not even exasperated. But she raised her voice so that the two older kids hovering in the adjoining room would know she had spotted the guilty party.

Baby Junior smacked his lips and exclaimed, "Yummy choc'it!" His voice was earnest, but sounded like he was parroting a line, and his hands were completely clean.

Mom clenched her teeth. Chocolate strawberries night was ruined, and it broke the spell of a hundred days passed with not a care in the wide world. She had an idea who was to blame for this interruption. As she counted down the seconds until the culprit made her appearance, Mom recentered herself on her happy thought.

Baby Junior never misbehaved. Ever. She clucked her tongue and smiled.

"What happened, Mom?" Jolie entered from the parlor with a seven-year-old's swagger. Her inquiring face darkened when she saw the injustice that lay upon Baby Junior's face.

Gemma bounded in behind her sister and gasped in surprise. "What did da baby do?" she cried, and Mom almost believed her.

"I mean I can't…I just can't believe he would do this!" Jolie stamped. "This is…this has to be the worst thing Baby Junior has ever done!"

"Yeah! The worst," said Gemma, huffing like her sister.

"He should get in trouble," Jolie resolved. "I mean,

because he got to eat all the dessert, and we got to have none."

Mom squinted at Jolie, the eldest child who stood opposite the kitchen island as Baby Junior's judge, jury, and executioner. There was the slightest discoloration on her flashing teeth. And the younger, Gemma, was busily watching the drama with a flush of fear and sugar.

Baby Junior repeatedly wiped his face and licked his hands with obvious delight.

Mom sighed loudly, "Quite the fall from grace." Bending upon the countertop, she indulged her cheery feeling with mock concern and hesitation as she asked the girls, "I wonder what his punishment should be."

Jolie didn't miss a beat. "Definitely time out. No toys. And an early bedtime. And probably extra brussel sprouts for dinner, because he got to eat so much chocolate it probably gave him a tummy ache. He can have mine. Really, I'm not that hungry."

Mom turned her gaze to Gemma, who wilted and glanced at her older sister. "Yeah, that's p'etty good punishes."

Baby Junior giggled. "Yummy 'prouts!"

Mom rose to a reasoning height. "Well, then. Why don't we have everyone show me their hands?"

Baby Junior took a pondering look over his fingers. The stains on his face he'd already wiped spotless, and any stray marks on his hands quickly found their way into his mouth.

Jolie surreptitiously wiped her palms on the back of her jean dress, then thrust her hands forward with confidence. Damp hands meant sweat or a recent washing—neither a good sign.

Gemma gingerly complied. As her fingers parted, chocolate-brown stains appeared between the creases like a magic trick, which she quickly hid by snapping her short fingers back together.

"How interesting," Mom observed. She was teasing them now, but such was the gamboling bliss of her life. "When I first entered the kitchen, Baby Junior's hands were completely clean."

"He must've washed them," Jolie insisted with a turned up nose. "You know how much he likes to wash his hands."

Mom bent down and sniffed Baby Junior's hands. "They do smell like chocolate, but they don't smell like soap." She turned to the girls. "How about your hands?"

Jolie took the tiniest step backwards, leaving Gemma frozen in the line of Mom's advance.

"Lavender," Mom remarked upon the smell, "and a *modicum* of chocolate."

Gemma stared terrified at Mom. "What's *modicum?*"

Mom grinned with good nature and brought her little game to an end. "I hereby pronounce Baby Junior guilty... of being in the wrong place at the wrong time."

"Guilty!" Jolie hissed in triumph.

"He will be sentenced to the spend the entire dinner... eating our strawberries."

Jolie's face grew long. "But those are for the family!"

Gemma pouted, near tears. "I wanted st'awberries!"

Jolie put her hands on her hips. "Fruit is not a punish-ment!"

Mom grew appalled at how they persisted and, in the effort to concentrate, blinked her eyes rapidly. "Do you think I'm being unfair?"

"Well, yeah," said Jolie. "If we ate the chocolate whip, we'd be in big trouble."

"How much trouble?"

Jolie caught herself before she answered, but Gemma spread her arms as wide as her guilty conscience.

Mom nodded, a little curtly. "Then it's a good thing I'm being unfair this time."

Gemma nodded too, understanding little.

But Jolie scowled at Baby Junior. "Why does Baby Junior get everything, and we get nothing? He never gets in trouble! You always give him new toys and fun rides and no chores! He acts like he's so good, but he doesn't mean it. And now he gets the fruit, too!"

A rush of adrenaline descended on Mom as she glared at Jolie. "I know what you did. Now go to your room, young lady!"

Jolie dug in her heels. Gemma sucked in a breath like it was the last time she would see her sister alive. Baby Junior held up a sage finger.

"That's a *no-no!*" he sang.

Jolie stomped off, up the stairs, and slammed her bedroom door.

Mom tried to shake out her own anger at Jolie's outburst, but couldn't shake the feeling that she'd missed something—some crucial detail that explained why Jolie blamed Baby Junior when she had clearly staged the entire event. Mom massaged her forehead, her thoughts nearing a breakthrough as the idea seemingly reached for her from the ceiling, when Baby Junior—the little scamp!—with his perfectly round face and toothy grin, clapped for Jolie's dramatic exit. Mom's heart melted.

Who could suspect that silly smile of anything but pure joy? Baby Junior was the perfect child—he made all of life perfect—perfect, since the day he turned two.

If only Jolie could act more like him.

After Jolie left, Gemma burst with confessions like a broken dam. "We ate-ed the choc'it, and Jolie smear-ded it on the baby's cheeks and told him to say, 'Yummy choc'it.'"

"Yummy choc'it!" Baby Junior repeated with a smile. How he relished following instructions!

t was a closed door meeting. The paper taped to the door said as much:

Gurls only. No babys!!
(and no moms too, jus kids!)

The agenda: Baby Junior.

By necessity, conference was held after breakfast in Jolie's room, as she was still grounded after last night's chocolate strawberry stunt. By necessity, Gemma was allowed in, but only by necessity, seeing as how she was the little sister and liable to wreck all of Jolie's things. But Jolie was getting desperate, and if matters regarding Baby Junior did not improve today, so help her, she was going to find a new family. She had already drawn up a list of possible candidates.

Gemma, for herself, gladly obliged to enter. Rarely was she allowed in so hallowed a room. And she would have been super distracted by it all had Jolie not conspired to lock the door by sticking eleven tapes across the inside door frame. A practically impenetrable barrier to entry. Gemma knew this was a super secret meeting and started paying attention.

"There's something VERY wrong with him," Jolie whispered.

Gemma shrugged. "Prob'ly he's a' alien."

Jolie paced the floor and acted out the scene from last night. "I gave him the whole bowl of chocolate whip, and he just looked at me and said, 'That's a *no-no.*' I mean, what two-year-old doesn't like sugar?"

"A' alien two-year-old."

"And Mom's impossible! She thinks Baby Junior is the best at everything. Best sleeper. Best eater. Best at walking and talking, peeing and pooping."

Gemma burst with a secret. "I hear-ed Mom on the phone say the baby's diapers didn't even SMELL bad."

Jolie struck her forehead with a palm. The sisters both remembered gagging at the odor of the diaper pail—it was their longest running joke together. Why did Mom remember it differently?

Jolie groused. "You'd think he won the Baby Olympics."

Gemma sat on the edge of Jolie's bed with her face scrunched in her hands. "Maybe he IS perfect, like Mom says."

"Mom is *di-luted*." Jolie peeled back a curtain and looked through the window. The backyard below was sunny, and Mom was lost in a hammock and a book. Baby Junior toddled on the grass nearby, contentedly returning the toys Jolie and Gemma had not picked up yesterday and leaving little nut piles for the rabid squirrels.

Jolie screwed up her face. "Mom doesn't know that Baby Junior's not a real baby."

"Prob'ly a' alien baby."

"Not alien—just fake!" Jolie tossed the curtain closed, crossed her arms, and hunched in the dark. "I mean, look at my room. It's a little messy."

The room was a tornado of dirty clothes and broken toys and forgotten forts.

"But," she continued, "the room you share with Baby Junior is super clean. Like, all the time. I know YOU don't pick it up."

Gemma flattened her lips sheepishly.

"All his blocks are in rows," Jolie complained. "All his books on the bookshelf face the right way. And when he learned his letters, he switched the books around so they were all A to Z! Why does everything have to be super perfect?"

Gemma had noticed how, every morning, Baby Junior stood on his tiptoes atop the toddler bed and nudged the corners of the picture frames so they were all perfectly square. "I kinda like it," she admitted. "It's nice and tidy."

Jolie rolled her eyes so hard her head fell back. "Of

course YOU like it, you don't have to do any of the work! But it's not real, Gemma. It's not *normal*."

Those pictures on the wall, Gemma thought, were from before Baby Junior's birthday, before Mom converted his crib and put him in Gemma's room. In the pictures, he wore dirty overalls, muddy shoes, and spaghetti sauce all over his face. It was weird. Baby Junior wasn't like that anymore.

Like Baby Junior wasn't Baby Junior anymore.

Gemma shrugged. So what if Baby Junior decided he didn't want to be messy anymore? Unless he really WAS a squeaky clean alien from outer space! Worry sent her legs kicking the bed frame. She wasn't sure Jolie was right, but she wasn't sure Jolie was wrong.

Gemma spoke up. "But you NEVER pick up your room."

"That's because it's *normal* to make messes!"

Jolie, super annoyed, stomped back and forth in search of a plan. She snatched a pack of colored pencils and a pad of graph paper off her desk, then tucked herself in a chair and started drawing.

"What's that?" Gemma hopped over and perched behind Jolie's shoulder.

"A trap."

Jolie drew a row of alphabet blocks. The J was missing—it was elsewhere on the page, under a laundry basket drawn so that it was propped up by a book. A kite string ran from the book to the edge of the page where two girl stick-figures stood waiting, holding the kite string, ready to pull.

Jolie stabbed the paper with the colored pencil. "It's his weakness!" she exclaimed and drew stick Baby Junior reaching for the missing block. "You know how Baby Junior freaks out if even one thing is messed up. That's how we catch him! But we won't let him out till he tells us who he really is."

"Or, it's time for lunch," Gemma added.

Jolie sighed and broke the tape on the door. "Just follow my instructions, or we'll get in big trouble."

Whenever the book fell on Mom's face, they knew Mom was sleeping instead of reading. And that's exactly how they found her in the hammock when they had finished rigging the trap inside the house.

Baby Junior was roaming free in the yard. He was coloring on the sidewall brick, coating each brick with red chalk so that every brick was the exact same color. Now he was washing his red hands in the birdbath, careful not to stain his little white polo shirt.

Gemma quietly scurried across the lawn to the birdbath and whispered in Baby Junior's ear. "I finded a block that's a *no-no* in the house."

He smiled. "I fitch it," and Baby Junior took his sister's hand. Together, they traipsed inside as Mom blissfully snored.

Gemma slipped away, leaving Baby Junior alone before the alphabet blocks on the coffee table. He clasped his hands together over the J, absent like a missing tooth. His eyes roamed from table to floor, until he saw the upturned laundry basket yawning over the errant letter. He stepped forward.

Around the corner, Jolie shushed Gemma as she made sure the kite string was taut. She'd tested it three times, but this time it had to work. But before Baby Junior plunged to retrieve the block, he went ahead and straightened the other twenty-five alphabet blocks so that their edges were perfectly flush.

It took an agonizing minute.

"What if Mom wakes up?" Gemma whispered.

Now Baby Junior crawled beneath the plastic basket,

and, as his fingers grasped the prize, Jolie yanked the string. The prop toppled; the basket tumbled over Baby Junior's head. The girls leapt from behind the corner.

"Gemma, get on top, quick!"

Gemma threw herself on top of the laundry basket. It was a wide basket, not tall, and Junior was too cramped inside to sit up, so he rolled on his side to see Jolie through the plastic lattice of his prison. In his hand, he held the letter J and looked longingly at the table and the missing tooth where the block belonged.

"Talk," ordered Jolie.

"Uh no!" he whined, shifting every which way for an escape. "Out now? I come out now?"

"You're not going anywhere." Jolie slid onto her belly to look the two-year-old in the eye. Gemma, laying on her belly atop the basket, dipped her head over the edge to stare at Baby Junior upside-down. The boy saw both their heads, one right-side up, the other upside down, and tilted his head in anxious search of the way it should go.

"Who are you?" Jolie questioned. "Tell us, and we'll let you out."

Gemma shared a room with Baby Junior and fancied herself the go-between. "What is your name?" she interpreted.

He blubbered, "I Baby Juner."

Jolie steamed like a kettle. "Not his name! We need to know if he's *human*."

Gemma asked, "Are you a baby alien?"

He whimpered, "A'lee'in?"

"I knew it," said Gemma, rolling off the basket. But Jolie grabbed the lattice and held it down until she kicked Gemma back in place on top. Their mission wasn't over yet. Baby Junior pushed against the basket with his bare feet, but there was no escape except through Jolie.

The eldest spoke with conviction, "You're lying to us. You may be perfect, Baby Junior, but I know you aren't a baby at all." She circled the basket until she was kneeling in front of the coffee table. "Tell us who you are…or I'm gonna start knocking blocks."

With a twist of her wrist, Jolie whacked the Z and sent it bouncing to the floor.

Baby Junior poked the lattice with his pudgy fingers. "Not letters! Not letters!"

"Then talk!" Jolie seethed.

"Um, Jolie…?" Gemma was looking out the window into the backyard where Mom was sitting up in the hammock. They were out of time.

Baby Junior silently looked at the gap in the letters. Jolie took the C and switched it with the B.

"Not letters!" Baby Junior howled. He gripped the J and looked almost ready to throw it at Jolie, but that would have been a *no-no*.

Gemma's eyes were wide as saucers as she watched Mom swing her legs out of the hammock in search of Baby Junior, and her confidence failed.

"Stay where you are!" Jolie commanded, but Gemma slid off the roof and fled the scene of the crime. Jolie lunged to hold down the lid on Baby Junior's prison. She looked at the little creature with menace. "I will always mess up the letters," she promised, "if you don't tell me who you are. Now."

Baby Junior looked frantic. He turned the J over and over in his hands. "OK. I tell."

Jolie stole a glance behind her. Mom was at the opposite end of the yard, checking the plants and calling for Baby Junior. If only Gemma had run out to distract her!

Baby Junior put the J upside-down on the floor. "I Two!"

"Not your age!" Jolie snapped.

"I Baby Two!"

He held up two fingers, and she squinted, trying to catch his meaning. Was this some play on his name, Junior, how he was named after Dad?

Jolie kicked her back foot and knocked off the L, M, N, O, P. Baby Junior burst in alarm and tried to explain it.

"I Juner Two. I fitch it. I fitch Baby Juner."

Fix Junior? Her eyebrows slowly lifted as his voice turned to sing-song.

"Baby Juner is a no-no!"

Her arms went weak with tingles. She thought about that silly dinosaur birthday party and Mom and Dad arguing and Baby Junior getting so mad he smashed his cake from head to toe. Then he'd clapped and Mom and Dad were smiling and Baby Junior went to the sink and washed himself clean.

Jolie saw Mom's shadow looming on the wall, but she couldn't let this go just yet. "You mean...there's two Juniors?"

"You fitch letters!" Baby Junior screamed.

But Jolie could only stare in his irises. The pupils were dark like the camera on Mom's phone. "Where's Junior One?" she whispered.

Baby Junior shook his head and knocked over the J to the blank side.

"You fitch letters, or I fitch you!"

Jolie only gripped the basket tighter. First, she had to tell Mom what happened to Junior One.

Then Baby Junior clapped. Jolie snapped out the back of her head. She dumbly watched her arms free Baby Junior and her hands collect the blocks off the floor—detached like a selfie stick taking a video of her from behind.

When Mom opened the backdoor and saw her eldest and youngest at play in the laundry basket, she smiled. She should have been furious, for Jolie had snuck out of her room and threatened again the endless joy that was her life as a mother—but seeing Baby Junior so rascally cheerful melted Mom's heart. Only moments ago, she'd thought she'd lost him forever!

Jolie was also quite chipper, and a happy thought crossed Mom's mind that maybe Baby Junior had rubbed off on her. Look at how carefully she arranged the letter blocks just exactly how Baby Junior liked them.

Mom gave her sweeties a hug. Baby Junior cooed with the same angelic grin he'd had since his two-year-old teeth filled in.

Later that night, when they were getting into jammies, Gemma asked Jolie what she had learned about their alien brother. Jolie laughed hysterically. Tears rolled down her face as she told her younger sister to just mind her own business and always follow Baby Junior's instructions.

ESCAPE

James T. Grissom

Tom looked around at his friends.

Not again!

Well, only Ed was a friend, the others were really *Ed's* friends. But when you move around so much, you kind of latch on to the first person that notices you and accept all of the unsaid rules that come with that new relationship. Like pretending to like the other people who had all known each other for years and years.

I wonder what it's like to have a friend that long?

Still, Tom wasn't about to mess up a good thing just because he really couldn't stand half of them. Ed was pretty popular, and Tom had never been part of that kind of group, so he laughed at Mike's stupid jokes because Ed did.

How could he possibly like both of us?

For some dumb reason, Dan thought it would be funny to throw his pickles at the trash can, trying to make them stick. Ed laughed and tried it himself, so Tom followed suit.

"Pablo has to earn that janitor money today," Mike said, throwing another and missing badly.

The covey of pimpled teens roared in comic agreement. Tom didn't laugh; his mother was a janitor at the church. Tom often helped her out after school, but it would be social death to let any of *them* know that. Ed noticed Tom's lack of mirth, and his smile slipped a bit.

"His dad's Mexican, numbnuts," Scott whispered to Mike.

Ed darkened a bit. He clearly hadn't thought of that either when he had laughed. Tom felt his stomach sink. Ed knew what "Momma Lois" did for a living. He stopped laughing for Tom's sake. Tom began to sweat. There was tension because of him, and now his whole standing was out of whack. He would be the weird kid eating alone again.

"Yeah, dummy," Tom said, with as real a chuckle as he

could muster. "My mom's on duty today."

I'm so sorry, Mom.

For a half second, everyone glanced at Ed, and cracked up all over again when he did. As the inane conversation continued, Ed caught Tom's eye for a significant moment. Balance was restored.

"Let's go check out Spencer's," Ed said. In a clatter of chairs, they all got up, no one bothering to pick up their trash.

"Y'all go ahead; I'll catch up." Tom said, pointing at his barely eaten burger.

Mike opened his mouth to make another idiot comment, but Ed cut him off. "Sure thing. See you there."

And that was that. Ed gave him a look over his shoulder as they left. A look both of thanks and apology.

The food court at High View Mall was always packed, so it only took a minute for them to be hidden from sight. The place had that strange smell from a conglomeration of people and ten different foods that reminded Tom of his dad's bachelor's quarters back at the Navy base in Florida. The one time he'd actually seen him in the last six years, he remembered with teen rage.

An old lady at the table next to him smiled as he picked up all the garbage the others had left behind and thrown about. He smiled back, thinking of his grandma who had taken care of him for a couple years between his parents' multiple divorces, and then sat back down to finish his lunch. Lunch alone was no new thing for him. He actually enjoyed it compared to faking for those jerks. If it weren't for Ed, he'd have stopped trying to fit in with them long ago.

"You're too nice for those boys," a sweet voice behind him said.

Tabitha Lopez. She was an absolute goddess. Her chestnut hair and rich brown eyes accentuated a face that could have been sculpted by Michelangelo.

"Oh, hey, Tab," Tom said, a bit shyly.

No, no. Girls want confidence!

He tried to steady his voice. "Ed's a good dude; it's the rest who need to grow up." That sounded better.

She smiled a smile fit to make the sun blush, and it sent heat through his entire being. "Can we share your table?"

Tom gave a bit of a start, and Brandi, whom he hadn't seen standing right beside Tab, rolled her eyes good naturedly with a grin. "Hi, Tom," she said, knowing full well he hadn't noticed her at all until that moment. He hadn't even noticed the trays. He glanced in the direction of Tab's salad and quickly back to her face. She wore a V-neck shirt that...hinted.

"Hey! Yeah, please have a seat. I think I got all the crap up." He pushed two chairs out with his feet, praying Tab would choose the one closest to him and hoping she didn't hate the word "crap." They sat their trays down, and Tom felt warm electricity as Tab's knee pressed into his leg as she pulled her chair into the table. The chair right next to him.

Breathe. Just breathe.

Brandi shook her head in amusement as he visibly struggled to decide whether he should move his leg away. "I forgot napkins," Brandi said." Her blond rings bounced as she walked away.

If she doesn't adjust, I won't either, Tom decided. And she didn't.

"Are y'all just hanging out?" He managed to say without stammering.

"We have to get ballet flats," Tab answered as she adjusted a bit in her seat, enough to where she could have moved her leg away from his but didn't.

Breathe!

"What about you?" she asked, looking him right in the eyes. He couldn't, didn't want to, break the spell.

Tom nervously picked up a fry with no intention of eating it. "Just chillin."

God, why did I say that!

"Are they for the spring musical? The shoes?" He asked. Her ruby lips parted again to reveal the glorious sun of her smile.

"Yep, next week we start rehearsing," Tab replied. "Do you sing?"

"Not like you. I sound like a frog." Oh, how that sun shined and melted him!

"Ribbit!" Brandi teased. Tom jumped in surprise, once again so immersed in Tab that he hadn't noticed Brandi's return. Tab gave a low, warm giggle, amused at his sweet discomfort. "I brought extra," Brandi continued, and handed Tab a stack of napkins as she sat back down.

"Thanks!" Tab said, looking away from him to grab them.

Tom yearned for her gaze to return, but was secretly glad for the break to compose himself.

"Need one?" She asked. "I think you used yours cleaning up their crap."

His fingers touched hers, mirroring the electric current in their still-touching legs. "Thanks," he said weakly.

Good. "Crap" is an okay word.

"That burger looks awesome," Brandi said, looking forlornly at her own salad. "Stupid dance tights mean stupid salad."

"Oh, sorry. I, uh...there." He spread a napkin over his food. They both laughed.

"No, please, eat! It's our own fault and we asked to sit here," Tab said. Brandi raised an eyebrow, then laughed. "Seriously, thanks; I'm just complaining to complain."

Tom noticed Tab had been fiddling with the dressing pack for a few seconds. "Do you need help with that, or are you deciding if it's too many calories?" Brandi giggled, and Tab chimed musical notes of amusement.

"Yes, please," she said, handing it over.

This day can't get any better!

The green field around them led to the small lake on one side, and the woods on the other, just a few feet away.

Green field? Wasn't I just in the food court? Tom's thoughts felt distant and vaguely troubling.

Ed and Brandi were trading jokes on the other side of the blanket. Tab set out the contents of the basket she had packed. Tom didn't really like subs all that much, but that thought was far away, completely unimportant in the moment. "Sorry it's just sandwiches, but it was the only thing on the way that wouldn't make a huge mess."

How does she read my mind? Tom thought with wonder.

"Yeah, and she was really careful to say no onions like fifty times," Brandi laughed. Tab actually blushed.

"No, this is great. Let me help." Tom tossed a bag of chips that Ed caught with a grin.

"What's wrong with onions?" Ed asked with a wink. Tom wished he could wear a sleeveless shirt as nonchalantly as his friend, but he was self-conscious about his hairy arms. Ed looked like a football player, but always joked that he could flirt in the stands with the cheerleaders while the idiots on the field banged their heads against each other, thinking they'd somehow make it into pro ball someday. Well, he had said that until he started dating Brandi. They were a blond-haired, blue-eyed power couple, even though she was a self-proclaimed drama nerd. Tom looked down at his Nirvana shirt, distaste twisting his mouth at the roll of fat, and quickly straightened to hide it.

Tab leaned in close and whispered, "I like you the way you are."

Again with the mind reading, he thought with amazement.

He kissed her cheek, his gelled dirty-blond Caesar cut crunching against her temple.

"You kissing me with onion breath is what's wrong

with 'em," Brandi quipped, making everyone laugh. "Those better be plain chips!" she said with mock severity.

They ate and chatted about the random things of teen life. School, projects at home, how unfair curfew was. Even Tab ate quickly. "How about a walk on the path?" She asked shyly, wiping her mouth on a napkin and throwing it and the wrappers in the basket.

"Hmm...you two go ahead, and we'll clean up," Brandi replied with a twinkle in her eyes.

The path wandered into the first ten feet of the woods and eventually all the way around the lake and back to the parking lot. As soon as the trees hid the two of them, Tab twisted her hand around in Tom's and positioned herself in front of him. She smelled like a rose garden. He had to bend his head down to lean his forehead against hers. He saw his hazel eyes reflected in her gorgeous brown ones. "How did I get so lucky?" He asked.

He forgot everything as she showed him, with her mouth against his, what she thought of that. Time faded while their bodies grew closer, hands exploring one another. He started to pull back, afraid he'd gone too far, and she shocked him by pulling him close, both hands on his own ample rear.

"Tab, you down here?" The stairs into the basement of the broken factory in the middle of the woods were still sound, but the door was barely hanging on.

Why would she be here? How did I get here?

He shook his head at the thought, which felt oddly like it belonged to someone else. He entered a small hallway with an empty office space on one side and a men's room on the other. The stench told him he didn't want to go in there, but a sudden churning in his stomach told him he had no choice.

The lights were on.

Why is that strange?

They flickered a bit. There was only one stall, and the

urinal had an *Out of Order* sign taped to it. The faucet made a constant, annoying drip into a dirty basin. Surprisingly, the toilet was clean, and there was paper on the roller.

Why is that a surprise?

He sat and went about his business.

When he flushed the toilet, he stared in horror as it began to overflow. He backed away, but the space was too narrow. Brown water soaked his shoes and the bottoms of his jeans. For some reason, he thought it best to take off his jeans and use them to mop the mess away as best he could.

Now what?!

Tom heard someone coming in the door with a jangle of keys. He looked out of the crack in the stall and saw a guard sit down at a desk.

Desk? What desk? In the bathroom?

Tom carefully, quietly backed away, and sat on the toilet, trying his best not to gasp at the cold mess that wet his boxers.

"When you come out, I'm gonna kill you," the guard said in a low Southern drawl. Ice shot up and down Tom's spine, freezing his marrow. The guard laughed, a deep rumble. Then he started to whistle.

For hours, the whistling went on. Tom was hungry, cold, and scared out of his mind. Eventually he drifted off in fitful sleep. His own snoring woke him. The guard cackled. "Tick, tock; tick, tock," he taunted in that horrible bass.

He woke again.

"I'm still here, piggy," said the horrible voice on the other side of the stall.

After what could have been days or hours later, Tom woke up again in a cold sweat and stared in horror at the men and teen boys across from him. In three rows, they laid on stone bunks, tied down, cords digging into the skin of their necks, backs, and legs. Heads were strapped down with what looked like filthy rags so that they were all forced to look away from the walls that must be against their other sides—just as he felt a rough wall on the side of him that he could not turn his head to see. They were all naked, but belly down, only their backsides were visible to confirm their lack of clothes. Tom opened his mouth, and they all glared at him, eyes popping at their inability, or unwillingness, to tell him to shut up.

He remembered this place, and with memory, a moan ripped out of him. The men and boys he could see clamped their eyes shut. Only one left his eyes open. One Tom didn't recognize, in a bunk he remembered being empty. That one struggled against the cords binding him. Where everyone else had dried scabs around their bonds, his bled. His eyes bled tears.

The Keeper walked into the room. He was clothed in gray rags, hooded except for a pasty face, sickly yellow where patches of skin covered the area that should have held eyes. His uneven *click-clack* footsteps echoed like a clock. A disturbingly asynchronous clock of metal and wood. A breeze stirred as the specter passed Tom toward the newbie, wafting a scent of mushrooms and death into Tom's nose.

The young man started to wail.

"Silence!" croaked the Keeper, in a voice like sandpaper on metal. He took one of the rags from his macabre raiment and stuffed it into the boy's mouth. Then he lowered himself and licked the tears off of the boy's face with a serpentine tongue and shuddered in ecstasy. "So sweet, the taste of despair."

Tom moaned, deep in his chest. Suddenly, the jailor at the young man's concrete bunk, now stood directly in front of Tom, his horrible eyeless face somehow looking right at him.

"You put that eyeball on me again, and I'll take it out!" the thing hissed.

Tom clenched his eyes so hard they hurt. The thing did not move. It stood there, breathing decay into his face.

Can't fall asleep. Not again. Please, not again. It just gets worse. At least let it be a nightmare. I don't want any more hope.

Tom looked around at his friends. Well, only Ed was a friend, the others were really *Ed's* friends.

Somewhere in the distance, he heard a moan that was somehow his own, and a laugh like ripping paper.

THE CAT

Christine Hand Jones

Grayson brought The Cat home the day after their first big fight as a married couple.

The fight was nothing. Mira had saved a single, dark chocolate peanut butter cup for herself as a special treat. It was her one indulgence, a fact that she would bet good money that Grayson knew. Yet he had eaten the chocolate, and when confronted, had protested ignorance. Mira knew it was a stupid detail to dwell on, but she couldn't let it go. They argued until bedtime, retreated in silence to their respective sides of the mattress, and avoided each other the next morning.

By the time Mira came home from work, she was laughing at herself over the whole incident. On the elevator ride up to their spacious loft apartment, she worked out all the details of her apology. But when the elevator doors opened, she found Grayson holding a scrawny black kitten, and, for the second time in her life, she fell deeply, irrevocably in love.

"Lucky" was the name the shelter had bestowed upon the cat. His fur was so black, he could easily be mistaken for a shadow or a trick of the light if not for his piercing green eyes and a single, white starburst spot on his forehead.

Mira was not the kind of woman who asked to hold babies or who teared-up at the sight of tiny suits with tiny bowties, but as soon as the cat crawled onto her shoulder and fell asleep, she understood all those maternal tropes.

She thought the name "Lucky" far too mundane, and after a week of deliberation, chose "Basil" instead, because he looked distinguished, like the British actor Basil Rathbone. "Hello, Basil," she cooed. But by then they'd gotten used to calling him "The Cat," so it stuck.

The three of them huddled together beneath Grayson's outstretched arm and smiled for a group selfie. Well, Grayson smiled his dazzling white grin, The Cat yawned, and Mira gazed down at his fuzzy head in adoration. Mira posted the picture with the hashtags #AndKittenMakes-Three, #BlackCat, and #FamilyPortrait, and watched the likes and comments roll in. *Adorable!* wrote her best office friend, Jen; *Disgusting,* wrote her sister; *Cute Kitten,* wrote a random blonde influencer named Sylvie; *Today a kitten, tomorrow grandchildren!* wrote her mother.

Mira stashed her peanut butter cups in a bright pink Tupperware container that she labeled in stark upper-case sharpie, and Mira and Grayson resumed their state of newly-wedded bliss. So on they went, the three of them, a happy little family.

The Cat continued to sleep on Mira's shoulder until he outgrew it within two weeks and transitioned to the center of her chest. At first, Grayson made a few light complaints about his new bedfellow, but Mira's answering glare silenced him. The Cat was his idea after all.

Besides, Grayson was often in the habit of working late into the night in his home office. He could hardly complain that his wife sought comfort with The Cat.

Four weeks in, and The Cat spanned the length of Mira's torso. Almost overnight, he had become a lanky adolescent, and Mira mourned the loss of her baby kitten.

"I thought you said he was six months old when you brought him home," Mira said.

"You're remembering it wrong," Grayson grumbled, and turned up the basketball game.

But her phone's camera did not lie. She pulled up their family portrait from three weeks ago and shoved it into Grayson's field of vision during the commercial break. "See? That's a six-month-old cat. Now look." She swiped to her latest photo, taken this morning as The Cat stretched in the rays of sun filtering through the patio doors and batted at a floating dust mote. "He looks like he's a year old already. That's not normal."

Grayson ran both hands through his golden hair, sighed, and faced her. "I told you, babe, he's a special breed, one-of-a kind. He's bigger than most cats, and he grows faster. You should have seen the mom. She was massive."

"She was?"

"Yes!"

"And you're sure you told me that?"

"Of course I'm sure."

"I feel like I would have remembered that, Grayson," Mira protested. But the game was back on, and the sounds of squeaking shoes and crowd noise drowned her out.

Mira scooped The Cat up and went back to the bedroom to watch Masterpiece Theatre.

The Cat had a habit of kneading Mira with his razor-sharp claws as he drifted off to sleep. The more Mira scratched his ears, the more he purred and kneaded, leaving miniscule needle pricks in her delicate skin.

"Why don't you just have him declawed?" Grayson asked.

Mira gasped in horror. "You know declawing is practically an amputation, right?"

"OK," Grayson said, "But you're only bringing the pain on yourself, you know."

Mira learned to pull the covers all the way up to her chin to protect herself at night. She bought an expensive cat tree with plenty of textured surfaces. The Cat loved the tree, and delighted in arching his back as he stretched and scratched its sisal-covered trunk.

Still, Mira awakened each morning with random pinpricks and small scrapes that she couldn't explain.

"Maybe I cut myself shaving and forgot," she mused,

inspecting a series of red marks on her thigh.

"Or maybe your cat is a menace," Grayson replied.

Grayson's long work hours paid off. His company sent him on a lavish business trip to wine and dine new clients in New York. Mira devoured Thai takeout, Rosé, and Hallmark movie mysteries every night while The Cat purred contentedly on her lap. Grayson posted glamorous photos of exorbitant dinners, red carpets, and gorgeous, sparkling women.

When Grayson returned, he glowed like a post-retreat yogi. He had never seemed fitter or more well-rested. Mira and The Cat, meanwhile, had become bloated and heavy.

"What did you feed him?" Grayson asked.

"Only the usual amount."

"Babe, you know you can't just leave food in the auto-feeder. He'll gorge himself."

"I know that, Grayson, I'm not stupid. I fed him myself, twice a day, like usual."

"Are you sure you didn't forget and feed him more than that?"

Mira searched her memory. She did have a tendency to lose track of time when faced with a never-ending stream of Hallmark movies. Not to mention the wine.

"I guess it's possible. I don't know."

The Cat made a mournful sound, rolled off the couch, and tottered to the corner, where he hacked up a hairball for a full thirty seconds. Under Grayson's smug stare, it felt like thirty minutes.

"Babe," Grayson said. "This is your cat. A gift from me. I thought that meant something. You should really take better care of him."

Mira decided to take The Cat to the vet. If he really was a unique breed, maybe his unusual girth was normal.

"Hello there, Basil," Dr. Choi sang as she pulled The Cat out of his carrier. The Cat let out a small, dejected "meow," then suffered himself to be poked and prodded.

"Well, Mrs. Hallward, it looks like Basil has put on a few more pounds than is normal for a cat his age."

Mira interrupted. "I know this is a stupid question, Dr. Choi, but what, exactly, is his age? He was a rescue kitten, and we really weren't sure."

"Except for this extra belly fat, Basil here looks like a normal two or three-year old cat. He's still a youngster."

Mira shook her head. "Two or three? But, Doctor, he was so tiny when he got him three months ago. That can't be right."

"A lot of strays are malnourished. Maybe that accounts for his overeating. Remember, he only needs a quarter cup of food twice a day."

"That's what I've been feeding him."

A tiny line appeared between Dr. Choi's eyebrows as she peered into The Cat's triangular face and offered him her hand. "Have you been getting into the trash, big guy?" she asked. The Cat responded by rubbing his cheek along the back of the doctor's fingers.

Dr. Choi looked from The Cat to Mira. "Sometimes those feral habits are hard to break. Make sure your trash-cans are secured, and monitor his eating. We don't want a diabetic cat on our hands, do we, Basil?"

The Cat purred.

Mira supposed it was possible that Basil had learned that the trashcan would open if he sat on the foot lever. If he was very quick, perhaps he could wedge a paw in before the lid closed. But why hadn't there been traces of trash around the apartment?

Mira sighed. Now she was in no mood to bring up the

scratches, but she supposed she should make the most of the expensive vet visit.

"There's one more thing, Dr. Choi. I think Basil might have a scratching problem. I keep finding these marks on my skin. I don't believe in declawing. Is there anything I can do?"

Dr. Choi ran through the usual litany: provide scratching posts, trim his claws, cover the furniture. Mira had heard it all before.

"I've yet to meet a cat owner without a few stray scratches," Dr. Choi explained. "But if it bothers you, you could consider these vinyl claw covers," she said, and took a box from her cabinet featuring a picture of a floofy white cat with a full-on pink manicure. Mira couldn't picture Basil with pink claws.

"Of course it bothers me, Dr. Choi. He's leaving some pretty serious marks." Mira pushed up her t-shirt sleeve to show Dr. Choi the three fresh lines near her underarm.

The line reappeared between Dr. Choi's eyes. "No cat made these marks, Mrs. Hallward." She leaned forward, assuming the expression of a daytime-TV-therapist. "Is there something going on at home that you need to tell me about?"

Mira stared blankly. The doctor tried again. "I can refer you to a colleague who specializes in psychology."

"You think The Cat needs a psychologist?"

Dr. Choi's forehead crease deepened. "No, Mrs. Hallward. I was talking about a human psychologist. Frankly, these marks indicate self-harm. I want to get you the help you need so that you," she scratched between The Cat's ears, "and Basil can have a happy, healthy life."

Mira dropped her eyes in shame. "Thank you for your concern, Dr. Choi. All the same, I think I'll try those claw covers, just in case." Dr. Choi shrugged, then pulled out a few more boxes in different color choices. The Cat sniffed curiously at the one labeled "cat house crimson."

When Grayson saw The Cat's dramatic new claws, he laughed so loudly that The Cat scurried behind his carpeted tree and crouched there for forty-five minutes.

But when Mira let it slip that she'd shown Dr. Choi her scars, Grayson's laughter dried up and his eyes turned dark.

"You showed the vet? Why would you show the vet?"

"I was only trying to…"

"Trying to what? Trying to make her think we have a rabid beast on our hands? Trying to get The Cat taken away to animal control?"

Mira hadn't considered that. "Well, you can relax, Grayson. She didn't believe that the scars came from The Cat anyway. She told me I should 'see a psychiatrist.'"

"Hmm," said Grayson.

"What?"

"Nothing."

"It's not 'nothing,' Grayson. You 'hmmed,' why did you 'hmmm?'"

Grayson turned to her, wearing the same concern Mira had seen on Dr. Choi's face earlier.

"Don't get mad, babe, but you have been under a lot of stress lately. Maybe Dr. Choi has a point. Maybe therapy would help."

Dr. Quill, the therapist, was kind. She served floral tea and tiny cookies, and Mira found herself drinking cup after cup and relaying her whole life story as Dr. Quill murmured 'hmms' and 'ahs' and gave nearly imperceptible nods. Mira spoke of the night she and Grayson met at the swanky bar in the financial district. She had slammed right into him, and he had spilled his cabernet sauvignon all over her dress. Grayson was probably the most attractive guy she'd ever met. He was certainly the most attractive guy who'd paid her any attention. She was smitten, her wine-soaked dress notwithstanding. They had talked all evening.

Dr. Quill interjected. "What did you talk about that night?"

Mira paused. *What* did *we talk about?* she wondered. "Oh, I suppose it was the usual small talk. Job stuff mostly. Grayson had just landed a big new client and was out celebrating with his friends. He talked a lot about his job—called himself 'a deal maker.'"

"And was he interested in your job?"

"Oh, my job isn't interesting," Mira said. Mira spent her days redirecting phone calls and signing for packages as the receptionist for a mid-size publisher. It was several rungs down the ladder from her true literary publishing dreams, but it was a start. She told Dr. Quill as much, and the doctor emitted her signature "hmmm."

"Anyway," Mira continued, "The next day, I got this delivery at work—red tulips and a brand new dress—to replace the one he'd spilled his wine on. It was the most romantic thing that had ever happened to me."

Dr. Quill cocked an eyebrow and leaned forward. "Have you ever heard the term, 'love bomb,' Mira?"

Mira shook her head.

Dr. Quill considered her, looked down at her notes, and then rephrased the question. "Does Grayson make these 'grand gestures' often?" she asked.

Grayson was the king of grand gestures. Mira relayed their engagement story, which had involved actual fireworks, and the first time he'd said 'I Love You,' when he had surprised her with tickets to Paris.

Dr. Quill nodded and relaxed back into her arm chair. "Love bombing is a common tactic in those with narcissistic personality disorder."

"You think I have a personality disorder?"

"No, Mira, I don't. If anything, I'd like to see you focus more on yourself and your own needs and desires. I'd like you to practice noticing your thoughts and emotions. Write down when you feel happy or peaceful or when something feels off. Pay attention to your gut. It might have something to tell you."

At the moment, Mira's gut was telling her to reach for another cookie. Dr. Quill saw her eyeing the plate and nudged it in her direction.

"I really shouldn't," Mira mumbled. "If Grayson were here, he'd…"

"He'd what, Mira?"

"He's just really into health and fitness, that's all. Like I said before, he's great. He takes care of me, goes out of his way to make me feel special."

"Tell me more," said Dr. Quill, and Mira told her about the chocolates and Grayson's gift of The Cat until Dr. Quill's phone began to chime. Their time was up.

Dr. Quill closed her notebook and stood. "Thank you for coming in today, Mira. I also offer couples therapy, and I'd like you to consider it."

"Couples therapy? So, you don't think I'm crazy?"

"No, Mira, I don't think you're crazy, but I do hope you'll be back."

Mira was ninety-five percent certain that she would not be back. She didn't need some psychiatrist to tell her what she already knew: Grayson loved her, she was *not* crazy, and she obviously just needed to have more long talks with her girlfriends.

She had to admit that it felt good to talk to someone, though. Just thinking about all the romantic things Grayson had done during their whirlwind courtship put her right back into that heady place of new love. That was the key to life: gratitude—counting one's blessings—and

Mira was certainly blessed.

At her post-therapy mani-pedi, Mira scrolled social media, enjoying the highlights reel of her life with Grayson. They were so good together, so happy and bright and attractive. And people were clearly jealous, as the comments section made all too evident, with its exclamations and heart emojis and the occasional eye-roll or puke face, all in good fun. One comment gave her pause, though.

Something's wrong with that cat, it said. It was that blonde influencer again—Sylvie Baine. No preamble, no laughing face to soften the blow, just a random insult to The Cat.

How jealous did someone have to be to lash out at an innocent kitten, even if he was a bit overweight?

Protective righteousness swelled in Mira's chest. She was so lucky to have her little family, so grateful. They didn't need couples therapy; they just needed to reconnect.

After the salon, Mira bought the ingredients for one of Grayson's favorite meals. At home, she wriggled into the red dress she knew he liked.

When Grayson arrived, the loft was fragrant with garlic and cheese, and he found his wife pulling a steaming pan of lasagna out of the oven. She poured them each a glass of wine. Grayson's eyes lit up as he surveyed the feast before him. He took a sip of the proffered drink, pulled Mira into his arms, and kissed her like a love-struck teenager.

The lasagna was a bit cool when they finally got around to eating it, but it was nothing the microwave couldn't fix.

The next morning, Mira awoke to the smell of bacon, coffee, and buttery toast. Grayson brought the feast to her on a gilded tray. He hummed and smiled, glowing with energy.

Mira could barely raise her head. The cat had settled on top of her and was purring like a motor, and when she finally succeeded in stirring him, he rose at a sloth's pace, practically stumbling off of her. Then he made a horrible gagging noise, tumbled off the bed, and threw up next to her slippers.

Grayson laughed and cheerfully cleaned the mess while Mira pushed herself to a seated position. She felt like she was swimming through oil. Her head pounded with a dull pain. The breakfast, which had smelled so delicious from afar, overwhelmed her, and the sight of the congealing yellow middles of the eggs sent her into a similar state as the queasy cat.

Then she spied water and aspirin on the tray. Grayson had thought of everything. She took her remedy gratefully, then picked at the toast. How was Grayson so chipper? He had easily doubled her, drink-for-drink last night, yet here he was, *whistling* while cleaning up cat puke.

Grayson returned for her tray. He raised an eyebrow when he saw how much food was left on it, but he didn't make any snide remarks about it. Instead, he brushed her hair from her forehead and planted a tender kiss on her temple. "My poor Mira, paying for last night's sins," he murmured, then whisked the tray away with the efficiency of a British butler.

Mira dozed for a few minutes, and, when she awoke, Grayson was clothed in full business attire, rolling suitcase in hand.

"My cab is here," he said.

Grayson was off for one of the biggest sales trips of the year with one of his wealthiest, most showy clients.

He turned to the cat, who was now curled up on Grayson's own pillow. "Take good care of her for me. Don't let her bring any of her boyfriends home."

The cat raised his head and let out a scratchy "mraow" in response.

And then Grayson was gone for a whole week.

Mira stretched out on the empty bed and luxuriated in

the soft sheets and the streak of sunlight coming through the window. The Cat stretched too. "You ok after your little throw-up?" she asked him. "I certainly hope so, because you have a big day coming up this week!"

Thursday was The Cat's neutering appointment. But today, they had no plans beyond rest, recovery, and re-watching *Bridgerton*.

Mira's phone dinged, and she opened the Instagram message before she had a chance to process who it was from.

DON'T TRUST THE CAT, the message screamed.

It was Sylvie Baine again, insulting her cat. Again.

Mira couldn't resist a peek behind the curtain. She tapped Sylvie's profile picture with her freshly-manicured forefinger.

This account is private.

She knew she should just block her and move on, but none of it made sense. Why would a beautiful influencer keep a private account? And why would she care about Mira's life? Mira decided on a more direct approach.

She typed out and deleted several messages, before she settled on *Please stop harassing me.* She hit send.

Her phone chimed a few seconds later. *Please, I know it sounds crazy, but your cat is not what it seems. You need to get rid of it. Now.*

Mira was intrigued in spite of herself. Her thumbs hovered over her phone for two weighty seconds before she typed out a hasty reply.

Ok. You have my attention. Tell me more.

The reply was almost instant. *Not online. We need to meet.*

Now Mira was miffed. *How stupid do you think I am? I'm not falling for your scam.*

No scam. Sylvie replied. *I used to date Grayson. We had a cat too.*

A n hour later, Mira nibbled half-heartedly on a chocolate croissant while her too-milky latte turned cold.
Sylvie was fifteen minutes late. Mira was about to
leave, when she felt a tap on her shoulder.

Mira turned and beheld the stylish, willowy blonde
behind her. Her face was obscured by enormous dark
glasses, but it was the woman from the picture.

She trailed a cloud of peony and rose as she came
around the table and settled herself opposite Mira. They
were both silent as she took the lid off her drink, inhaled
the scents of ginger and turmeric, and then downed half
of it with determination. Then, she took a big breath, let
it out, and whipped off her glasses, staring Mira straight
in the eye.

Mira's breath caught loudly in her throat. She couldn't
help it. Sans glasses, Sylvie was at least thirty years older
than in her picture, and she had to be twenty years older
than Grayson. She looked good, though. She had the
glowing skin and hair usually reserved for celebrities,
and judging from the immobility of her lineless forehead,
she'd had some work done. But her glittering blue eyes
held a lifetime of sorrows, her crow's feet cracked at the
slightest grimace or grin, and purple circles peeking out
from her concealer belied insomnia and stress.

At Mira's unsubtle gasp, Sylvie winced, but held her
gaze, and began her tale.

"I've never told anyone this story. I believed I was crazy, or perhaps temporarily insane or blinded by love, but
when I saw your picture with Grayson and that...*thing...*"

"Our cat, Basil."

"You shouldn't have named him," Sylvie scolded.

Mira felt chastened for no good reason and hurried to
add, "Well, we mostly call him 'The Cat' anyway."

Sylvie cleared her throat. "*Anyway,* when I saw the cat

I knew I had to say something. I could have just assumed that you had posted the different photos well after the cat had grown, but something was off. The plant in your photo—the Christmas cactus—"

"Vincent?"

Sylvie paused. Her forehead struggled to move. "You named your cactus Vincent?"

Mira shrank into her chair.

"So this...*Vincent* was blooming in both photos. Unless you took them a year apart, it just wouldn't make sense. I had a cat like that once. So I knew I had to say something. I knew your life was in danger."

Mira downed her coffee and grabbed her bag. "You obviously need help, Ms. Baine, and I'm sorry I can't give you any. Have a good day." Her chair scraped loudly against the wood floor as she stood.

"You wake up with scratches, don't you?" Sylvie said.

Mira paused, then plunked back down in her chair, still clutching her bag. "Have you been talking to Dr. Choi?"

Sylvie pushed back her flowing linen sleeves to reveal a row of silver scars, long-healed versions of Mira's own.

"I would wake up with mysterious scratches. Bite marks, sometimes, too. Grayson laughed at me, said I was too cozy with Cocoa, our cat, said we should get rid of him. But I loved the cat. I knew it couldn't be him. But I grew weaker, started hearing and seeing things. I had heard the old tales of crazy cat ladies, of cat-scratch fever, but I thought that was just prejudice, disguised as science. But I started looking up the symptoms. I had them all."

Mira put down her bag, transfixed by the tale and the oddly charismatic storyteller. Sylvie looked vaguely familiar to Mira, as if she had seen her some time in her childhood. She was certainly old enough. Encouraged by Mira's attention, Sylvie continued.

"And there were other signs. Strange signs. The rapid

growth was the strangest of course, but I noticed other things. Cocoa would get sick for no clear reason. He developed unseemly infections. He would grow listless and—I know it sounds strange to say, but he would be depressed. Or so I believed. Grayson thought I was crazy, and to be honest, so did I...This was twenty years ago. I had just landed my role on *Days of Our Lives*."

Mira remembered why Sylvie looked so familiar. Mira's mother loved soap operas, and when Mira would stay home from school when she was sick, she would eat soup and crackers on the couch and get lost in the glamorous, improbable lives of the characters. It was a definite upgrade from the daily drama of middle school. Indeed, Mira had gotten 'sick' a lot during seventh grade. A name sprang to her lips: "Victoria!"

Sylvie smiled sadly. "You were a fan?"

"My mother was," Mira said.

"Ah, yes, you're a bit young to have been invested in my one and only season on daytime television."

"But how...how were you and Grayson...?" Mira began, frantically calculating in her mind. Grayson was only a few years older than her. He would have been seventeen or eighteen when Mira was watching soaps with her mother. "He was a teenager twenty years ago."

"Was he?" Sylvie looked at her with something like pity.

Mira reasoned that it was possible that a 28-year-old actress would get involved with an 18-year-old guy. Maybe Grayson had sophisticated tastes. Maybe Sylvie had poor taste.

"All I know is that when we met, Grayson said he was in his thirties. Maybe he was mature for his age. Or maybe he's been lying to you. Whatever the case, I'd love to know his secret. Korean face masks? Injectables?"

She wasn't kidding. Sylvie's eyes glinted with envy.

Mira cleared her throat. "So, what happened?"

"I lost it, ok? Total breakdown. You may remember Victoria's sudden off-screen death on *Days*? They had to cut me—fast. I ended up in the hospital. When I got out, Grayson and Cocoa were both gone."

Mira rose to leave. "I'm sorry that happened to you, Ms. Baine, but I don't see what this has to do with me. Lots of people have cats, you know."

Sylvie clutched at Mira's arm, her gel manicure carving half-moons into Mira's skin. "But not like *that* cat! Not pitch black with a white star on the forehead—not with the rapid growth and the scratches and all the rest! Don't you see? I wasn't crazy! It was the cat! It was *always the cat!*"

The coffeehouse had fallen silent. A couple of people held up their phones, recording.

The young manager trembled as he approached. "Ma'am? I have to ask you to leave."

Sylvie whipped her head toward him, blonde locks flying, bared her teeth, and hissed.

Mira spent an ordinary week without Grayson. At work, she answered the phone with her cheeriest "Lipincott Publishing, how may I direct your call?" At home, she fell asleep to the sounds of Jane Austen's witty dialogue and The Cat's heavy purrs.

The video of Sylvie's coffeehouse breakdown began making the rounds on the internet. "Crazy Cat Lady" was well on its way to becoming a classic meme. Thankfully, Mira's face was turned away from the camera.

Finally, Mira's curiosity about Sylvie's story got the better of her, and she ventured into Grayson's holy of holies: his walk-in closet. Of the two of them, he had the bigger closet, featuring rows of pristine designer suits and Italian shoes, silk neckties and coordinating handkerchiefs, gleaming cufflinks and tie pins. And, she knew, a heavy black box, pushed to the back of his underwear drawer.

She'd seen it only once, when Grayson had lost his favorite tie pin. He'd accused her of laundering it, of being careless with his things. She'd searched the whole apartment and found the pin inside a blazer pocket. Now, she returned to the drawer and slid the box from its secret place, gingerly avoiding the rows of meticulously-rolled overpriced underwear. She wasn't even sure what she was looking for, but if there were any clues about Grayson's past, any inkling of evidence for Sylvie's story, a mysterious black box seemed like a good place to start the search.

The box was wooden, painted a rich black, and the lid creaked open to reveal a luxurious, blood-red velvet lining. And staring up at her, right on top, was the photograph of their little family of three: Mira, The Cat, and Grayson.

Mira was touched that Grayson had taken the time to print the photo out, that he cherished it enough to keep it among his prized possessions. He had written *Basil* and the date on the back, in his precise, slanting print. Mira felt foolish. She had gone looking for some outlandish subterfuge and found only that Grayson was sentimental.

She picked up the photo, admiring its details, and then her mouth went dry.

The next photo in the stack was nearly identical: A stunning redhead beamed up at the camera. In her arms was a tiny black kitten. Grayson held a protective arm around them both.

The name of the cat was Soot, the date, 2017, the year she and Grayson had met.

"So what?" Mira said aloud to The Cat, who had nosed his way through the cracked closet door and was now happily rolling around on top of Grayson's old Nikes. "So he was seeing someone before we met. No big deal, is it Cat?"

The Cat burrowed his face into the sneaker, purring furiously. Mira returned to the stack of photos. The next picture, labeled *Oscar, 2012*, featured more of the same, this time with a brunette and a bigger version of The Cat. In 2006, he posed with a cat called Ganymede and a bespectacled librarian-type, hair pulled into a tight bun. And in 2001, Grayson grinned next to a twenty-something Sylvie Baine and a black kitten wearing a bright red bow—*Cocoa*. Grayson looked the same as always: golden hair, glowing skin, blinding smile.

As Mira flipped through the photos, they turned grainy, from Kodachrome to black and white, to the brownish tones of a daguerreotype—one of those silly novelty photos they sell at tourist traps, no doubt: OLDE-FASHIONED PHOTOS HERE! MAKE A MEMORY YOU'LL NEVER FORGET!

Only the women and the names of The Cat changed: Henry, Oscar, Lucifer, Algernon, each cradled in the arms of a besotted woman. Grayson remained constant.

"What's going on here, Basil?" In light of his various doppelgangers, she thought she should address The Cat by his proper name. The Cat ceased his frantic shoe rubbing and looked right at her with his wide, green eyes.

"Are you not a rescue at all? Did you come from a breeder? From a long line of special cats?"

The Cat blinked.

"So, your cat dad had a lot of girlfriends before he met me. But it's really not any of my business, is it, Basil?"

The Cat flicked an ear in response, then zoomed out of the closet.

Mira sighed. "Look at me, interrogating a cat. The next thing you know, I'll be hissing at some hapless coffeehouse manager."

That mental image frightened Mira enough that she picked up the phone and made another appointment with Dr. Quill.

The Cat had complained loudly from the minute Mira put him in his carrier to the minute she left the vet's office for his neutering procedure. Now, Mira sipped nervously at her lavender tea as Dr. Quill settled in the armchair opposite her.

This time, Mira resolved to tell her everything, so she started with the fateful peanut-butter-cup fight. But before she could even get to The Cat, Dr. Quill stopped her.

"When you confronted Grayson about the chocolate, what did he say?"

"He said that I was remembering wrong, that I had eaten the chocolate."

"And was he right?"

"No! At least—I don't think so? I was so sure that he was wrong, Dr. Quill. I knew I didn't eat that chocolate. But now...? I'm not sure about anything." Before she could stop herself, Mira was crying all over Dr. Quill's green velvet sofa.

Dr. Quill put down her notebook and handed Mira a box of tissues.

"I believe you, Mira."

Dr. Quill sent Mira home with a pamphlet called "Loving a Narcissist." Reading it was a bit like looking at a funhouse mirror: she both recognized and rejected the image she saw. She learned terms like "countering," when the narcissist questions a person's memories, and "trivializing," when they invalidate another's feelings. She learned about gaslighting and covert narcissism and Dorian Gray syndrome and malignant narcissism. And as she read, the bits and pieces of her relationship with Grayson began to fall into place.

And Sylvie's story made sense, too. If Grayson really had this narcissistic personality disorder, it might explain

Sylvie's breakdown. He had gaslit her into thinking she was crazy. And he was trying to do the same thing to Mira.

She was interrupted in her musings by a call from Stephanie, the receptionist for Dr. Choi. "We couldn't do the neutering procedure today. Basil has an infection."

"What kind of infection?"

Stephanie paused. "You'll need to talk to Dr. Choi about that, Mrs. Hallward."

When Mira arrived at Dr. Choi's office, The Cat was asleep in his carrier. Dr. Choi's face was grim.

"I've never seen anything like it, Mrs. Hallward. Our staff is stumped. If it didn't sound crazy, I'd say it bears all the markings of—well—a human STI."

Mira blushed. "I can promise you, Dr. Choi, Basil is *not* that kind of cat."

Dr. Choi squeezed her eyes shut and pinched the bridge of her nose. She let out a big breath before responding. "I said it bears the *markings* of an STI, not that it *is* one. Frankly, I've never seen these exact symptoms in a cat. Can you think of any changes, anything unusual at all in Basil's lifestyle or diet?"

Mira shook her head.

"Well, we can't perform the procedure if he has an infection. We put him on some antibiotics, and we gave him something to help him sleep. Keep an eye on him, and let us know if anything gets worse."

Mira took the Cat to the front desk and handed over her credit card. The exorbitant fee cut only mildly through her mental haze.

Unseemly infections, Sylvie had said.

Surely it was coincidence, nothing to worry about. Everything was fine.

But Dr. Quill had urged her to listen to her gut, and her gut was not fine.

Something was bothering her about Sylvie's story, about the dozens of identical cats in Grayson's past, and about what she had read in Dr. Quill's pamphlet.

This was more than ordinary narcissism. Mira suspected that she was married to a sociopath.

At home, Mira tore through Grayson's underwear drawer until she found the black box, reading the names of the cats again and again. *Henry, Basil, Oscar*—they all seemed so old-timey and familiar, like family names. And then she came to the faded brown photo, the one that reeked of fairground novelty. But if this was a fairground novelty, it was the best facsimile she'd ever seen. And on the back, in Grayson's handwriting, she found a faint inscription: *Sybil and Romeo, 1891. Love, D.G.*

The fragments juttered together in Mira's mind. Sybil, Basil, and Henry were all characters in a novel: Oscar Wilde's *The Picture of Dorian Gray*.

And everyone told her an English degree was useless.

"Grayson, we need to talk."

Mira sat serenely on the couch, stroking The Cat coiled in her lap. Spread out in front of her on the coffee table were the pictures.

Grayson sighed like a put-upon teenager. "Babe, I just got home. Can't this wait?" He kept talking from the bedroom as he deposited his bags. "You always want to 'have a talk' when it's convenient for *you* and inconvenient for *me*." Mira heard the shower faucet sputter on.

"Grayson!" she called. Then, in a voice she'd only ever heard her own mother use, she called again, "Grayson Hallward. I know what you are!"

The running water jerked to a halt.

"Seriously, Mira?" Grayson grumbled, as he rounded

the corner to the living room. Mira's heartbeat picked up at the sight of his shirtless state. She knew there was a reason she'd married him. "Can't you let a guy shower in peace for once?" he demanded. Then he caught a glimpse of the photos arrayed on the coffee table and turned stone-still.

"You went through my personal things?" he growled.

Mira cleared her throat and rehearsed her talking points. Dorian Gray syndrome took up only one paragraph in Dr. Quill's pamphlet, but together with some of the other details about narcissism, Mira had formed a pretty clear picture about Grayson's particular disorder. She had prepared for an intervention.

"Grayson, you know how much I love you—"

"So *that's* why you went through my private things, to show your love? You always do this, Mira—you never respect my boundaries—-"

"Grayson." Mira said, using her stern voice again. "I do love you, and that's why I need to tell you that I know what you are, and I want to help."

Grayson stood stunned for a long moment. Then the silence broke with a snort and a cackle. He was laughing at her.

"Grayson, this isn't funny. A personality disorder isn't something you choose. I want to help you. Let me help you!" Mira pled. As Grayson laughed, Mira stood, letting the Cat lope away (was he *limping* now?), and she walked toward Grayson, arms outstretched.

"You think you know what I am? You think you can help me?" Grayson scoffed, still bent over in laughter.

Mira touched his shoulder. "Please, Grayson."

Grayson caught her wrist in his hand and pulled her against his chest. "Oh, pretty, sweet, insecure Mira. I think you've helped me as much as you can."

An icy jolt shot through Mira's spine. This was not how the intervention was supposed to go. "Please just

listen to me, Grayson. I know about your past relation-
ships, about your obsession with youth, with beautiful
women and nice things. You're so obsessed you only keep
one kind of cat that you get rid of after they get too old.
You even name them after that Oscar Wilde story, *Dorian
Gray*. Because you need to control things, to feel special,
to feel powerful. You're so obsessed that you keep all their
photos, just like the story, as if photographs can somehow
preserve your youth. I know all about it, Grayson! But you
can get help—*we*—can get help."

Grayson observed Mira for a moment, considering the
stream of word vomit she had just hurled. Then his eyes
softened. He released his grip on Mira and slumped onto
the sofa, raking a hand through his golden hair.

"I'm sorry you made me lose my temper," Grayson said.

Silence roared between them.

Mira couldn't breathe; she couldn't speak. Instead, she
sputtered.

"You're sorry *I made you* lose your temper?"

"Babe, don't take my words out of context," Grayson
said. "Look, if it will help you calm down, I'll go to couples counseling, ok?"

Now it was Mira's turn to laugh. "You want *me* to calm
down?"

Then Mira calmly gathered the photos splayed on the
coffee table and calmly carried them to the fireplace.

"I'm sorry *you* made *me* do this," she said, and tossed
the whole pile into the flames.

Mira wasn't sure what she expected to happen. She
knew she would hurt Grayson by burning his sa-
cred photographs, but a piece of her also hoped that
this drastic action would make him admit his problem. In
some secret place, she almost believed that there was a

dark magic to the photos, that destroying them would kill the monstrous narcissist in her husband.

She didn't expect more laughter.

He laughed until he cried, until he shook, sending The Cat sulking on the highest perch of his carpeted tree. Mira slid to the ground beside the fireplace, mouth open in disbelief.

When he was done laughing, he poured them each a large glass of bourbon and put the glasses, the bottle, and an opaque prescription bottle on a tray, which he placed on the coffee table next to Mira's crumpled form.

"Have a drink, babe. And maybe an antipsychotic or two."

"Grayson, Dr. Quill didn't prescribe me any—"

"You have to be crazy to believe that story you just told me. You thought the photographs held mystical power, like some kind of cursed Victorian portrait? Seriously insane. I'm worried about you."

Mira was shaking. She reached for her glass and took a tiny sip, then gathered her courage. "I'm not crazy, Grayson. I know you have a—a *pattern*. I talked to Sylvie Baine—"

"The cat lady from the internet?"

"She's a *person*, Grayson, a person you used to date."

"She's way too old for me, babe. Now I *know* you're crazy."

Mira gestured wildly toward the blackened, curling photographs. "You kept the evidence!" she yelled.

"Evidence that you burned, Mira, and why? Because you think I made some deal with the devil for the photos to age while I live? Well, the pictures are gone now, and I'm still here."

Mira drank, willing herself not to respond to his ridiculous accusation, until she could no longer keep from defending herself. "I didn't really think that, Grayson, that's just made-up."

"Especially the portrait part," Grayson murmured. "That was Oscar's idea."

Was it just Mira's imagination, or had Grayson's voice changed? Why did he sound like he was trying to pull off a bad British accent? She shook her head. "The whole *story* was Oscar's idea, Grayson, it's a work of fiction."

"Not all of it," Grayson replied with a smirk.

Mira's head was beginning to swim. "What do you... what are you talking about?"

"You see, *babe*, only life can prolong life. Oscar chose a portrait to make some statement about art and beauty; that was his invention. But when I made the deal, the demon clearly explained that only living creatures can carry the sins of other creatures. And Lady Wotton had a cat."

"Romeo," Mira whispered.

"Sybil named him that; she fancied herself a real actress. Poor Sybil."

Mira's vision blurred. The drink was strong. Too strong. "Poor Sybil...and poor me and poor Sylvie Baine... why?" Mira could barely form words, nevermind coherent sentences.

"Why the women? Well, for one thing, it's fun. You can't say we haven't had fun together." He smirked and knocked back the rest of his drink. "But since you'll be in a psych ward soon, I may as well tell you that the demon I made a deal with is an incubus. I give him what he wants—women, blood—he gives me what I want: eternity, youth, my sins cast into the bodies of a distinguished feline lineage."

"The scratches were never from the cat..." Mira managed, through the looming fog.

"Very good. I knew you were a smart one," said Grayson.

"And the cat's blood line...you need his bloodline. I guess we got lucky with his neutering procedure..."

Grayson froze. "His what?"

"I took him to the vet to be neutered, but—"

Before Mira could finish her sentence, Grayson was on top of her, his hand gripping her throat. "I told you The Cat was special, Mira, one-of-a-kind! Do you know what this means? Do you know what I'll have to do if Basil is the last of his line? I told you to stay out of my private business, Mira."

Grayson's normally fair, glowing face was an unnatural shade of red, flanked by darkness encroaching at the edges of Mira's vision. Mira grabbed frantically for some weapon until her fingers closed around the fire poker. She swung it with all the strength she could muster.

Grayson stopped the blow, easily taking the sharp instrument from her weakened hands. He gripped it like a spear and lunged.

It was at that moment that The Cat leapt from his scratch-tree and pounced onto Mira's chest. He made himself huge, arching his back and baring his teeth in a hiss. He was fast. Faster than Grayson, faster than Mira's frantic attempts to push him away. She felt something warm seeping into her shirt. Blood.

Grayson's mouth hung open in shock, and his eyes went wide with an emotion Mira had never seen on him: fear. "Stupid Cat!" he yelled. "Stupid, stupid cat!"

Mira beheld the limp figure in her arms, felt its shuddering breaths, and she cradled him to her chest, trying to stop the bleeding.

"He's still alive!" Grayson yelled. He scrambled for his phone. "What's that vet's number? We can still save him." He was panicked, fumbling. "My stupid hands won't work." He muttered. "What the—" He dropped the phone, staring open-mouthed at his gnarled and twisted fingers. *Arthritis.*

Mira looked at him and gasped. His silky blonde hair had gone white, and his hairline had receded. Wrinkles cracked his forehead; brown spots appeared on his arms and hands. He sank to his knees.

"Mira, please. Help me. We have to save Basil."

Mira wanted to save Basil, but all she could do was hold him and stroke his face. She watched his green eyes close, saw, from the corner of her eye, Grayson shrink to the ground in pain. Both bodies became very still. Then she watched in horror as Grayson's skin peeled away, rotting before her eyes, until only bones remained.

Then, all she saw was darkness.

Mira emerged from her chemical haze still clutching The Cat's furry body. He felt lighter in death, though he was still warm. Still…purring?

Basil was purring.

Basil was alive.

The shock of it cleared her vision. The Basil she held in her arms was a fuzzy, round six-month old, and he was purring. He opened his eyes as if from a deep sleep and let out an adorable kittenish yawn.

On the floor beside them, the bones of Dorian Gray dissolved into dust.

THE NURSERY

Autumn Swindoll

12:57 AM

The night's darkness nestled everywhere, disrupted only by the pool of yellow light in this corner of the nursery. Marielle could faintly see the upstairs banister in the unlit hall beyond the open door. She sat in the cushioned glider, her feet extended, exhausted, on the ottoman. On the dresser beside her sat a basket heaped with burp cloths, nursing pads, lanolin and empty bottles. She breathed slowly and deliberately, just like the birthing coach had taught her. *You only have to get through this moment,* she told herself. *And this moment. Inhale. Now this moment. Exhale.* She tried to loosen her clenched jaw.

It turned out that she needed the breathing almost as much now as she had the day before yesterday. She had breathed through each wave of birth pains, through the torrent of the delivery itself. Now she breathed through the feedings.

The tiny newborn, Pip, nestled in her arms, was still figuring out how to eat the most primitive of foods. Who knew such miniscule jaws could practically suck the lifeblood out of you? Dribbles of milk ran down his cheeks, onto the flannel blanket her grandmother had embroidered for him.

Then without warning, Pip pulled his tiny mouth away from her breast with a yank.

Marielle winced with the searing pain. She attempted a slow, mindful breath. She attempted not to squeeze the baby too furiously. And then that mouth, too small and uncoordinated even to maintain its own eating, opened wide and let out a piercing wail. The creamy stillness of the air turned into a wavering buzz. Marielle's breath caught in her throat. Her body, fatigued, achy, and mis-shapen, shuddered in the onslaught of soundwaves. Her stitches stung. She felt a contraction seize her chest. She gripped her shrieking, blanketed child with the intensity of survival. She tried to remember not to shake it, or throw it out the window, or scream right back at it. *Exhale,* she reminded herself. *Exhale, then inhale. He's just a baby, he doesn't mean any of it.*

"Shhh, shhh," Marielle toned to the baby, shoving her cracked nipple back into his ever-demanding little cavern of a mouth. She felt like she might fall in and never quit falling.

1:34 AM

Pip finally fell asleep. Marielle already dreaded his next feeding.

As she mustered the energy to place him back in his crib, she glimpsed an edge of light outside the nursery doorway. She looked, and there in the hallway landing, she saw it—a great, golden beast resembling a lioness standing at the top of the stairs. Long, pointed horns stretched from either side of its stately head. Traces of yellow light glinted on its silky haunches and flickered in its eyes. Behind it, to one side, the edge of the landing dropped off to the first floor below. To the other side, the hall led to several doors, all shrouded in the dark.

The gleaming beast peered into the nursery as though it knew something. Marielle leapt to her feet, thrusting Pip onto the ottoman. His tiny form swayed on the footrest while she stood entranced.

The glowing eyes peered toward her from the hallway, gently watching from between its broad horns. Marielle stared at those eyes, her sight roving over the creature's bold, sturdy muscles, the twitching tail. Its glistening coat seemed to suggest that it took good care of itself. A forepaw mewed at the carpet. Leaning forward as if to peer through an apparition, she met its eyes. For all its wild shape, its eyes were surprisingly serene. *I must really be losing it,* Marielle marveled.

"You figured I was close enough to the edge to say hello, didn't you," Marielle whispered. "So you came to meet me here."

The beast dipped its stately chin. It curved its neck and stepped, blinking slowly, to rove the landing once more, its coat catching the yellow light in glistening streaks. Marielle watched it in wonder. It was such a grand creature, and strong. Were such creatures common sightings in these night watches?

The shadow of the listing ottoman swayed on the nursery wall. Marielle looked around. Everything was calm and quiet–even the baby for this liminal moment. The cubbies of onesies and the board books from aunts and uncles lined up impeccably on the designer shelves. Everything looked Pinterest-perfect, she thought. Everything except for the baby, herself, and the beast.

When she brought her eyes back to the doorway, she saw the beast bent forward. It wrangled a mass of flesh, which hung from its mouth. Its muscular jaws tore chunks of pink meat from between tufts of fur and strands of white connective tissues. *Ugh!* Marielle's stomach turned. "If you're not even real, why do you have to do that here?" she implored. She wondered what unfortunate creature from beyond the borders of sanity had suffered to become this meal. She only ever wanted to see meat in tidy cuts, packaged in plastic at the grocery store.

The baby whimpered, and in an instant, the beast and its dinner disappeared into the darkness.

Marielle shuddered. She turned to Pip, still on the ottoman, lone and afloat in space. His tiny eyes blinked between incomprehension and wonder. She thought he looked so small and fragile, so surrounded by empty air. She felt the air and lamp-light all about herself, too, like an amniotic bath. She too was afloat. The endless waves of feeding, pooping, sleeping, and soothing had eroded all the familiar shorelines. It was just her and this needy babe, adrift together on this vast new sea of being alive. She scooped him up gently and set him down in his crib.

3:40 AM

Too weary to walk downstairs to her own bed, Marielle kept vigil from the glider in the corner. She let out a long exhale and watched the patterned curtains sway in her vision as she rocked. Her gaze tracked the fabric's interlocking petals from the floor to overhead, to the shadow cast by the valence on the wall. It drifted to the crib, where the peaceful rise and fall of the swaddled bundle indicated that Pip was finally asleep. Content that the baby slept, Marielle let her arms slump on the armrests, and her heavy eyelids began to sink.

In her slumber, Marielle became aware of a strong odor. Stirring from sleep brought the sting of her stitches back to full force. She groaned. The smell wasn't the mild stench of newborn diapers she'd become so familiar with in the past two days. It was pungent and briney. She dreamt twice that she was opening her eyes, but found they remained shut. Then she heard Pip's hungry grunts, and her eyes shot open. When they did, she saw the source of the smell.

A huge winged creature perched on the crib's edge nearest her. Its gray claws grasped the crib rail and its great white wings flapped above. From its face extended a horrible, enormous beak. Marielle sat motionless, wondering if she was dreaming or had truly lost her mind. Pip began to cry in earnest. At the sound, the great bird cocked its head and let out a piteous screech. It bowed its beak to its breast with a gouging pluck and heaved with exertion as spurts of blood shot like projectile milk over the crib. Plumes of feathers scattered into the air above the babe.

Marielle leapt from her seat. Crimson splattered all

over the crib sheets, the bumpers, and on little Pip himself. "Stop!" she yelled, lunging into the spray. She seized the great fowl and shook it, shoving it off the crib rail. Blood gushed on her. Spattered, she snatched up her child. The bird, too weakened to right itself, lay limp on the nursery floor.

Marielle, too, collapsed on the carpet with Pip in her arms. She crouched around him, frantically running her hand along his little face all covered with blood. Her fingers left streaks where she tried to wipe him clean. An image of him freshly born flashed in her mind. He was coated from forehead to toes. A spurt from the bird, still bleeding where it lay, splashed on her right cheek and across her forehead.

"What is…all this?" She gestured wildly at the gore.

"This is my blood," the bird replied.

Marielle recalled a stained glass she'd seen in a small chapel while touring Europe. It depicted a mother pelican hovering over her starving young, letting her own blood to feed them. She thought about her own blood stain on the glider seat, the soaked linens in the delivery room, the traces of red left in her nursing pads.

She looked at the grand bird, its brilliant white feathers matted red. "Oh God," she whispered. She felt as depleted as it looked, drained of every life-giving fluid.

Her eyes blinked, and she saw the carpet pale and clean. The bird was gone.

She realized her hand was still roving restlessly over the face of her babe. She gasped, seeing his pristine face. He was sleeping peacefully with a milky haze about his mouth, no trace of blood. She climbed back up into the glider and collapsed, exhausted, clutching the infant near. Two trails of milk and blood seeped down her shirt.

AN UNLICENSED HUNT

Michael Hustead

D id the Arugula in my salad just yell, "Don't eat me"?

No, of course not.

"Arugula doesn't yell anything," I said. I glared at my salad, daring it to contradict me. It didn't. I stared at it for another moment, just to be safe. Nothing happened.

"You've been working too hard, Matt, I said, looking around my dingy office. Being a game warden was tough, especially with deer season newly underway. I'd been working long hours, mostly at night, for the last week. No wonder I was hearing things. I picked up my fork and went to take a bite.

"Stop!"

I screamed. Hey, it was a manly scream; more of a barbaric yawp, really. You'd scream too if your lunch started talking. I gave my food an experimental poke with the fork. The salad yelped and jumped. I yelped and jumped. My knee struck the card table which toppled backward, spilling my lunch across the floor.

"Crap!" I surveyed the ruins of my lunch, scattered across the dirty floor of my office, and sighed. That was less than ideal. Or maybe ideal? Nine out of ten doctors say you shouldn't eat your food if it's talking to you. The tenth doctor just has you committed.

"Salad? Are you talking to me?"

Silence, even from the arugula, which was probably the best possible outcome.

But then, "Are you stupid?"

That definitely came from the salad.

"Probably." I conceded. "Or at least insane." As a Game Warden, I'd been called every name in the book, but to be called stupid by salad was proof that I'd reached rock bottom.

"It's good to know what your options are," the salad replied.

I crouched down and glared at my scattered lunch. "Since when does arugula talk?"

The arugula let out a long, drawn out, world-weary sigh. "Look, just relax, ok? I'm coming out."

The leaves shifted, and a creature crawled out from under my lunch. I blinked. It was small, only about four inches tall, and covered in coarse brown fur with two stubby horns poking out of the top of its head. There was a second shift of greens, and a piece of arugula fluttered to the side as the thing's tail rose up behind it.

My first thought was, *Oh thank God, my salad isn't talking to me; maybe I'm not going crazy after all.* Then I realized a tiny demon-monster had just crawled out of my food, and that didn't seem much better.

The thing moved toward me, a tiny spear clutched in its hands.

I backpedaled, reaching for my gun and then stopped. I didn't want to start blasting away in my office. The paperwork would be a nightmare. I snatched an umbrella from the floor by my desk instead and brandished it at the creature. "Freeze!"

The monster froze.

"Good," I said. "Just stay right there."

Now what? Hold the demon-monster-thing here until…when? Who do you call for this? The government? That's no help. I work for the government. No one knows better than me how useless *they* are. A priest then? Don't they specialize in demons?

The monster moved, and I jumped, nearly dropping the umbrella.

"Don't move, demon," I warned. "I'm going to call a priest and he'll…send you back to Hell or something."

"I'm not a demon," the creature snapped, shaking its spear at me.

"That's what a demon *would* say. I think. If you were a demon, would you admit it?"

The creature tilted its head. "Probably not."

"Aha!" I reached for my cell phone. Where do I find the

number for a priest?

"But...if I *weren't* a demon, would I claim to be one?"

I frowned. The thing had a point. "What are you then?"

"I'm a Heinzelmannchen."

"Bless you."

"What?" The creature frowned, its furry brow crinkling up. For a demon it was surprisingly cute, although I didn't particularly care for that spear. It was only a few inches long, but it looked sharp enough to take my eye out.

"Nothing," I said, not wanting to anger the thing. "What is a Heinzel-what-have-you?"

"A kobold," it said, standing up straight and thrusting out its chest.

"Oh," I said. *What the Hell is a kobold?*

The creature noticed my confusion and sighed, its shoulder slumping. "A house spirit."

"Like a ghost?"

"What? No! A kobold is a guardian spirit." It stared at me expectantly and then slammed its spearbutt on the floor and stomped its furry feet. It would have been more impressive if the creature didn't so closely resemble a gerbil. With horns. And a spear. The creature muttered to itself for a moment...something about ignorant Americans? It composed itself and tried again, speaking slowly and distinctly. "A kobold guards the home from intruders and evil spirits."

Great. The weird demon-rat-thing's talking to me like I'm an idiot.

"So a house spirit. Shouldn't you be in a house?"

The kobold's face went all twitchy, and I realized it was about to cry. *Great job, Matt. You reduced the spirit-rat to tears.* Maybe this is why I lived alone. Now I knew what to tell my mother next time she asked.

"Look," I said. "It's no big deal. It was just a question."

The kobold collapsed in a despondent pile on the floor, its spear clattering to the ground at its side. "I have no home. The Old Country has changed too much. No families keep guardian spirits anymore. I immigrated looking for work, but it's not like anyone makes want ads that say, 'Needed: Experienced Heinzelmannchen.' It's not a thing."

I let out an explosive breath and put down the umbrella. Whatever this critter was, it didn't seem to be a threat. I flopped into my desk chair, which groaned in protest. I stared at the kobold; the kobold stared at the floor. The silence quickly became uncomfortable. *Say something encouraging, Matt.*

"Um…" *Brilliant start. Try again.* "Do you have a name or something?"

"Johann Friedrich Konrad Horst Heinzelmannchen," it said, still staring at the floor. "The thirty-sixth."

"Oh," I replied, a little dumbfounded. "So…Joe it is."

The kobold ignored me. I leaned back in my chair and drummed my fingers on the desk. What to do? Somehow calling a priest didn't seem as helpful now. What would I tell him? Yes, Father, a house spirit. I call him Joe. Would you make him go away?

"Look here, Joe. This is a government office. I'm a game warden, you see." I pointed helpfully at the little wooden sign on my desk. It read, *Matthew Hardy: Game Warden.* "I can't really have a kobold here. It's…ah…against regulations. Pets in the office and all that. You'll have to leave."

The kobold ignored me. Maybe it didn't understand? I stood up and walked to the office door hoping it would take the hint. The moment my hand touched the handle the kobold let out a blood-curdling shriek.

"NO!"

I froze, my hand on the doorknob. "What's your problem?

"Don't open the door!"

I rolled my eyes and turned the doorknob. This was getting absurd. I wasn't going to be trapped in my office with some bossy little house spirit. I heard a soft whistling sound and then pain exploded in my hand. I yelped and jumped back. The little monster's spear was embedded in the back of my hand.

He threw his spear at me!

"What's the matter with you?!"

"I warned you," Joe said, leveling a finger at me. " Step away from the door or feel the wrath of the heinzelman-nchen."

"Feel *your* wrath? Listen here, you little rat, you've just assaulted a police officer. I can…"

I stopped. What could I do? Arrest him? The park didn't exactly have a holding cell for kobolds. Maybe those plastic buckets I used for snakes would work?

"Ok," I said, trying to calm down. "I'm sorry, but you really can't stay here. And you can't go around throwing spears at people either."

"I can't leave this place. It's not safe."

I sighed and stepped away from the door. Clearly, Joe wasn't going to be reasonable about this.

It's ok, Matt. He's hardly the first unreasonable person you've dealt with. Deep breaths. Just keep him talking.

I walked over to my desk and pulled out the first aid kit. The spear may have been small, but it was sharp. The stupid thing was stuck deep in the meat of my hand, and I winced as I pulled it out. Blood trickled down my wrist. I snatched a tissue off my desk and pressed down on the wound until the bleeding stopped.

"So what's your deal?" I asked. I took extra care disinfecting the wound since God only knew what was on that spear.

"I'm being hunted," Joe said. He scuttled across the floor, snatched up his spear where I'd dropped it, and dashed under the cover of my desk.

"Hunted? By what?"

"An elf."

I froze, a band-aid in my hand, and peered under the

desk. Joe was crouched in the shadows as far back as he could get. "You're kidding."

"No."

"A real elf, like *Lord of the Rings*?"

"Lord of *what* rings?" Joe asked.

"You know," I said, waving my hand in the air. "Ancient magical creatures that are all wise and sing songs and stuff."

"Sure," Joe said. "Except less singing, and more eviscerations."

"Oh," I swallowed. "And one of these things is after you?"

"Yes," Joe retreated deeper into the shadows. "He's been hunting me for weeks."

I finished bandaging my hand and put the first aid kit back on the shelf. "Why is this thing after you? What'd you do?"

"Nothing!" Joe protested.

I frowned. I'd heard that a lot. People never did *anything*. It was always the other guy. "So this elf-guy is just chasing you all over the state for fun?"

"He wants my fur for a trophy!"

"Is that legal?"

Joe shrugged. "What difference does that make?"

I bristled at that. I couldn't help it; poachers made my blood boil. Occupational hazard, I suppose. Besides, this wasn't just killing a deer out of season. Joe was a sentient creature; you couldn't just kill him for the fun of it.

"So that's it then? He's hunting you for sport?"

"Yes," Joe chirped. "And…the other thing."

Ah, there it was. I bent down and peered under the desk. "What other thing?"

Joe swallowed and looked around, refusing to meet my gaze. "I might have borrowed something from him. Without permission."

Of course. There's always more to the story. I stood,

grabbed my hat from the desk, and headed for the door.

"Where are you going?" Joe squeaked.

"Out."

"You can't!"

"Yes, I can," I snapped over my shoulder. "I have work to do. I've no time to deal with mythical creatures and their feuds."

There's a sentence I never thought I'd say. For the first time, dealing with a drunken deer hunter without a license seemed like the *preferable* option. I sighed. No one's life is as hard as mine.

"Stop!"

I ignored him and yanked the door open. Something blurred across my vision.

Thwack!

I froze, staring stupidly at the arrow quivering in the door frame next to my head. It was massive. A yard long at least, and lined with strange golden-red feathers I'd never seen before. Behind me, Joe shrieked. I blinked and then threw myself on the ground as another arrow struck the hat off my head and nailed it into the wall behind me.

"Ack!" I screamed and kicked the door shut as hard as I could. Something thudded into the door, and an arrow punched through its point, stopping an inch from my eye. I crab-walked across the floor and took refuge behind the card table, careful to keep my head clear of the windows.

"What did you steal from this guy? He seems really pissed."

"Just some stuff from his castle. Gold and things, nothing important," Joe said from beneath the desk.

"Nothing important!"

"He wasn't using it," Joe protested. "And I needed it to pay my way here. Do you know how much it costs to immigrate?"

"Can't you give it back?"

"I spent it all. Why do you think I'm hiding here?"

"Great," I muttered, peeking around the corner of the card table. A murderous poacher-elf was lurking outside my office because a European house spirit had stolen his treasure to pay for a new life in America. "How does this crap happen to me?"

I could hear my mother now. *Should have gone to law school, Matt. You could have married a nice girl, had a fine career.* Instead I'm hiding behind a card table while an elf shoots arrows into my office.

"I'm getting out of here." I drew my gun and crawled across to the small window to the left of the door. I peeked over the edge of the sill and looked out. The narrow lane that wound past my office was empty. Across the road the trees grew close and thick. There was no sign of the elf. I saw a flash of movement in the underbrush and another arrow crashed through the window into my office. I swear I felt the breeze as it passed over my head. I crouched down, swearing under my breath.

"Ok, then. At least we know where he is." I turned around, careful to keep my head below the window. "Joe, there's just one of these guys, right?"

"Yes," the reply came from the shadows under my desk.

"Then out the back we go."

I crawled across the floor on my hands and knees, forced open the window in the back wall and kicked out the cheap screen.

"Wait for me," Joe called. The kobold dashed across the floor and leapt, catching hold of my belt as I rolled out the window.

I came up in a crouch, gun in hand, and scanned the woods. Nothing.

"So far, so good." I briefly considered running straight into the woods and hoping to lose the elf in the under-growth, but the last thing I wanted was to play hide and seek with this nutcase.

I took a deep breath, leapt to my feet and ran around

the side of the building to where my truck sat parked in the little gravel lot. I dove behind my truck and fumbled for the keys, expecting at any moment to feel an arrow between my shoulder blades. My breath hissed between clenched teeth and I dropped the keys twice before I was able to open the truck. Naturally, the state couldn't splurge for a new truck with automatic locks.

"Come on, Matt, come on," I said.

At last I got the truck open. I threw myself into the cab and started the ignition. An arrow struck the rear window of the truck. I screamed as cracks spider-webbed across the glass. I couldn't see anything. I threw the truck into gear and jolted onto the road as a second arrow struck the window. This time, the glass broke filling the cab with little shards. I hunched down and floored it, sending the truck bouncing down the lane. I took the winding park road at full speed, shrieking around corners until my office was far behind.

At last I pulled over, parked, and collapsed in the seat, panting. I needed a moment to collect my wits. "You alright?"

Joe sat up on the seat next to me and shook out his fur. "I think so. Did we lose him?"

I looked out the broken rear window, but couldn't see anything except the cloud of dust my truck had kicked up. I shook my head. "I don't know. Maybe? We should keep moving though."

I drove out of the state park and down the highway to my house, checking the rearview mirror constantly. I wasn't sure what I expected to see. An elf clothed in shimmering white chasing me down the road on the back of a unicorn? Or flying through the air on a dragon with a flaming sword?

I saw none of those things, and we reached my house without incident.

"This is it?" Joe asked as I slowed to a stop at the curb.

He didn't seem impressed.

"Yep," I said. "It's not much, but no one's shooting arrows into it, so it could be worse."

There's a comparison I never thought I'd make, but that's life, I suppose. The house wasn't impressive; it was one story, and fairly old. I winced a bit looking at the grass, which had really needed to be cut *last* weekend.

"Come on," I said.

I led the way up the sidewalk and unlocked the front door. Once we were inside and the door was securely locked behind us I relaxed and breathed easily.

"This is it," I said, gesturing at the faded furniture in the living room. "Make yourself at home."

I started to walk in, but stopped. Joe was still standing by the front door, looking unnaturally still.

"You alright?" I asked.

"Do you mean it?"

"Umm...mean what?"

"What you said before," Joe squeaked. "You want me to make myself at home?"

"Sure?" I wasn't sure what to say. Just being polite. Honestly, what's the protocol when entertaining a mythical creature after another mythical creature has just tried to turn you into a pincushion?

Joe's eyes filled with tears. "Thank you," he whispered. "You won't regret it."

The little kobold dashed into the kitchen and disappeared into my pantry. A moment later he was back, wearing a flowered apron of all things, and clutching a little broom. Before I could so much as blink he was sprinting through the house, sweeping as if his life depended on it.

"Where did that apron come from?" I asked. "And where did you get a little broom?"

"No time," he answered breathlessly, and continued to clean.

"I know this day could probably get weirder," I said,

watching Joe sweep. "But I really can't imagine how."

I peered into the pantry, half expecting to see a stash of miniature cleaning supplies waiting in there, but there was nothing but a few cans of vegetables and the rather sad looking remains of a loaf of bread, long gone stale. I sighed and went to the fridge for a beer, deliberately ignoring the pile of dirty dishes in my sink. Dishes could wait; I needed a drink.

I opened the beer and collapsed onto my couch. The kobold had abandoned his broom, and was busy dusting the mantle.

"Is this some sort of stress relief thing for you?" I asked, taking a drink of the beer. "You can relax. We're safe from your elf friend."

Joe stopped and stared at me, his gaze incredulous. "What makes you think that?"

"We got away, didn't we?"

The kobold shook his head in disbelief. "He's tracked me all the way from Europe, and halfway across this country. We drove, what, ten minutes down the road and you think we're safe?"

I set my beer down as a pit of ice settled into my stomach. "But he can't come inside, right? Not unless I invite him in? Isn't there supposed to be some kind of threshold thing in effect? I think I saw that on a show once."

"Oh sure," Joe said, returning to his cleaning. "He won't be able to work any magic in here unless you invite him in."

"That's good," I said, taking another drink of my beer. "I've got plenty of sick days stored up. We'll just wait him out. With any luck I can miss most of deer season, too." That thought cheered me up. Cloud, meet your silver lining.

"Of course, he can just set the house on fire and wait for us to run outside," Joe said. "Or come inside and beat us to death with his bare hands."

I sat up straight. So much for silver linings. "We have to leave now!"

"And go *where?*" Joe asked. "If we go outside then he *can* use magic. Not to mention the arrows." He finished his dusting and started scrubbing the tiles in front of the fireplace. Was that a tiny bucket and sponge he had now? Where did he get these things?

"So we just sit here and wait for him to burn my house down while you clean?"

"Don't worry, I have a plan," Joe assured me, scrubbing away.

Great. At least I'd die with a spotless house. I shook my head. There wasn't time for this. I knew one thing for certain: I wasn't putting my faith in a kobold wearing a flowery apron.

I hurried into my bedroom and stuffed clothes into a backpack as fast as I could. I threw in a large buck knife, some deodorant, a toothbrush, and my phone charger as well. The sun was starting to set, and I was ready to get out of there. I checked my gun, stuffed two spare clips and a box of ammunition into my bag, slung the whole thing over my shoulder and headed back into the living room.

"Joe," I called.

The kobold didn't answer. I looked around the living room. There was no sign of him. The room was spotless, though. I blinked. Literally spotless. The tile shone. This place hadn't looked this good since I moved in. Even my beaten up living room set looked like something from a showroom floor.

I heard a thump from the kitchen, and I hurried in, my hand on my gun. Joe stood on a stool in front of the sink, which was now filled with soapy water.

"What are you doing?"

"Saving our lives," he replied without looking up. "What does it look like?"

"Saving our lives," I repeated, "...by doing the dishes?"

He stared at me, soapy water dripping from his left horn. "It's not about the dishes, Matt."

"Right," I said. "Ok. Look, you do all the dishes you want. I'm getting out of here before the psycho death-elf shows up."

I turned on my heel and stalked out of the kitchen, grumbling to myself.

I should have made my living selling shrimp out of a van. Fishmongers don't have days like this.

I threw open the front door. The elf was standing on my front porch. He was tall and lean with gray skin and a face like a hatchet. I yelped and slammed the door shut, but he kicked it back in my face. I reeled backward, and the elf came through the door, a knife in his hand.

I screamed as he stabbed and thrust, forcing me back down the hall.

"Joe," I cried out. "A little help here."

I didn't know what the silly kobold could do to help me, but I wasn't thinking too clearly. A deranged elf trying to perforate your bowels will do that to you. I drew my gun, but the elf lashed out with the knife, slicing across the back of my hand. I cried out, and the gun tumbled away.

I roared and charged forward, barreling into the elf's midsection. He grunted in pain. Or maybe it was just surprise at the stupidity of my charge, because without missing a beat he brought his elbow down onto the back of my neck.

The blow drove me to my knees, and I landed on the floor coughing and choking. I rolled to the side just as the elf tried to stomp on my head with his boot. I kept rolling, trying to get clear, but the elf stayed on top of me, his knife flashing as I struggled to regain my feet.

"Enough!"

The elf and I both froze at the booming voice. The elf looked over his shoulder toward the kitchen, his expression puzzled.

Joe stood in the kitchen doorway, still wearing his flowered apron, a soapy ladle clutched in his tiny fist like a staff.

"You will leave now," Joe said, menacing the elf with his ladle as soap dripped on the floor.

The elf scowled, and stepped away from me, his knife held low.

"Look out," I cried as the elf stalked toward the kitchen. I lunged for the gun, praying I could reach it in time.

The kobold stared down the elf as he drew closer to the kitchen. With a tiny bellow, Joe brought his ladle down and struck the ground.

Soapy plates sped from the kitchen like bullets, hammering into the elf's chest. The plates shattered on impact sending bits of pottery shrapnel everywhere. I yelped and dove for cover behind the couch.

"Take that," Joe said, thrusting with his ladle. "And that! And some of *that!*"

With each thrust, pots and pans flew through the air battering the elf across the head. He dropped his knife and crouched, struggling in vain to protect himself from the offending cookware.

Joe leapt into the air with a squeaky roar and brought his ladle crashing down onto the kitchen floor. A thunderous crack sounded throughout the house, the tile split down the middle, and the ladle shattered into tiny fragments. A burst of light filled the room, and the entire house shook. I screamed and squeezed my eyes shut against the blinding flash.

The light faded away, and I blinked my eyes open. My living room looked like a tornado had blown through. The furniture was thrust against the walls. I stared stupidly at my spilled beer lying in the middle of the floor, the carpet turning dark as it soaked up the liquid.

How did this happen?

I looked around. There was no sign of the elf. After a moment, I spotted Joe crumpled in the doorway from the kitchen.

"Joe!" I ran to the kobold's side and turned him over. "Are you alright?"

He moaned and opened his eyes, though it took him a moment to focus on me.

"What happened?" I asked him. "Where did the elf go?"

Joe stared at me for a moment and then a weak laugh burst from his lips. "It worked. It really worked."

"What worked?"

"He's gone," Joe replied. "I banished him. He can never return to this house as long as I'm here."

I sat back, dimly conscious that my mouth was hanging open. "You were hiding in my salad just this morning. How did you banish him?"

Joe waved his arm in the air, gesturing at my spotless but now disheveled house. "I'm a heinzelmannchen. My power is tied up with a home."

"So?"

Joe looked at me like I was an idiot. I frowned. This was becoming obnoxiously common for him.

"So," he said. "You told me to make myself at home, and…I did."

"You mean all that cleaning…"

"Exactly," he said. He clambered to his feet, wincing at the movement. "Before I was a heinzelmannchen without a home. Powerless. Lost."

A sinking feeling filled my stomach. "And now?"

"Now," Joe said, a grin splitting his face from ear to ear. "I'm *your* heinzelmannchen. This is my home, and I have the power to protect it. Good news, Matt. It looks like I'm staying."

"Oh," I said, staring around at the ruins of my living room. "Lucky me."

TOOTH FAERIE

Amber Helt

J amie stared at his brother, shivering in the firelight. *It's going to kill him.*

The newlywed's small cabin was oppressively hot, even through the late autumn night. Jamie hadn't been in here since Sarah moved in, but he could already see her touches around the single-room home. Elk furs draped over freshly varnished chairs, dried herbs hanging from the rafters, a new oak wardrobe with dainty carvings of faeries and selkies standing next to Oisin's more familiar heirloom chest. But this heat...the heat sucked all the lovely warmth from the air, replacing it with a desperate, smothering heat of a young wife trying to keep her groom from dying.

Sarah sat on the edge of the sickbed, moved now from the loft to the fireside. She stroked Oisin's sweat-plastered hair. The fire made the copper strands dance with shadow. Oisin looked back at her, but Jamie knew his brother wasn't truly seeing her. Those were fever eyes. Their eldest brother, Finn, sat near the cracked window, idly whittling a child's toy.

"Let me see it." Jamie leaned closer to Oisin, and Oisin obediently rolled his head across the pillow and opened his mouth.

The hearth's roaring fire tossed Oisin's dirty face in sharp planes. The fever had sucked a lot of the life out of Oisin's cheeks, highlighting the swollen pocket on his jaw line. Jamie gingerly took his jaw and tilted his brother's head so the firelight could reach down his throat. The folly tooth was partially erupted but mostly obscured by swollen tissue. The white of the tooth stuck out of the back of his gums like a maggot caught on an apple.

Jamie released Oisin's jaw and took a step back, gagging from the sickly-sweet rot. He wiped the sweat off his own face and retreated to the other end of the bed.

"Well?" Finn asked. The skittering knife crissed and crosshatched across the whittling wood.

"Looks to be to the bone by now."

"What should we do, Jamie?" Sarah gripped Oisin's hand tighter. Her lip trembled.

That was always the question these days. Jamie was always looked to for decisions, even before their father died. What to do with the harvest. Where to bury the gold. When to slaughter the last pig. Where to bury the body.

Bale. Floorboards. First frost. The pasture. Relatively easy decisions, but this was different. It was Oisin. Little Oisin, the artist. Little Oisin, the softhearted. Little Oisin, the dying. Father had fled this world like a swallow before the frost, and he'd left Jamie alone to save his family from the shit-stained world.

"...Healer?" rasped Oisin.

Jamie turned to his little brother, pulling his mind away from the winter-wet grave newly occupied in the pasture. Oisin shivered in the fireside's heat.

From his corner, Finn grunted. "Corin's not come back from Strandsberg yet. Maybe one's on their way."

Jamie exchanged a look with Sarah, and he gave a small shake of the head. No one was coming. No one would want to come. The village had had a healer, once. A fae had gotten him a year or so back, and no one in the valley had been able to convince another one to move this close to the forest. Not even to visit. Now the valley was left to the farming families with roots too deep in the soil to ever consider leaving.

"What we need," growled Finn, slamming his whittling knife down, "is for that over-optimistic bastard to tell us when he's got a tooth ache so we can pull it *before* the infection spreads. And for you—" He glared at Sarah. "To tell us when your man's been laid out in bed for two days, instead of smothering him with your fancy city pulps."

Oisin's breath hitched, and he let out a low groan. A quiet moment later, he was softly snoring.

Sarah sniffled. "I'll get him another cool cloth." She

ducked out of the cabin, the door slamming behind her.

Jamie rubbed a hand over his face. "He's past cooling cloths. This fever *will* kill him. Maybe tonight."

"Same as Pa." The chair squeaked in protest as Finn leaned back and scratched his neck beard. "He's been too hot for too long. No one has any medicine in town. Corin's not bringing a damned healer this close to the forest."

"I know." Jamie cursed. This gaunt, Oisin looked like Father on his own deathbed just last week. Damn him. Oisin should have said something before it got this bad. The farm couldn't lose another hand.

Finn got up from his chair and approached the bed. He eyed his sleeping brother thoughtfully. Carefully. "We could summon one, you know. It'd gift him healing in return for the tooth."

Jamie looked up. "There's no way to guarantee the bargain will be healing. Fae are unpredictable. We're just as likely to end up with a shiny coin and a dead brother."

"Not necessarily unpredictable, just...clueless. But if you left the tooth in, let the faerie extract it himself, it'd know Oisin's strongest need. It'd gift him healing, I'm sure of it."

Jamie froze, his arms prickling with goose flesh. Summon a tooth faerie, invite it into the mouth of their brother...no. No, they couldn't do that. Not to Oisin. Not to the village. The valley.

The door swung open again. Sarah entered with the freezing night air, wet rags dripping in her hands. She put one on Oisin's face. The chill made him jerk, but he didn't wake.

Finn continued their talk. "I don't think we have any other options, Jamie."

"We do that, and you'll get us all killed. No."

Sarah looked between the two of them, confused. She pulled her night shawl closer over herself. "What does he mean, get us all killed? Do what?"

Jamie opened his mouth to explain, but Finn spat, "Tooth faerie. It could heal Oisin instantly."

Sarah frowned. "I thought tooth faeries only liked children's teeth?"

Finn laughed, but Jamie shot him a dark look. "Not the time for teasing." He turned to Sarah. "Tooth faeries are primarily drawn to children's dropped teeth, yes, but they'll come for any tooth your mouth no longer needs— or no longer can house."

Sarah brightened. "Then, wouldn't we want that? We could summon one. It'll take the rotted tooth and boon Oisin with good health. It'll solve all our problems." She stood, looking around the room. "Where's the boarwax? We could do it now."

Jamie sometimes forgot Sarah hadn't grown up in the valley. She didn't understand the risk that illnesses, full moons, and firstborns brought to the mortals—especially this close to the Twinning.

"There's always a cost with the fae, Sarah." Finn tossed another log on the fire. "Costs we're not willing to risk, which is why there's a process to summoning a tooth faerie. You have to pull the tooth, boil it, and leave it under the mattress of the one who lost it, but only after the wound has had a chance to heal thoroughly. Most wait three nights before lighting the boarwax candle."

Jamie eyed Finn wearily. He was one of the valley's more...fascinated residents. There was a reason their grandmother had given the boarwax candle, silver bells, and other fae relics to the eldest child of her only daughter and not one of her own sons. Finn knew more than most about the fae, but Jamie worried his fascination was too eager, not cautious enough.

"Why?" Sarah asked.

Finn tossed another log on the fire. "Because if a tooth faerie smells blood, they'll taste flesh."

"And a tooth faerie that tastes flesh will turn into a

bone fae," Jamie said.

The room was quiet. Jamie ground his teeth, thinking.

Bone fae. Of all the nasty things to live in the cursed forest beyond their valley, the bone fae were one of the most harrowing. Not because of their size, or strength, or even their method of feeding. It was the personal nature of their predation. Bone fae didn't just want to eat the bones of the one who made them. No. Fae were too old and proud for such narrow-minded appetites. They wanted to taste the heritage. The bones of not just of their maker, but of their maker's line. Father had always said that if he had to choose between meeting a bone fae or a Dullahan on a dark path, he'd choose the demon Dullahan.

Sarah wrapped her arms around herself. "But...we don't have three days. The fever..."

Jamie looked at Oisin. He really did look like Father when asleep. Grief tore at him. He couldn't lose Oisin, not right after Father. He was too young, too full of life.

Jamie glanced at Finn. Finn and Jamie weren't enough to run the farm. If they lost Oisin, they very well might all starve this winter anyway. Finn gripped the knife at his hilt with a tight nod. They'd protect their youngest brother, no matter the fae cost.

Jamie rested a hand on Sarah's shoulder. "It'll be okay. We won't let it get to Oisin." He pulled his own knife from his belt, then crossed the room and took his iron scythe off the wall.

Deep breath.

"Get the boarwax candle, Finn."

There. The decision. Jamie slumped in his chair, lost in thought while Finn went to his own house to get the boarwax; hopefully to warn his wife and child to stay inside for the night. Damned Oisin. This tooth must have been bothering him for weeks now. He remembered his own folly teeth coming in when he was a young man. As soon as he'd felt the one tooth inflame, he'd had Father cut it out of him. That day. His own tooth faerie reward had been a miracle calf from their single remaining cow the next week. *That* was how you handled a bad tooth in the valley. Not this.

Sarah sat next to Jamie, watching him sharpen the scythe with a whetstone.

"Can we kill it?" she whispered.

Jamie sharpened the rusting iron blade for a few more passes. Oisin stirred in his sleep at the sharp sound. "Not all fae can be slain the same way. Iron may kill one but only bind another."

"Church bells?"

Jamie shrugged. "Not all fae are Christ-scorned demons. The best bet is to stab it through the heart with iron. Finn will know. Don't worry, we'll find a way. Before it turns."

"What's going on?" Oisin's eyes were open. His glassy eyes found his wife's, and she rushed to his side.

"We're going to heal you, Love," she said, wiping his wet hair. "Finn's gone to get a boarwax candle."

Oisin's eyes focused. "A tooth faerie? Jamie, it—"

"We know. It'll be okay." Somehow.

Finn banged the door open. He had a black box tucked under one arm and a struggling chicken in the other. Cold autumn air swept into the small cabin, kicking up hearth ash. Without a word, Finn crossed the room and slammed the black box onto the only table. The chicken clucked and flapped in panic, strewing feathers over the threshes.

Jamie stood. "Wait. The wards."

He set his scythe down and went out of the cabin. The cold night air bit his face, the starlight twinkled at him like laughing spirits. Stomping his feet at the cold, he took his knife and hacked at the runes carved into the doorway, distorting the time-worn charms against fae and evil. There'd be no point in the summoning if it couldn't get through the damned door. The last done, he yanked the iron bells from their place above the door and made to throw them into the dark, but he hesitated and shoved them into his pocket instead.

Back in the cabin, Jamie tucked the bells in Oisin's chest. "Ready."

Oisin was sitting up. The first he'd been able in days. "I don't want to. I'll be okay. It's just a sweat."

Jamie clapped his hand on Oisin's shoulder and gently pushed him back down. "You're dying, Oisin. We'll get the faerie's boon and you'll have peace."

"But—"

"Shut up, Oisin." Finn took a flaming log from the fire. "And sit still."

Sarah sat on the edge of Oisin's bed, holding his hand in hers, watching with morbid curiosity what the brothers did. Jamie himself had never summoned a tooth faerie before; it was something his parents had always done in another room while he slept with his brothers. Finn's own boy was not yet old enough to lose a tooth, and the boarwax candle had sat untouched for many years in Father's home. But they all knew the ritual. You don't grow up next to the fae forest and not know these things.

Jamie opened the black box, revealing the warped, oily boarwax candle within. He took the ebony candle out of the box and placed it on the table, then took the flustered hen from Sarah's lap, holding it by the neck. His heart thundered in his chest, closing his ears against the hen's protests. He locked eyes with Finn and gave a sharp nod.

Hand shaking, Finn lit the candle with the log then tossed it back in the fire. The four of them watched in silence as the candle sputtered to life, the unnaturally tall flame sparkling from yellow to blue to white. When it flashed green, Jamie took his knife and sliced the hen's throat, forever silencing its squawks. Sarah yelped. The blood doused the boarwax flame with a sizzle.

In the heavy silence, everyone stared at the candle

smoking on the table. For a breath, nothing happened.

With a roar, the cabin's air sucked toward the candle, squeezing their lungs until Jamie's eyes watered. The cabin rumbled, a low groan of supplication, then the air fell still. The hen's blood bubbled, frothing thicker and thicker until it rose to cover half the table. A scratching filled the air, like insect legs behind the woodpile. Jamie took an instinctive half-step between the table and Oisin.

Out from the boiling blood rose a tiny blue hand. Soon the rest of its body followed, ripped through time and space into the cabin from wherever in its world it'd been prowling. Finn took a long step back, his face paling at the sight of the little fae.

The blood quieted and settled into a black, glassy puddle.

And there stood the tooth faerie.

Whoever had carved those faeries in Sarah's wardrobe had clearly never seen a fae. The tooth faerie was small, about the size of a large rat, with membranous wings that draped to the table's shiny surface. Its skin was translucent with a hint of blue. In the firelight, Jamie could see the naked faerie's many veins and organs pulsing under its skin. And its face . . . Jamie shuddered, glad his parents always summoned the tooth faerie after he'd fallen asleep. Where the tooth faerie's body was slim and twiggy, its face was swollen and shiny, its beady eyes almost obscured behind folds of bloat. Its mouth was too wide, its ears too sharp under its matted moss hair. Jamie wasn't sure how it managed to hold its own head up.

Behind him, Oisin whimpered. The sound caught the faerie's attention. It snapped toward him, cocking his head. Sniffing.

"Oisin," Jamie muttered, "open your mouth."

Oisin shook his head, his prone body shaking from fever and fright. Sarah put her arm around him, her own expression now uncertain.

Jamie took three slow steps over to Oisin's side. "Finn, help me."

Together, the brothers pinned Oisin's arms to his side while Sarah moved to sit behind Oisin, supporting his head and stroking his hair. Oisin's skin was like fire. Jamie wrinkled his nose. The heady mix of boiled blood with diseased air was enough to churn his stomach.

The tooth faerie skittered on the tabletop, pacing back and forth as it watched the humans. Sniffing, grunting. Whining.

"Open, brother," Jamie said. "It'll heal you."

Oisin whimpered again.

Sarah kissed her husband's feverish brow. "Are we sure it's safe?"

"Yes." Finn smiled. "We'll kill it after the boon."

It was the wrong thing to say.

The tooth faerie snarled, opening its too-wide jaw. Fangs like a snake sprang out, a long, black moth tongue unrolling down to its knees. The tooth faerie leapt across the room and flew straight for Finn. Finn yelped and dove to the ground, but just before the tooth faerie could land on him, Oisin gripped Sarah's hand and opened his mouth wide.

A putrid, rotting odor rolled from his infected tooth. Sarah gagged. The tooth faerie shrieked in delight and pivoted mid-air, diving into Oisin's mouth.

Jamie stared in horror at the little blue legs kicking out of Oisin's pale lips. The tips of the faerie's wings tickled Oisin's nose. It looked like Oisin had stuffed his mouth with an overlarge cricket that was fighting its way down his throat. Oisin gagged, whipping wildly under Jamie's grip. Finn jumped up from the floor and helped Jamie hold him down. It was the most strength Oisin had shown in days.

And then the screaming started. Jamie could hear the faerie slurping, smacking his lips and tearing at the tender gums as it fought to dig out its prize.

"Make it stop!" Sarah screamed. "Make it stop! Get it out!"

"Don't bite it," Finn warned. "Let it finish."

Jamie wanted to close his eyes. He wanted to never see the blind panic in his brother's eyes again. Never see his stream of tears dilute the blood dribbling from the corner of his mouth, dripping off his chin. But he didn't. He stayed steady, holding Oisin in place, praying to every god buried in the valley for his brother's salvation.

After what felt like hours, the faerie ripped itself free from Oisin's mouth. It flapped lazily back to the table and pulled a huge, bloody tooth out from under its arm. It started licking it, dancing from one foot to the other as it did so.

Oisin slumped back onto the bed. Eyes closed, breath ragged and shallow. Sarah was sobbing. Finn retched across the threshes, adding to the unholy atmosphere the fire's heat only magnified.

Jamie kicked Finn, never taking his eyes from the gleeful fae. "How long do we wait?"

Finn stood and wiped his mouth. "When we know the boon's been done."

Faerie gifts weren't always immediate, though. It had taken Jamie's folly tooth's miracle calf a week to arrive in the barn. Who knew how long they had now. Jamie watched with horror as, with every lick, his brother's blood spread through the tooth faerie's tiny veins, clouding its translucent blue skin, darkening its pulsing abdomen to a solid, deep crimson. Still the fae continued to gnaw at the tooth. It looked too preoccupied for gift-giving.

Sarah coughed and choked out, "Is...is it working?"

Jamie turned to look. Oisin's face was covered in blood, but Jamie thought the swelling had gone down. Oisin raised a shaking hand to his face and felt along his jaw. The corners of his mouth were slightly ripped, but Jamie thought Sarah could probably sew those up.

"Rotting gods," Finn cursed.

Jamie spun back around and let out his own curse.

The faerie had swallowed the tooth. It choked and gagged, used its twiggy arms to help shove it further down its own throat until with a wet *plop*, it landed in its destination. The faerie pulled its hand out of its mouth and turned its buggy eyes toward the humans. With a wicked grin, it straightened, sighed, and fell back off the table into the glassy pool of chicken blood.

Finn and Jamie rushed to the table.

"Where'd it go?" Finn roared.

Jamie flipped the table. He kicked the threshes and searched the shadows for the imp. But the faerie was gone.

"Maybe it's fine," Sarah said. "Maybe it was happy with the tooth."

Oisin hiccupped a hysteric laugh. "Maybe Father's at the door."

Finn paced the cabin, searching for the escaped little fae, but Jamie remained still. He could feel it. A heavy evil pulling at him. Pulling him forward, toward the blood, just as whatever lay at the bottom of that weight was dredged up the depths to this world. With each small step, he could feel it closer.

Everyone stopped to watch the puddle.

Oisin whimpered. "It's here."

Jamie leaned forward over the puddle to examine it. He jumped, his heart in his throat.

Just beneath the glassy black surface, a skullish face grinned up at him. It was like Jamie had come across a submerged body in the valley's bog and the corpse was laughing at him. The bone fae raised a spindly hand from the depths and stroked the underside of the blood, as if caressing it.

Then it pulled itself out of hell.

If the tooth faerie was primitive and impish, the bone

fae was preternaturally refined. Crouched on all fours, its shoulders stood taller than Jamie, taller even than Father. Its soft body from before was now covered in a thick, abominable carapace made up of dozens of skeletal portions from unearthly creatures to create a monster with unnatural joints and angles. Like a man who had been dissected and reassembled in the dark with too many pieces. Jamie thought he counted eight rib cages braided together. Along its back, the heavy wings glittered in the firelight with thousands of tiny human teeth.

Dread clawed up Jamie's spine. How could they get iron to its heart through all that bone?

Its presence filled the cabin, dousing the fire's heat in a cold, deep chill that uncurled like mist tendrils into Jamie's very bones. But it wasn't the chill that iced Jamie's veins. No, it was the face. It had Oisin's face. Or rather, it wore a stylized ivory death mask inspired by Oisin. The mask had carved, unknown runes contouring its hallow shape. The mouth—Oisin's mouth—was stretched back in a too-wide smile with carved teeth too sharp to be human—all except for one very human, rotting folly tooth. Firelight danced with shadows across the little runes, mirroring the very real tears now found on Oisin's ripped lips.

It fanned its wings behind itself, shaking clotted blood across the threshes and splattering the elk furs, then turned toward the four humans huddled together. Jamie couldn't see anything of the true face beneath except for the eyes. Burning, flickering.

Hungry.

Jamie clutched the snath of his scythe. Bone fae built their legacies by consuming the marrow of their makers and their maker's makers and any semblance of relation beyond that. Bone fae didn't just prune a family tree, they eradicated the whole damn thing. They'd spend decades in the mortal world dedicated to this pursuit.

Lucky for this fae, its entire fare was all standing in

one small room.

A knife behind Jamie clattered to the floor. From the corner of his eye, Jamie watched Finn flee to the door. He threw his weight against it and fled into the night.

"Finn!" Sarah cried.

Jamie was too stunned to react. The coward. The damned, bastardly coward. The bone fae flickered its attention toward the door, but it didn't move. Its eyes remained locked on Oisin. Jamie could practically hear his brother's marrow sing out to the fae.

We're too late, Jamie thought. *Too late, too late, too late. It turned. It's here. No one survives a bone fae. I failed.*

"Please," sobbed Sarah, "Please. Heal him."

"Sarah!" Jamie hissed. "Don't bargain."

"Please," she said. "Leave us alone. Please."

A voice hushed through Jamie's mind, crackling under the fire's embers, hidden under their thoughts. *Tooth booned to bones ground, marrow maker and skull breaker.*

The fae cocked its mask from one side to the next. Its sniffing drowned out the crackling fire as it took a short step forward and stepped on the discarded hen. The fae bent to pick up the limp carcass. It held the hen delicately between two spindly fingers, sniffing louder, as if considering a wine.

The fae removed its mask.

Sarah screamed. Jamie's mind could not comprehend the horror that made up the bone fae's true face. Every time he tried to register a detail of its inhuman, ghastly visage, his mind immediately blacked it out. His mortal mind was too limited, too predictable to allow something so clearly from another plane to take hold in memory. All he could focus on was the teeth. The rows and rows and rows of teeth of all shapes, lengths, and purposes that stretched unnaturally wide and swallowed the chicken whole. Wet crunching, as quickly as it'd started, and the hen was swallowed. The fae took a low bow to Jamie, then returned the bone mask to its face.

It was like a spell broke over the humans. It didn't have to be too late. He could get them out. If Sarah could get Oisin across the field, past Finn's entry door with the protective runes, the fae would be barred from entry. It could buy them time.

Marrow...maker...

"Sarah," Jamie muttered, "get to Finn's."

Sarah scrambled off the bed, pulling Oisin with her. Now the bed and Jamie stood between them and the fae. Oisin slouched against the bed, his own face close in matching the bone mask's deathly hue. She'd have to drag him.

Skull...breaker...

Jamie gripped his iron scythe. "Hey, beast!"

The Oisin mask swiveled between Oisin and Jamie. Too many vertebrae in the motion. Jamie swung at it with the scythe, and the iron tip scratched one of its moist bones. The fae screamed. It was claws on glass, steam in an over-pressured kettle ready to burst. It rounded on Jamie, pulling itself up to its full height. It struck Jamie to the floor, knocking the wind from his lungs and sending the scythe clattering across the room. The glowing mask leered over Jamie, a dark tendril of drool dripping down the chin of the mask onto Jamie's face. Jamie struggled for air as it leaned down—

A clear bell rang out.

The bone fae threw itself to the floor with a howl. Jamie rolled just in time to avoid getting impaled by one of the snapped bones that spiked the creature's arms. It screamed and rolled as another light tinkling split the darkness.

Sarah stood protectively over Oisin, the cluster of iron bells gripped in her hands. Jamie scrambled to his feet and raced across the room to them. Iron may not kill it, but it was still fae. It could still be hurt.

Sarah picked up the dropped scythe and handed it back to Jamie. "You okay?"

"Yeah," Jamie panted. "Take Oisin. Get him out."

"It's calling me," Oisin whispered. The bloody corners of his mouth cracked. A fresh trickle started. "I can hear it inside of me."

The fae had recovered. Sarah rang the bell again, but this time the fae only shuttered and staggered at its power. Jamie squinted, watching it swing its head back and forth. Had it...it had. The crown of bones at the top of its skull had melted and hardened around the fae's would-be ears.

Sarah rang the bells louder, harder, the cluster swinging wildly in her hands. The fae swayed with each ring, its joints stiff and locked. The new carapace crown kept the bells from incapacitating the fae, but still the iron song slowed it.

Jamie hoisted Oisin over his shoulder and began to drag him toward the door, but the fae stood, blocking the way. Jamie had to protect Oisin. He *had* to. It was his job; he was his older brother; he let Finn talk them into summoning a tooth faerie. They robbed Oisin a peaceful death out of selfishness for the farm, and Jamie couldn't live with that.

Jamie glanced between Sarah and the fae. She couldn't carry him as fast as Jamie could, but she wasn't equipped to kill a fae. She couldn't even brave jumping the flames at the Grianstad festival. If there was any chance in saving Oisin, he'd have to do it.

"Love you, brother." Jamie kissed the sour tang coating Oisin's forehead, then stood his brother against the wardrobe. He turned back to the fae, no longer trembling.

"Come on!" Jamie screamed at the fae. He circled it, trying to lead it away from the front door. The fae cocked its Oisin face, hissing at the iron blade. Jamie swung, and the fae reared. It hissed, low and throaty.

Tooth booned to bones ground.

The bells paused. Jamie and the fae both swiveled to catch Sarah putting her arm around Oisin. "Oisin, help me," she sobbed. "Please, we need to go."

Sarah struggled to hold her husband upright. Her city upbringing didn't lend her the strength other wives in the valley carried. She dropped the bells.

The fae lunged.

"No!"

Jamie jumped in front of it and swung his scythe. The scratch of iron to bone made bile rise in Jamie's mouth. Jamie swiped again, and quick as a whip the fae lunged, caught the scythe, and threw Jamie across the room.

A snap in Jamie's leg colored the world white. If he screamed, he couldn't hear it over the thunder of pain rolling through him. Bone speared through his trousers at the thigh.

Sarah grabbed a glass lamp from atop the heirloom chest and threw it at the fae. The fae hissed, flaring its wings as the glass shattered against its chest. The wings' powerful stroke threw Jamie against the opposite wall and extinguished the cabin's fire with a burst of embers.

It was dark.

The low red glow of the embers cast deep shadows all around the small cabin, the only shapes clearly defined were made of bone and tooth.

The iron bells sang out, their soft music cutting through the heavy darkness. It was a ward, and a beacon. The fae slunk toward the cowering humans, struggling against the iron song with each step. Jamie struggled for consciousness. With every blink, the world tipped one way and then the other. The front of his brain pounded against his skull, and nausea swam with the shadows.

It grabbed Sarah first. She screamed, and in the darkness Jamie watched the fae drag her away from Oisin.

Jamie shouted, "Give him the bells! Give him the bells!"

Sarah flung the bells to Oisin, the iron glittering in the

fading ember's light, just as the fae flung her body across the cabin. She landed with a heavy, final thud.

"Ring them, Oisin!" Jamie yelled. The world pitched itself over a ledge, and Jamie clung to the swaying floor-boards. Red flashed across his vision.

The bells rang, furious and urgent. Jamie propped his elbows under himself. He'd crawl to Oisin. He'd claw to him. He'd tear that fae apart bone by bone, and—

The bells fell silent.

"Oisin!" Jamie screamed. He dragged himself forward an inch, fingers digging into the splinters of the floor, his heart pounding against his ribs, his temples. "Oisin!"

A sickening *CRACK* rang out in the darkness. Time stilled. For a horrible, wrenching moment, Jamie couldn't breathe.

Then the ripping began. Wet, low, velvety yet sharp, something was torn in the darkness. Iron filled the air, stung Jamie's nose. He retched.

The fire was out now. No light entered the cabin save for a small sliver of moonlight through the seam of the window curtain. It was barely enough to outline the pale contours of the bone mask, discarded on the threshes.

The fae ate. It munched, slurped, sucked, nibbled, and lapped in a macabre feast in the darkness. Jamie collapsed against the floorboards. He wanted to die. He wanted to be anywhere but here. No matter how he pushed himself into the floor, he couldn't escape the sounds, the smells, the mocking sight of Oisin's death mask glinting in the moonlight.

The cabin fell quiet once more. Then something horrible happened. It started in Jamie's jaw, then trickled down through his chest, his groin, his legs. The blood in Jamie's bones began to warm, to quicken.

His marrow was singing. Calling.

The darkness shifted. The cold, the malice, it focused its weight on Jamie.

Tooth booned to bones ground…Maker's elder, join in melder.

This had been Jamie's decision. He had chosen to bring this evil into this house. He had thought he could protect his brother, lead this family of the valley through pain and death. It would hunt them all. It would hunt Finn, Finn's child, until it had the bones for trophies. It would start with Oisin, the youngest, and feast its way up the line.

The cabin door burst open, and in strode Finn.

"I've come to make a bargain!" Finn cried over a solemn bell toll.

Finn wore an iron breastplate and swung a single heavy church bell in one hand, a bright lantern held high in the other. The church bell's ring struck the fae like an external force, knocking it flat on its back into the slick floor. The lantern drove a bloody light into the hellhole, dazzling Jamie's eyes as it bounced off Finn's dented iron plate. Jamie refused to look at the fae, at the soft wet pile of discarded skin bleeding just behind it. Instead, his eyes found Sarah, slumped against the wall. She was breathing.

Finn caught Jamie's eye and crossed the room to stand between his hunted brother and his brother's bones. He struck the bell again. The masked fae wailed under its weight, but it was getting back up. It had grown, Jamie realized. A new, spongey rib cage sprouted from its chest.

"You want to taste a mortal's heritage through our bloodline, right? To consume our marrow and taste mortality from ages past?" Finn struck the bell like a whip at a dog. "What a sorry bloodline you've chosen, fiend. Our father's roots grow deep in this valley, rich with fae magic and darkened, doomed life. But he is dead—buried this past week. His father is gone too, and all his siblings. Your quest for knowledge of this mortal world stops here on this branch, with us thr—two brothers. Our mother died long ago, and she was not of this valley. My bones and the bones of my brothers are diluted, less true."

Jamie couldn't follow Finn. The blood loss at his leg

was pulling ice into his fingertips. Finn struck the bell again, and the fae screeched in frustration.

"I have a bargain for you, fae," Finn yelled over the din. "Bone for bone, and we'll be done. Cease this hunt, and I'll give you the bones of our father. A richer thread in our line, with the valley's heart in the marrow. Follow our marrow song, and you'll never taste this piece of our history. You'll be unsatisfied. Starving."

Finn grabbed the bell clapper, cutting off the holy notes and dousing the room in silence. Jamie trembled. The bone fae got to its feet, raising itself up to its full height. It still wore Oisin's face. Jamie's stomach roiled just as his marrow sang. He laid his head back on the floor to keep the darkness from swallowing him.

Bones of maker's sire for my thirst's desire. The fae's head snapped up, and it growled at Finn. *No mortal offers freely to bone fae. It is not the way.*

"Will you accept the bargain?"

The fae considered a moment. The quiet was broken only by the skittish flickering of Finn's lantern and a muffled, digestive gurgle from places Jamie refused to consider.

A shudder rippled through the cabin, and Jamie took a deep breath. It was like someone had opened the window of a stuffy room. His head cleared a bit.

Finn nodded. Keeping his eyes on the fae, he backed to the door of the cabin. Jamie held his breath as Finn—and the iron—disappeared from view for a heavy heartbeat before returning with a muddy sack. Finn kicked it to the fae.

The pack was dirty and moist. The bone fae rose, wary, but it sniffed the pack and ripped it open. Inside were bones. Human bones piled together and clinging to chunks of soil-stained flesh.

"The bones of our father," Finn stated. "Take these, taste our family's roots in its marrow, and be done with us."

The bone fae picked up their father's skull. Jamie stared. Held in its hand, his father's skull blended with the spindly bones of the fae's hand. Their father's skull seemed to smile at Jamie, as if it knew. It knew their need, and he had come to help one last time.

The fae crushed the skull in its hand. It sprinkled the bone dust over the mask, and the runes carved within began to glow. The bone fae purred, amused. *This I will accept, maker's elder.*

The fae scooped the remains of their father into its arms. The bones clattered together, the final words Jamie's father would ever give him. With a final sniff toward the brothers, the fae lumbered through the cabin's door and into the night. It spread its wings and launched itself into the cool breeze, disappearing into the cursed forest beyond the valley.

Jamie took a deep breath. His marrow's song had quieted. All he felt now was pain, and as blinding as his broken leg felt, it was a simple pain. A human pain.

His vision flickered—no, glittered. Glittered?

Finn swore. Jamie blinked, focused, and gasped himself. Oisin's remains had vanished. Sarah's wardrobe shimmered in the lantern light, conspicuously clean and polished compared to its surroundings. The floral faerie carvings had been replaced with carvings of the bone fae, the wooden doors now inlaid with gold and bordered with studs of tiny, pearly teeth. Finn crossed the room and opened the wardrobe. Inside, Oisin's ivory mask rested on a small mountain of gold—stack upon stack of gold coins glittering in the lantern light like a pyre for a king.

ON THE WAY TO THE NEW JERUSALEM

Cody Ramer

Consciousness surged upon Lucinda Wells for reasons she did not immediately apprehend. Fitful sleep had become the new norm in her most recent stage of aging, which was her least favorite as of yet, but the immediate panic that seized her suggested something beyond the typical failures of her body.

She first noticed that the window had been opened, something she would have never done of her own accord in the summer. Upon this realization, she wanted to open the bedside drawer to retrieve her pistol, but could not bring any part of herself to move. Lucinda had no choice but to continue sitting upright against her headboard and listen for the presence of evil in the dark.

Moments went by. There was some solace to be taken in the fact that whatever had opened the window had not yet brought her any harm, and Lucinda's resolve began to take shape. Slowly, she rotated her right leg over the side of the bed. It was as her hand reached out for the drawer handle that she heard the voice for the first time:

"Do you ever wonder what Christ meant when he said unclean spirits go out into waterless places?"

Lucinda did not register the question. She opened her mouth as though to yell, but only a dry, crackled gasp came forth. She was parched. The sound had come from directly above her, a detail, which like many others at the moment she had only loosely grasped. But the observation was now taking shape: *What could possibly be above her?*

"I'm only looking for a place to be," the voice spoke up once more.

Lucinda found her voice. "Well I can't help you—there's one bedroom in this house, and it's mine. There ain't no reason for you to be here, and I'm willing to make that point clear if I need to."

Lucinda opened the drawer, firmly grasped the .38, and pounded the hammer back with confidence. She stood up, fueled by rage at the prospect that her home was being violated. "I done told you to leave my house!"

The response came this time from the corner of her room, above and behind her this time, much closer than before.

"The Lord will return like a thief in the night, the Scripture says, and be met by the barrel of a .38 special."

Turning and pointing her gun to obliterate the cobweb infested corner of her home, Lucinda screamed righteous-ly: "YOU AIN'T THE LORD!"

But there was no blasphemer to shoot. There was no man in a black ski-mask inhabiting her ceiling like a large spider as she had vaguely expected. No, she saw nothing at all. Her trembling hands, both still grasping the pistol firmly, fell down in front of her lap. Only half-resigned, she wondered how she might be able to fight someone she couldn't see.

"What do you want from me?" She asked.

"I already told you. I need somewhere to be—some-body to rest with."

It was the strangeness of this response that finally led Lucinda to the conclusion: "You're a demon, ain't you?! Trying to get in the head of a God-fearing woman, visiting me here to take the words of our Lord in your mouth in vain and deceive me."

No reply came. Lucinda's righteous indignation over-came the feebleness of her flesh. She straightened her back and pulled her shoulders back, as though to get down to business. With a casualness that resembled arrogance, Lucinda tossed the pistol onto the bed. She knew the Lord would protect her from any demon because she belonged to him. But she would not stand for the presence of evil—she would flee it. She grabbed the truck keys from the dresser.

"I'd shoot you seven times over if I could," she said.

Barefoot, pajamas dragging the ground, Lucinda walked with purpose out of her bedroom, unharmed by the thing that hovered beneath the ceiling of her home. In the brief moment it took Lucinda to walk from her bedroom to the front door, she heard from behind her:

"How do you know I ain't the Lord?"

Lucinda carried on as though she had heard nothing.

"**B**rothers and sisters, there will be no music in this morning's service. Last night, I received a call from our sister-in-Christ and piano player, Mrs. Wells, that chilled me. Now, as you all know, Mrs. Wells is a level-headed lady. She's here every Sunday morning and evening with a smile on her face, ready to serve the Lord. She has been a member of Pine Grove Holiness Church for now over twenty years, and I've never seen her tell anything that even resembled a lie. Since the day I met her, I've known Mrs. Wells to be nothing but a decent woman and a fine Christian." The pastor paused to give room for the already swelling response of the faithful.

"That's right, Preach!"

"Okay now, tell it like it is."

Though the content of this morning's message was already different than the norm, Brother Jeffrey had quickly gained command of his ever-attentive and loyal audience. "I need all you kind folks to keep these things in mind, now, when I tell y'all this next thing."

As the words ceased from his mouth, Brother Jeffrey's eyes drifted slowly from one side of the chapel to the other, making direct eye-contact with each member of his flock. This had become a habit of his as of late. Fifteen, he counted. These fifteen people before him would one day stand before the good Lord in heaven and bear witness to the work he'd done on this mortal plain. As the shadows of life lengthened, he relished more and more his calling to the people in front of him, for he knew his reward was great.

"Now friends, this shouldn't come as any shock, as the Good Word tells us that our struggle is not against flesh and blood, but against spirits and principalities—against Satan, that terrible and real Prince of the Air. Now, ain't that right?"

A chorus of amens reverberated against the chapel's dusty beams.

"Well last night, Mrs. Wells, she tells me, was asleep in her own bed when she heard someone in the house. And as you all know, Mrs. Wells lives alone in that old house, so she was rightly frightened. She says she saw the window open and grabbed her gun looking for a burglar. Instead, she hears this voice—this strange, ungodly voice coming down from out of the ceiling."

Brother Jeffrey's voice grew hushed. The congregation leaned forward with a singular, spooked anticipation.

"And this voice didn't give its name or show itself. It just sat right up there and spoke blasphemous and horrible things against our Lord and taunted Mrs. Wells. But don't be alarmed—Mrs. Wells has *the Lord*. She's a strong woman. And that being the case, she picked herself up and walked right out her door. She's at Sister Millie's house this morning, recovering from the fright."

There was horror and shock across the faces of the flock, but no trace of disbelief. Though they had not known of any such haunting in their little community, somehow everyone knew it had always been a possibility. And no one had known Brother Jeffrey to speak anything but the truth. The chapel and its inhabitants rested in an uncharacteristic silence.

"Now, brothers and sisters," the silence was broken by the boldness belonging only to preachers. "The good news is that Mrs. Wells is safe; I spoke with her just this morning by phone. However, the bad news, as I'm sure you're all realizing, is that there is evil in our midst.

"I don't know what's caused it, but you folks know from God's Word that such evil doesn't come about without a cause." Brother Jeffrey paused, welcoming back the dense and terrible silence from before. He began again: "And y'all know I ain't one for accusing. The Lord alone knows the heart. But God didn't put me here—or you here, for that matter—to just watch the Evil One do his bidding. No sir!

"That's right!"

"Tell it, Brother!"

"And so this morning, we're all going to do something a little different: We're going to get down on our knees, and we're going to tell the Lord what we've done. We're going to search out what we might have done to bring such a thing upon Mrs. Wells—'cause we know it's not the Lord who sends such evil. Your sin breeds sin, brother. Evil is our doing—beg his forgiveness!"

"Lord, have mercy!"

"Jesus, help us!"

"Come quickly—come on, Lord!"

Brother Jeffrey was looking more and more like a dog with its hackles raised, manic with the single-mindedness of instinctual anger. His voice had picked up, hovering above the swelling chorus of "amens," other cries, and the one or two beginning to chatter in unknown tongues. Looking on the glory, he momentarily quieted himself once more, basking in the reality that he still had it in him to rouse his congregation after all these years.

"Yes sir," he began again. "We're going to get on our knees and beseech the Lord to take away this wretched presence from among us and the sin that brought it here!" The swelling chorus had turned increasingly into a singular wail. The preacher had warned them of the terrible consequences of hiding their wickedness, and finally the Lord had brought them a terrible revelation. What was happening in Pine Grove—what was happening in their won souls—that they had failed to notice? Somebody had found them out.

Confessions, tongues, and the occasional plea for Mrs. Wells's soul sung out past noon. Holy disorder had descended upon the congregation. It was only after people's throats had become so uncomfortably dry from participating in the great cry that silence began to gradually overtake members of the church, one-by-one, over the course of half an hour. Slowly, wet faces and penitent eyes looked up to the reverend for direction.

At 1:30 pm, three-and-a-half hours after their initial gathering, Brother Jeffrey began to give his final instructions, his voice hoarse from prayer:

"Brothers and sisters in Jesus, you know that the work is never finished. It's not enough to be sorry for your sin—you got to stay sorry for your sin. It's not enough to ask the Lord—you got to keep asking him. Don't let your guard down!

"Now, my encouragement to everyone would be to go home and to leave Mrs. Wells alone. She needs to rest. We'll be back here at 7 pm for our evening service, and I hope to have some clarity from the Lord on the situation by then."

At their pastor's direction, the congregation went to their homes, quietly struggling to not cease from prayer.

Millie had been thankful for the company. At her stage in life, she so scarcely had opportunities to play the host—a role she dearly loved. And though she had her own private opinions about what had befallen Lucinda the night prior, she had of course looked on her sister-in-Christ with love and given her a place to stay. In her old age, she now scarcely left her bedroom, and she had seized the opportunity to visit with an old friend.

After church, Brother Jeffrey dropped in to visit Lucinda. The three of them passed the time mostly in uncomfortable silence, but the two involved parties arrived at the important conclusion that what was in the house would need to be confronted as soon as possible. Brother Jeffrey insisted that this, being far from his first exorcism, was merely a part of the job. Lucinda had believed him, but found herself increasingly ill at ease. She had scarcely ceased from trembling since she had woken up and had spoken little of what passed through her mind.

Parting from the table, Millie hugged Lucinda and her pastor, who she saw less and less of, being increasingly homebound. She watched on with a disinterested skepticism as the two headed for Lucinda's little white pickup.

Lucinda had always preferred to drive, and Brother Jeffrey consented, citing how the folks at church had wore him down that morning. The drive was a familiar one. Lucinda visited Mille to sew and gossip at least twice a week: Three minutes to the general store where she worked, a right at the stop sign, and another three minutes down State Highway 59 before she was back home. They were on the highway before either spoke a word.

"You know, Preach, last night, in the moment, I felt brave…strengthened. I was scared at first, you know, but there was something about realizing I could stand up to wickedness that made me feel bold for the Lord." She paused, not expecting a response and then continued. "But I don't feel that way right now. Last night, I would have shot that demon if I could. Now, if it weren't that I had you here with me, I'd just as soon never go back home. The voice I heard last night was strange, besides being wicked, and I can't stand for nothing wicked, and I don't like nothing strange."

Brother Jeffrey rolled the bottom of his jaw up toward his bottom lip. Lucinda had long called this the pastor's "thinking face." Though—and she never told anyone this—

she often wondered if it was the remnant of an old tobacco habit. She had never seen him make the face in church. The pulpit came naturally to him.

"Have you prayed for courage yet?" The pastor asked the question with authority.

"Jeff, my husband died six years ago and left me in a home in the country with no job and no kids. I ain't stopped praying for courage; you know that." It was hard to tell whether Lucinda was offended.

The truck slowed down as it approached the driveway. It slid ever so lightly as the front wheels made initial contact with the gravel.

"The battle's won, but it ain't ever over. Is it, Mrs. Wells?"

She nodded.

"I think the Lord has a nice place for you up there. Better than this place, for sure. Ain't no one poor in heaven and ain't nothing strange. Yes ma'am, you're on your way."

Lucinda parked the truck a respectful distance from the home. The mood in the vehicle shifted as the truck rested. Lucinda noticed something near delight on the pastor's face. He had been quiet, but clearly excited. He wore a smirk, held his shoulders high, and stared at the little house, not as if searching, but perceiving.

"Mrs. Wells, this ain't your fault. I think the Lord is testing me." Within a few seconds, he had opened and closed the passenger door.

This wasn't exactly the encouragement Lucinda had hoped for from her pastor. Getting out of the vehicle, she wondered if her growing confusion at the situation was justified. She followed after Brother Jeffrey, who was already twenty yards or so ahead, making no effort to catch-up.

Brother Jeffrey stopped at the screen door, his face still radiant with determination. Lucinda arrived at his side. He could hear her trembling breath and her muttered prayers. In spite of all that he had told his congregation that morning about her uprightness before the Lord, he was beginning to wonder with all pity if she was wavering. Had she put her hand to the plow and turned back? He began to wonder why he hadn't thought to tell her to stay at Millie's.

"Mrs. Wells, I think it's best if you go back to the truck. Ain't no use in traumatizing you twice."

The thought was not repulsive to Lucinda, but somehow, she had been imagining herself there with the pastor all along. "Are you sure? I mean, it is my house..." She trailed off for a moment, gradually coming to the conclusion that she had no energy or cause to pursue a dispute. "I'll let you handle it, Preach," she said. Avoiding eye contact, she turned back towards the truck, wondering if it was really her who needed to be delivered, and not her house.

The reverend laid his hand on the screen door and opened it without haste or hesitation. He did the same with the front door behind it. Before him opened up the living room and kitchen of Lucinda Wells's home of thirty years. He vaguely remembered the place from his first and only pastoral visit to the home six years ago. He noticed that the windows were closed and that the air was blowing strong from the window unit. At the two-seated dining table, situated in the middle of the space between the kitchen sink and the singular sofa, stood two sweating glasses of ice water.

"Are you thirsty?" The voice came from across the table, as though it were in Lucinda's room. The question, unexpected and unsettling, caused Brother Jeffrey's soul to burn. The sound of a lit match falling on soaked coals filled his mind. Yes, he was thirsty; the thought had never occurred to him. At the renewed sight of the condensation pooling all around the glasses, with no coaster to protect the table, the resolution needed to perform an exorcism melted into the deep passion of longing.

"My hope was that Lucinda would offer me a drink, but I had to go to the tap myself." The voice's words brought back to mind the pastor's goal, though his thirst persisted. He was only about a foot inside of the little house and dared not move for fear that he might make a break for the table if he did. He wrestled within himself for what it was that he had come there to say.

When the words came forth from the pastor's mouth, they were loud, but not commanding and controlled as his words to his congregation had been that morning. What came forth was a frantic, spit-less scream that scarred the back of his throat:

"By the power of Christ in me, come out from this place, you filthy spirit!"

Silence.

"I said leave!"

The house was still and quiet, but the pastor knew he was not yet alone. His arms shook beside him in anger; he could feel a blood vessel pop in his eye.

The spirit, after some time, replied a little quieter than before, "How do you know it's Christ that is in you, and not just a stranger?"

The question brought about fiery rage once more in the pastor's soul. He would not stand for the presence of evil, and he—an experienced man of God, a shepherd of God's people—would not stand for such disrespect. Without realizing it, he had slammed both doors behind him and was heading for the truck.

Lucinda had been too spooked by the passion of Brother Jeffery to question him on the way back to Millie's. His jaw moved furiously up-and-down and side-to-side as the truck eased down the two-lane roads. Lucinda did not know what to think.

By the end of the drive, however, it was clear that the pastor was no longer so at unrest. The look of triumph so common to his disposition had not yet returned, but something akin to resolve had taken the place of his rage. Lucinda pushed the shifter into park, looking up at her pastor of twenty-two years for something to orient herself to.

He returned her look with a question, finally seeming to quiet himself: "Mrs. Wells, how often do you think about heaven?" His voice was hoarse, as though he'd spent a lifetime yelling at the devil.

"Often enough," she replied. "My husband and my Lord are there."

"So you'd probably know better than most folks that that's where the real treasure is, right? You know that the things of this earth—the physical, the flesh—they're passing away, in the blink of an eye. You know that, right?"

She nodded in response.

His jaw settled down, and his eyes narrowed, focusing on something far away. "The New Jerusalem," he said, "the New Jerusalem will be our home. And what I love about the New Jerusalem is that it's a city—it's a place for folks to live and belong. There'll be things to do and work to be had. I imagine there'll be butchers and farmers, maybe even firemen and police officers—though their jobs will be much easier. Yep, there will be speed limit signs in the New Jerusalem, but everyone will obey them. For now though, we all got to forsake the things of this world."

The heavenly city seemed as far away to Lucinda as the home she felt she had just lost. Had the preacher taken but a moment to look into the confused eyes of his faithful congregant, he might have reconsidered his approach. But his gaze never wavered from whatever it was that lay beyond the glass of the windshield.

"Well, Sister, I best be going."

By the time the last word had left his mouth, Brother Jeffery was already on his way out of the truck—he didn't even bother to close the door. Lucinda went into the house, crying and uncompelled by the thought of a New Jerusalem. Her sobs were so dry and harsh that there was something comforting about the water running down her face. She was exhausted. Someone else could play the hymns at church tonight.

At 8:30, roughly the time the congregation would normally return to their homes after the evening service, a collection of aging sedans and pickup trucks descended upon the house of Lucinda Wells. From them poured seven men dressed in flannels and jeans, six women dressed in dresses that touched the ground, and two little blonde-headed boys, ages four and seven—all led by the pastor of their church, Pine Grove Holiness. In each of his hands he held a red, plastic container full of gasoline.

He had not told Mrs. Wells about his plan to eradicate the evil from their midst; he had simply taken her word that she had no regard for the things of this life. Surely, she could sleep on someone else's couch if she needed a place to be.

At his command, the menfolk unloaded a host of firewood from the back of one of the trucks and made stacks alongside the west wall of the quaint pier-and-beam home, making sure to factor in the wind. The evil specter would be carried away by the breeze. The womenfolk and the little boys picked up sticks and pine straw to serve as starter, singing praises as they worked to eradicate the discomfort inherent in the task before them:

> *There's a land that is fairer than day*
> *And by faith we can see it afar*

For the Father waits over the way
To prepare us a dwelling place there

In the sweet by and by
We shall meet on that beautiful shore
In the sweet by and by
We shall meet on that beautiful shore

One-by-one, each brought their offering forward until the task was complete. Brother Jeffrey, looking over the work, continued to think on the persisting thirst in his soul and in his body. With quiet hatred, he thought also on the glasses he assumed were somehow still sweating in the house. No one would again be troubled by the monster that had so troubled him. He was good to his flock.

When the time came, he doused and lit the fire. The house, dry and old, roared to life. The pastor stood triumphant in its glow, hand-in-hand with the fifteen faithful there with him, watching the smoke go up into heaven.

GRAVE DIRT

E. S. Murillo

Rue was a dark and stormy night.

Being that she was…dark, stormy, and older than dirt.

Literal dirt, as it were. Older than the sediment not seen since the foundation of the deep and the dust that formed the first ribs and the muck that slammed on top of every coffin in the graveyard that night. Older than the clay in the bricks she'd casually encouraged the mortals to use on the Tower of Babel…if only they had been more subtle, the fools. Man's insistence on crowing down unnecessary attention to himself from the heavens proved the bane of her unending existence.

She was absolutely so much older than the dirt from which an oozing, properly expired finger was trying to poke out of just to the right of her. She glanced over in annoyance. This was supposed to be her night off. As the hand attached to the finger attempted to emerge with it, she wrinkled her nose and pressed the appendages back into the mud with the silver tip of her cane. At her behest, the mud swallowed them up with an undignified *sploot*.

Forever a smartass, the dirt.

The gravediggers did not see the stabby motion or hear the simultaneous twelve other sploots around the cemetery, but they felt the slight tremor beneath the earth (a part of the gig that OSHA was nigh fifty-some-odd years off from addressing) and began to dig faster. In their line of work, you learned quickly that if your intention was to fall asleep sober and with your soul firmly intact, then you had better not be asking a lot of questions. Darwin's theory had already claimed more than a few of their number in recent days. Not these diggers, though. These knew precisely when to say their Hail Mary's and pretend an old widow was nothing but an old widow.

Rue whipped a man's timepiece (and a fair amount of wrinkled arm skin) around on her wrist to check the time and pouted. Dean had always laughed at her when she grumbled about Jamie being late. "Your Jamie is forever Jamie, sweetheart, and he has no plans to change. I'll just start carving the turkey without him. He'll turn up in time for dessert." Dean had died without knowing just how much truth his words held. It was not for nothing that Rue had missed the crowning of Queen Esther.

"Not to beat the metaphorical dead horse, but I truly don't know what you saw in that one," came a voice from just out of sight.

She flicked the watch, and the skin, back to their proper places and hid a grim smile before turning around.

Jamie was smoking one of those cigars, which she hated and he loved so much. His other gloved hand was tucked snugly inside the pocket of a jacket made from some type of dark leather, which looked suspiciously like one the German bombers were notorious for wearing. She recalled he had taken a liking to the jackets even while their owners kept him very busy. She squinted (the cataracts had been an unfortunate shapeshifting oversight), and he responded sarcastically in kind. When Jamie had fallen, he had fallen in Norway, and as such, his long blonde hair was fairly glowing in the moonlight. He carefully brushed a stray bit of ash from the arm of the jacket. Knowing Jamie, it was highly likely the jacket was a Luftstreitkräfte original.

"You're late."

"You're old."

"You...look ridiculous in that jacket."

Jamie's smile widened around his cigar and his crystal clear eyes sparkled. He could always tell when she was lying. It came with the territory.

She hated that.

He looked her up and down and grimaced dramatically for effect. She lifted her chin toward him and cackled in response. If there had been flying monkeys adorning the trees, they would have circled down at the sound of that cackle and offered her their immediate services. As it was, the crows simply watched from the branches with muted interest.

She had come to the graveyard as her old self one last time for the occasion, for Dean, so the two of them made quite a pair standing in the moonlight. Anyone (who was not a crow) foolish enough to be corpse-watching under these circumstances would assume the couple consisted of a doting grandson and his spectacularly great grandmother. Her insistence upon fake aging had been a point of contention between them since the Great Flood, one of their few, beyond Jamie's tardiness. She kept in step with whatever husband, gladiator, or fellow coven members she had picked up that century, which forced Jamie to at least appear to age right along with her for the holidays. Despite all his lamenting, he hardly fell on his sword for the ruse, just some greying around the temples (barely visible in his light hair) or added laugh lines around the eyes. These attempts to mollify her without sacrificing too much of his sizable ego would continue for as long as he could reasonably get away with it. As medical advancements increased, so did the ages of her...gladiators, along with his grumpiness.

He pretended to stamp out his cigar in the muck, covertly crushing a mutinous forearm beneath his heels while the gravediggers dug on. With a murmured word from Jamie, there was another sploot. The souls were restless tonight. The Mayor of Chicago could blame the virus for his moratorium on funeral attendance all he wanted, but the gravediggers knew the truth. Rue grinned a grin of the senile and long-dentured (dentistry had come so far this century, bless the humans and their capacity for creativity), and Jamie heaved a long-suffering sigh. A few more silent Hail Mary's went up from their left.

Jamie was nearly impossible to be around from his fake-sixties onward. Dean had lived well into his eighties, and Jamie was threatening to pull the plug himself (a phrase he coined long before electricity, and he was quite pleased with it). Although, in the end, no metaphorical plug pulling had been necessary. The poor bastard had succumbed to the Spanish Flu all by himself, along with half the neighborhood.

"A terrible loss. You know, the whole thing really…and, uh, whatnot." Jamie's face appeared quite solemn as he and Rue watched the gravediggers lower Dean's casket into the empty grave. He was a handsome young man now with just a few tasteful laugh lines creasing the corners of his eyes again.

"Stop it—you barely cared." Rue grimaced when the flimsy wooden box hit the bottom of the hole, and the dirt—at its most sardonic on this, of course, a full moon—didn't waste any time filling it. Suddenly very tired, she dabbed at her own faded blue eyes with the sleeve of her coat and sighed at both the living and the dead as the diggers shoveled more dirt onto the casket.

Having lifted their eyes quite against their will upon his arrival, the gravediggers did not allow themselves to stop watching Jamie as they buried Dean. At no point would OSHA have a lot of helpful advice to offer up for that one. It was almost late enough at night to be early in the morning…they were fortunate to have gotten enough wood for a casket and an official hole at all, given the year they'd collectively been having. Jamie was too busy watching with a weather eye for the un-entirely-dead (who sensed one of their caretakers atop them, nights off be damned) to care that the diggers were staring.

She pulled her coat tight around her. The ground had not frozen yet, but if poor Dean had held on a week or two longer, they might have had to make very different arrangements.

Jamie took a step closer to her and made a face of genuine disgust. "Ugh. Is that…mothballs? Rue, please, enough of this…"

It was the little touches, she always said, that kept this game amusing.

One of the gravediggers sneezed with one eye open so he could continue to keep it pointed at Jamie. The sneeze caused his compatriot to flinch and duck his head away as the offender wiped at his nose with a filthy sleeve, but Jamie still didn't bother with a glance in their direction. Stares and sneezes and plagues were of little concern to him, insofar as the first affected him not at all and the others merely affected his caseload and not his life expectancy. He considered the flu to be a pleasant reprieve from that business in Europe, anyway. He was not particularly affected by human suffering, but that one had started to wear on him after a while. The diggers stared and shoveled on. He always had this unsettling effect on humans. Rue could blend in seamlessly, but no matter how hard he pretended to try, the mortals always watched him. He could not have been putting in much, if any, effort to deter their stares. He enjoyed the attention too much.

Rue was over it. All of it. The night was iron and dirt and blood and the remnants of that cigar still smoking upward from the ick. Everything smelled damp and sick, and when they had poor Dean good and buried, the gravediggers hastily crossed themselves and turned to start digging another hole for a much sturdier looking casket than Dean's. The graveyard stretched out in front of them, not a crumb of dirt unearthed but for the final plot they were about to begin. Whoever had wrangled a fancy carved coffin in the last plot left in the cemetery must have had better connections than even Rue, and Rue's Connections were, as such, the best.

Jamie tapped her elbow lightly and turned to walk away just as she dropped an Amaryllis and her cane on top of the mound of dirt now covering Dean. The diggers shuddered and crossed themselves again as she hurried by. She followed him through the graveyard and across the street and caught the warm leather around his arm just as it crooked to light another cigar. He held it steady and looked down at her with approval.

"Red-headed this time?"

"I thought it might cheer me up."

"Amber. You even smell better."

A light snow began to fall as Jamie slid his hand over her small gloved one and dropped a kiss on the top of her head. They reached the sidewalk, and he held her steady as she lifted her dress and scraped the offending grave dirt off of her new boots. She had been coveting this particular style for years, but didn't feel that an eighty-seven-year-old could believably pull them off. They looked every bit as good on her once-and-again twenty-five-year-old feet as she had long dreamed they would.

"Dean would have appreciated this look on you."

She batted ginger eyelashes that were already dusted with snowflakes. "Maybe he would have. Maybe not. It doesn't matter now, I suppose."

They walked in silence. "Who handled him at the end?" Jamie asked after a few blocks. Her eyes were young and dark now, but the tears sprung up in them anyway.

"Not one of ours."

"Mmmm." He smiled gently as he steered her down a dark stairwell toward one of the few remaining pubs still open in this all-forsaken city. "Good man."

She held his arm until they reached the bottom of the steps, then he opened the door for her in a gentlemanly fashion. Warmth and light poured out of the pub and into the frigid night air. Their favorite barma...ah, bar-being, was working that night, and he smiled as he turned to pour Rue a whisky sour. Jamie waited until she had settled in and then he excused himself back out into the cold.

"Just for a moment, darling," he assured her, as the bar-being complimented her new legs, "Do save me a drink."

The pub door closed behind him, taking the warmth and light with it, as he adjusted his jacket and turned to walk back up to where he could smell the gravediggers heading home for the night. "I haven't had my dinner yet."

THE DOOR WAS OPEN

Abigail Pickle

The artist flicked her wrist for the final stroke. Gray-brown liquid splashed as she plunked the brush into the cup of murky water with the twenty other brushes she had used in the day's session.

Kala stepped back and folded her arms to scrutinize the painting. Her right hand came up and cupped her chin, index finger tapping her cheek and smudging her pale, freckled skin with the sludgy colored paint.

In the painting, a figure sat before a high window open to a vibrant, futuristic cityscape.

Kala had spared no energy on the details of the room in the painting: wainscoting stained green but with the woodgrain still showing, cracks and smudges on the cream-colored plaster walls and ceiling, gleams and shadows in the wood floor, dirt and stray fluff from the sheepskin rug. The figure sat on a wooden chair with a patterned cushion and simple carvings. The cityscape too, was a mass of distant detail: suspension bridges and glass windows and metal spires and cathedral steeples and industrial towers.

In contrast, the figure bore almost no detail to distinguish it. It gazed out the window so that only a sliver of the suggestion of a face was visible. The dusk lighting from the window made the skin-tone impossible to discern, revealing only gray highlights and shadowed hints. The figure was neither skinny nor fat. It was a human-shape that could have been of any race or of no race. It could have been male or female, or neither or both. It was full grown, but it was impossible to tell whether it was young or old or somewhere between. Simple clothing draped vaguely over the ambiguous form.

Kala let herself indulge in a slow, hard-won smile.

She had done it: an expression of the pure human essence, a vision of a humanity made up of individuals who could encounter each other without meeting difference.

Particularity caused difference, and difference caused

conflict. Thus, to depict the pure human essence, she had painted a human who had transcended particularity. It was a perfect portrayal. The hope of a world without division or conflict.

Kala strode over to the studio sink, turned on the tap, and snatched the bar of soap into her fist like it was a trophy. As she scrubbed the suds over her hands and wrists, she closed her eyes and imagined the articles of gushing critics, the spotlights of televised interviews, and the painting on tour, starting local at the Dallas Museum of Art, then moving on to be displayed on a center stage wall of every prestigious museum in the country.

Snapping those daydreams to the back of her mind— tucked away for the future—Kala dried her hands on the coarse cotton towel, pulled her phone from her back pocket, and tapped the name of her agent.

Jule stood by the doors of the Dallas Museum of Art, facing the contemporary gallery and resting their hands on their round hips beside their holstered stun gun and flashlight.

It was 12:30 a.m. Jule had spent the first half hour of their shift, checking all the doors, the main lobby, and the gift shop. They liked to follow a different path each night; security guards with discernable patterns were the easiest to exploit—at least, that's what Jule had decided after seeing all those spies in movies pull off incredible heists. The night before they had started around the African mask display, so tonight they were starting in the contemporary section.

The after hours lighting didn't leave anything dark enough to call a shadow, but there were soft, low-light areas between the islands of brightness. Jule preferred this to the full lighting when the museum was open, and they stood in the places of softer lighting whenever they could.

Jule shifted and scanned the gallery. It was a new exhibit called *Communal Core*. It featured quite a few contemporary artists. There were seventeen paintings, three sculptures, and one assemblage of recycled items that sort of looked like a tapestry. Jule often counted the things they were guarding; it helped keep them focused. Most of the paintings were abstract, and a few were surrealist representations of city life.

One kept drawing Jule's gaze.

It featured a nearly photo-real, cozy room with a window looking out on a futuristic city skyline. But it was the figure that kept tugging at Jule's attention. It sat in a chair before the window, gazing out at the city. Its posture was human. Its proportions were human. But Jule couldn't call it human. It was obscure, like a thief crouching in the shadows. But it wasn't in the shadows, and it wasn't crouching. Jule squinted, searching for a detail, wishing it would turn its head so they could see its face and make sure it wasn't malicious or some sort of criminal. But they couldn't make out a single detail to anchor their mind; the face was turned toward the window.

Jule shook their head and looked away. It wasn't a thief. It was just a figure in a painting. It creeped them out, though, and they couldn't help glancing over at it every few seconds.

"Stop it," Jule muttered when their eyes flinched over again. "It's a painting, not a thief, and you've seen lots of paintings that were creepier."

The museum didn't pay them to like the art, just to guard it.

Motion in the corner of their eye caused Jule's gaze to dart again to the featureless figure.

Had it moved?

A primal instinct deep in Jule's body said the figure had moved, said it was dangerous. Their pulse sped up.

In the still, quiet museum air, they could hear their heart beating quick warning thumps within their ears.

"It's a painting," Jule said firmly to their pounding chest. "Time to walk around. That's the best thing to ward off The Jumps."

Jule walked northwest down the slope along the high-ceilinged corridor toward the main entrance. A third of the way down the hall, at the white stone sculpture of the reclining Assyrian queen, Semiramis, they banked left and took the stairs up to the Asian art section. They counted the calligraphy scrolls and painted screens, the little figurines, and the vases twined with friendly dragons.

Pausing beside a dark bronze sculpture of a seated, meditating Buddha, Jule felt their shoulders relax and their heart rate slow. They didn't know much about religion, but something about the Buddha's posture and expression calmed them down.

What was it?

The look of acceptance in the eyes? Something about the nose that made it seem to be inhaling breath? An overall sense of centered humanity...

Jule wanted to reach out and put their hand in the Buddha's upturned palm.

They caught themself, ran their fingers through the bristly short side of their thick black hair.

"You're acting weird tonight, Jule. Come on."

They turned from the sculpture, scanned the surrounding hall, and started walking again. Their palm tingled with the strange feeling of wanting to touch the Buddha's hand. Jule ran their hand over the short side of their hair again to try to brush the feeling away.

The other side of their hair was two or three inches long, spiky, and tipped with green and blue. Jule sometimes wondered if their hairstyle was what had landed them the job guarding the art museum. They forced a little laugh and looked at their hand. Their skin was a rich bronze with a red undertone, but their fiancé always said it was caramel-colored. *"Sweet and strong, like you."*

Jule smiled a real smile and kept walking.

They patrolled a circuit of the whole second floor, counting the objects as they went, and by the time they returned to the stairs, they had forgotten about the Buddha and about the painting in the contemporary gallery that had given them The Jumps.

Jule started heading down the stairs, intending to patrol through the European art wing next. But when they neared the last step, they heard something from further down the hall, from the contemporary gallery.

It sounded like a person moaning.

Jule's hand went reflexively to their stun gun. They bounded to the foot of the stairs and strode briskly up the slope of the hall toward the contemporary gallery, darting their eyes all around, listening as well as they could without stopping, and trying to keep their footfalls silent.

The moaning stopped right as they stepped into the gallery.

Jule's eyes went immediately to that painting with the vague figure. Their vision seemed to swim, and again they thought the figure had moved.

They blinked hard.

When they looked again, the figure was as it had been before: seated at the window with its face turned away.

Jule checked carefully through the whole gallery, but didn't find anyone or anything that could have made that moaning sound.

"Did I imagine it?" They whispered. "I've got The Jumps bad tonight."

They left the gallery and continued up the hall to check the southeast-facing doors. Secure. They cupped their hands around their face and peered through the glass to look outside. No one in sight. They went back to the gallery and did the same with the northeast-facing doors there. Again, secure and no one in sight.

Jule sighed. "Maybe it was the wind, or the pipes, or the building shifting..."

They shook their head. It hadn't sounded like that. It had sounded like a person, like a person sick or in pain.

The back of their neck prickled. Jule whipped around and looked at the figure in the painting.

Of course, nothing had changed.

"It could've been anything combined with my imagination."

Jule walked away to another section of the museum.

But later in the night, three different times, they thought they heard moaning near the contemporary gallery.

The soft shadows and the normally relaxing quietness of the museum at night slowly transformed into a dread-filled isolation.

Jule had never been so relieved to reach the end of their shift.

Taiwo flipped back the cover of his work tablet, held it screen-up propped on his left forearm, and logged in to his DMA employee account as he strode out of his office.

"Anyone want to make bets on whether the curator will touch his chair today?" Shelby, the communications coordinator, called through her open door.

"Ha!" Taiwo kept walking, but answered, "Maybe for lunch."

"Gotta get your steps in, huh?" Shelby chuckled.

Passing her door, Taiwo said, "It is my way."

"Yeah, yeah, we all know you come with all the high honors and..."

Taiwo turned into the main hall and didn't catch the rest of what Shelby was saying.

She wouldn't mind—Shelby was as good at monologuing as Taiwo was at avoiding his desk. He knew curators who could spend whole workdays in an office, but Taiwo worked by instinct, and that required walking the halls and feeling out how the pieces and exhibits were interacting with each other. Seeing the reactions of the guests helped too; he found that observing the way other people talked about and looked at the art helped him compensate for his own blind spots.

After a short aimless stroll around the museum, Taiwo sat down on the bench next to the Miztec representation of the rain god, Tlaloc.

The statue faced northwest toward the Hart Window, the high, floor-to-ceiling windows, which, adorned with Dale Chihuly's glass flowers, let the main entrance and the cafeteria bathe in rainbow-colored morning light. Taiwo took a moment to appreciate the way the seven hundred year-old ceramic sculpture beside him stared out toward the modern glass sculptures and beyond the city to the sky. For Taiwo, the arrangement represented the past looking toward the future, ancient toward the modern, and both facing the sky with its cycles of sun, moon, and stars: the modern was new and yet repeated an old tradition. The history of human sacrifice surrounding the ancient sculpture made the symbol even more poignant. To Taiwo, it seemed to ask, *Are we, as humans, progressing toward something better, or are we merely repeating the cycle of violence in new ways?*

Perhaps the answer was an aching *both*…

Clapping his cacao brown hands together once to break from his reverie, Taiwo reopened his tablet and started responding to emails.

Half an hour passed amid the soft murmuring of echoes in the high-ceilinged space: voices and footsteps, doors closing and opening, the sounds of movement and contemplation and life, and sometimes the sound of air sighing.

A scream.

Taiwo stood, listened.

Another scream and a clamor of footsteps.

All in one motion, Taiwo closed the tablet and broke into a jog along the balcony, down the steps to the main lobby, and to the left up the sloping hallway toward the source of the screams.

Several guests ran past him toward the exit.

He saw terror in their faces.

Somehow the terror didn't touch him; he was in motion, forward. That forward motion brought him to the contemporary gallery. He heard a groaning and stopped.

A figure slumped, folded forward on its knees with its palms to the ground. Its shoulders heaved. It groaned and groaned.

Now that he was standing still, Taiwo felt the fear. Cold sweat started at the back of his neck, soaking into the short twist-braids of his dark, kinky hair. He glanced at the painting behind the groaning figure. It was Kala Kenney's new piece, *Unnamed Essence*. He looked briefly at the detailed, cozy room and the window opening out on the futuristic skyline. He looked at the chair in the painting. The chair was empty.

A shock of breath.

Taiwo's eyes locked on the heaving, groaning figure. He felt like he was falling: a pitching in his stomach, a sensation of upward rushing in his arms and legs.

The figure staggered slowly, heavily to its feet. Took one step. Another. Toward Taiwo.

Taiwo shivered, but didn't move.

Looking at the figure made him feel like his eyes wouldn't focus, made his eyes feel blurry, his mind feel blurry. He blinked. Shook his head to try to shake off the blur.

The figure staggered forward.

Taiwo searched for a face, for an expression to understand.

But the figure had no face. The front of the figure's head was a blank oval of gray smudges. No nose. No eyes. No mouth.

The gray jaw worked. The chin strained down, left to right. The figure groaned. The chin jerked down. With a sound like clay sucking, the gray skin where the mouth should have been stretched, snapped, ripped and tore open into a ragged slit.

The figure threw back its head and screamed.

Taiwo's instincts reeled. Terror. He didn't move.

The figure staggered, stood straighter, walked, gaining speed, leaned forward into a barreling run.

Taiwo hopped backward just before the figure collided with him, and the figure ran past him, down the hall toward the main entrance.

Again Taiwo's eyes landed on the painting with the empty chair.

He heard screaming.

His mind snapped from the daze.

He spun and opened his tablet as he ran after the figure. Now that its back was to him and it was moving away, his terror turned to excitement. Taiwo opened folders through the tablet touchscreen, scrolled as he glanced back and forth from the screen to the hallway and the figure ahead. Surely he had the artist's phone number in his records.

He tapped, scrolled, searched.

There.

He tapped the number for a video call. The artist wouldn't believe this without the video, without seeing it. Taiwo didn't even believe it, and he *was* seeing it, chasing after it...

Ahead, someone walked into the main hall from an adjoining gallery. The figure, barreling forward, collided with them.

Figure and human tumbled to the concrete floor.

Taiwo ran forward.

When he got close, he saw a tangle of vague limbs and tan limbs, vague body and body clothed in jeans and a blue t-shirt. The woman in the blue t-shirt made a guttural sound of revulsion as she struggled, then, getting her arms free, punched the side of the figure's faceless head.

"No!" Taiwo shouted. "Don't hurt it."

The woman paused and stared up at Taiwo with a mix of confusion, anger, and fear in her tan face. She shoved the figure away and jumped to her feet. The anger won out and solidified in her expression. "It was self-defense! You saw that monster attack me, and you just stood there!" Her brown eyes smacked at Taiwo's.

"It didn't mean to." Taiwo looked away and watched as the figure staggered slowly, groaning, to its feet.

The woman flinched and jumped behind it and out of its reach.

"It is confused in its first moments of life," Taiwo said softly. "It is the same for all of us, entering the world."

"What?!" the woman snapped.

The figure moaned like a wounded bear and bowled forward into a wobbling run.

The woman turned and ran the other way toward the rear exit.

Taiwo followed the figure.

Kala Kenney wasn't picking up. Instead of trying to call again, Taiwo switched over to the tablet's camera app, swiped for the video setting, and hit the red circle. He tried to walk smoothly and keep the figure in frame. It was picking up speed. Taiwo had to sacrifice smooth cinematography to keep up.

The figure came to the main entrance, running faster.

Faster. It barreled into the cafeteria. Tables and chairs screeched and clattered on the concrete floor as the figure flung them aside and kept running.

And kept running.

Straight toward the floor to ceiling windows.

It charged.

Leaped.

Its head and shoulders clipped the lowest of the Dale Chihuly flower sculptures. Green and yellow glass shattered over the figure's shadowy gray body and fell to the concrete floor with the sound of bright rain. A deep boom with a wider shattering, and the whole lower window pane broke outward.

Taiwo winced. Those sculptures were made in the 90s and, at the time, they were the largest pieces of blown glass ever created. There were larger works now, of course, but the history—

History was happening right now. Right in front of him. A painted figure out of its frame and alive.

Fortunately, the figure seemed unharmed—Taiwo couldn't even find a cut or blemish in the blurry surface of its form. It landed in the bushes amid the raining shards of glass and staggered forward across the concrete, trellis-covered patio.

Taiwo stopped following at the edge of the shattered glass, but he held the tablet up and kept filming.

Near the broken window, the summer heat rushed in and wrestled with the air-conditioned cold. The prickle-scent of exhaust mixed with the fragrances of summer flowers and mist from the little sprinklers in the grass.

Taiwo kept the figure in the tablet's frame and zoomed in as the nebulous form staggered across the driveway.

The figure crossed over grass and pavement and stopped before the brightly colored 1950s mural by Miguel Covarrubias.

Genesis, the Gift of Life.

Taiwo gasped and held his breath. He made sure the tablet was steady and still filming, then watched the figure with his own eyes from a distance, feeling as if time itself was holding its breath for this moment.

The figure walked closer to the mural, paused. It raised both arms slowly and put its palms to the red hand in the mural, the hand holding the seed. The figure pressed with its palms, threw back its head, and howled.

The sound made an icy shiver run up Taiwo's spine. He lost track of filming. The figure ended its howl with a shriek. It tore right and sprinted east, its speed and stride now potent and powerful as an Olympian's. It turned, and the next second, the corner of the building blocked Taiwo's view.

Heels clopped on concrete as Shelby walked up and stood beside Taiwo. A red bruise on her forehead stood out bright against her pale skin, and there were jagged stand-up tangles in her long black hair. She held a phone to her ear.

"Now it's turned right on Harwood," Shelby said into the phone.

"Who is that?" Taiwo asked.

Shelby turned toward him and covered the bottom half of the phone with her hand. "The police." She uncovered the phone, stepped gingerly over the glass, and peered out the window. "Yes...no," she said into the phone. "It's going fast...I can't see it anymore."

"No!" Taiwo shouted.

Shelby covered the phone again and glared at him.

"They won't understand," Taiwo pleaded. He didn't understand it either, but he wanted to. "They'll shoot without even trying to—"

"Did you even see that thing!?" Shelby gestured wildly to the broken glass.

"Yes," Taiwo said. His voice softened. "It's a...miracle."

"It's a lawsuit waiting to happen," Shelby snapped. "It

knocked over three people."

"Was anyone injured?"

"Not really, but that won't stop..." Shelby trailed off as her gaze landed on the screen in Taiwo's hands. "Wait. Are you recording?" She started striding toward him. "Delete that right now, before—"

"I will not." Taiwo raised his arm and held the tablet high over his head, far out of Shelby's reach. "This is a historic day for art and for all of humanity."

"You're crazy! That thing's messed up. Didn't you feel it? When it was coming toward me—" Shelby hugged herself with her free arm and shuddered.

"I did feel the fear, but then..." Taiwo stared out onto the tree-lined street where the figure had gone out of his sight. "I must follow it," he whispered. And without another look at Shelby, he turned and sprinted for the parking garage.

Kala Kenney rubbed a rag with gray blue wash over the canvas, applying the base tone, setting the foundation. Reviews for *Unnamed Essence* had been coming in left and right. Glowing reviews. The critics loved it. Half of the laypeople who commented about it online didn't like it, but Kala could ignore the uneducated masses. Everyone who knew what they were talking about praised the work and its artist:

"A masterpiece."

"A work of true genius."

"Transcendent in both form and concept."

Kala let these praises play to a beat in her head as she applied the wash. No interviews yet, but they would come. She just had to keep the buzz going. If she did nothing or moved on, it would die down in a few weeks. But if she made this concept into a series...

Her heart sped up. The pressure was on now. Kala smiled fiercely through the weight of stress and anticipation.

She set down the rag and stepped back to let the foundation dry. As she washed her hands, she closed her eyes and kept them closed, reaching things on the familiar studio sink without sight, envisioning the backdrop of the new painting. A vast view of a city from the roof of a highrise and, beyond the city a landscape of rolling hills beyond to represent hope for humanity. In the foreground, a group of figures would stand facing that view, looking out toward hope together.

Kala reignited her fierce smile, opened her eyes, and crossed the room to the shelf where she had left her phone.

There was a missed call from the curator at the DMA.

"Huh." That was odd. The painting had only gone on exhibit a day ago. Better call him back.

Watching the screen as she unlocked the phone, she opened the door and stepped out into the late morning summer heat and onto the shaded sidewalk. The city smelled like asphalt and coffee, cigarette smoke and a mix of foods cooking, hot tires and the bark of elm trees.

Kala leaned against the cool, west-facing brick and tapped the name on the phone screen to call.

But just then, a cold buzzing shivered through her sternum, between her shoulder blades, and up her spine along her neck to the base of her skull.

With a flinch, Kala shot her gaze down the street to the left.

Someone was standing at the corner, shoulders slumped, staring at her.

Kala canceled the call. She didn't want her voice to sound ruffled when she spoke to the museum curator. Shivering, she shoved the phone into her back pocket, faced down the street, clenched her hands into fists, and tried to widen her shoulders and look confident.

The figure snapped into motion, charging right toward her.

Kala's breath turned fast and shallow. She didn't really know how to fight, but reflexively, she widened her stance and tried to get ready to throw a punch.

As the figure got closer, she realized she couldn't make out any details about it: no clothes, no face, no...Her mind slipped. A strange nausea started in the core of her throat.

The thing halted a step away from her. It stared at Kala's face and groaned a pained guttural sound that tugged something from the pit of her chest, from within quartet chambers that kept her heart beating. She knew this creature. It was her figure, *Unnamed Essence*.

How?

"A work of true genius."

Her creation had come to life.

Kala beamed a full, open-mouthed, victorious smile.

The figure howled, lurched toward her, and gripped her shoulders.

Its hands were cold.

Kala's smile dropped. Fear clenched her heart.

The figure groaned, shaped sounds with the jagged tear that made its mouth, sounds almost like...almost like words...

Kala strained to listen, to understand.

It *was* speaking.

"What..." the figure groaned. "What...am I?"

Kala felt like she had swallowed a pitcher's worth of ice cubes, like she had been trapped in a freezer far, far from the summer heat.

She swallowed, stoked the feeling of victory back into her throat, and tried to project all that confidence into her voice. "You are the unnamable essence of humanity. Transcending race, gender, class, or any other category, you represent every human who has ever existed."

The figure slumped, moaning, gripped her shoulders

tighter. "Name…" it groaned. "…my…name?"

"You don't have a name," Kala said firmly. "That's the point. You represent something beyond words, beyond definition."

The figure screamed and lurched, shook her with its left arm and clawed at her face with its right.

Panic took over. Kala shoved the figure away, scrambled back into her studio, gripped the knob and yanked to slam the door.

Just before the door closed, a colorless arm shoved into the gap.

Kala yelped. Her pulse hammered her whole body. She couldn't think.

The figure shouldered into the studio, screaming like something tortured and prehistoric.

The door swung on its hinges. The heat and the smells of the city mixed with the cool and the studio smells of wood and lacquer and paint.

The figure charged over to the easel, grabbed it by the support behind the canvas, and hurled it across the room. The easel clattered to the concrete floor, and its aluminum legs filled the room with a cold, hollow ringing. The canvas snapped and crumpled.

Kala shouted a wordless protest.

The figure stood in the center of the studio exactly where the easel had been, stared at Kala, and stamped its left foot.

A sharp, brittle sound.

Hairline cracks webbed out in the concrete floor around the figure's foot.

Kala clenched her fists. She knew what the figure wanted. It wanted her to paint, to change the figure here, which…would it change the original?

"No. I won't," Kala said. Her voice felt hard in her mouth, edged with scolding. "You are already finished. You're perfect. The critics are all saying so. You may even become the new symbol for world peace."

The figure screamed, leaped, collided with a shelf, snatched up a handful of paintbrushes and flung them at Kala's face.

Kala blocked the assault with her arm.

The brushes pattered and rolled over the floor.

The figure threw back its arms, thrust its neck forward, and shrieked.

"Stop!" Kala shouted. "Throwing a tantrum like a spoiled toddler isn't going to change my mind. You're alive. You're a masterpiece. Calm down and I'll make the right calls and announce you to the world. We'll both be famous. We will solve—"

The figure lunged, throwing its arms around Kala's shoulders, hurling its weight against her chest. Kala's knees buckled. She toppled backward.

The floor shocked the air from her lungs.

The figure landed on top of her.

It screamed in her face. Kala flinched and shuddered. The breath from the rip of its mouth smelled...terrifying, stale and airless, like a vacuum-sealed vault abandoned for centuries.

The faceless head of the figure stared down at Kala. It stopped screaming and paused like a lost traveler at a fork in the path, unsure which way to go.

Kala struggled, but couldn't budge. The figure was much heavier than a human of its size. It felt like a boulder was sitting on her chest.

She looked frantically around for something to fight with.

The easel!

Kala strained her arm sideways.

The figure shuddered, groaned, reached forward, groped its hands over Kala's face like it was searching in the dark.

When its hand touched her nose, Kala smelled something electric, dry and heavy, but buzzing, like lightning on stone.

Kala stopped straining to reach the easel.

What was that smell?

She recognized it.

She had never breathed it with her nose, but…somehow she felt like that smell had been inside her before… or like she had been inside it, surrounded, overwhelmed… the smell of a storm brewing, electric charge over asphalt, the smell of the potential for lighting, the—

That was it!

Potential. It was the smell of potential. It was the smell of an idea, and she remembered being caught up in that smell and in the feeling of full focus as she painted the idea to life.

It had been like that while she painted *Unnamed Essence*. She remembered that smell while painting the city outside the window. She remembered it while painting the room and the rug and the chair. She remembered it—but no… she tried, but whenever she thought of the moments she had spent painting the figure, she couldn't remember that smell. Surely it had been there. She racked her memory and only came up with daydreams of interviews and fame.

It wasn't there.

She had painted the figure without that smell.

The figure slumped, the side of its face against Kala's. It moaned and shook like someone sobbing.

Kala breathed the smell of potential lightning.

Her right hand twitched, aching to hold a brush.

The figure's sob cut off. It raised its faceless head and stared down at her. Its hands gripped her arms like she was a rope leading out of dark and tortured waters.

Kala swallowed through tension in her throat.

If she changed it, the painting would become mediocre—nothing. No one would notice a painting of a person looking out a window. Laypeople might like that painting for a minute, but they would forget about it the moment they walked away. And the critics would write about the change. She imagined the new quotes that would come: *"Artist capitulates to the status quo." "Once riveting painting sinks to the level of cheap hotel art." "Masterpiece ruined." "Transcendent to uninspired."*

Uninspired…

But she had painted the figure without the potential lightning. Could a painting without that spark be called inspired? Could she call it finished at all? And if she refused what her art begged her to give, could she even call herself an artist?

She imagined interviews discussing *Unnamed Essence* as it was. She would state her vision to portray a humanity unified and transcending difference. But knowing now that she had painted it without the spark of potential lightning, all those grand statements of purpose would feel like lies.

The figure stretched its ragged mouth-opening and made a rasping sound like something struggling to breathe through sick lungs.

The blood in Kala's heart seemed to expand, stretching the tight muscle chambers until every beat ached.

She could be an artist and obey the potential lightning, or she could be famous and leave her art in pain, half-alive and rasping for breath.

Kala sighed. Her heart stretched and ached. Shutting her eyes, she let her imagination swell with the interviews and photographs and fame. She sniffed.

Those visions smelled like stale perfume.

Kala grimaced, shut her eyes tight, and let those bright-flashing daydreams fizzle and fade, let her imagination fill instead with the unfinished figure, let her nose fill with the smell of potential lightning.

Her stomach pitched like she was falling. Her stretching heart seemed to split with the pain of loss.

She relaxed her fisted hand.

Maybe that hand would never hold a microphone or an award.

But it would hold a brush.

Kala tried to force a bitter smile. She couldn't manage it. With the pain of loss in her mouth, she met the figure's eyeless gaze. "Let me up. I'll paint you."

The figure cut to silence, then hummed a sound that mashed pain and hope together. It climbed off of Kala and returned to the easel's place in the center of the studio.

As Kala got up and rummaged around between the counter and the shelves, gathering rags, the scattered brushes, paint tubes, oil, and her palette, the figure watched her with a birdlike pose, like at any moment it might jump from its perch on the floor and fly.

Kala piled her supplies on a little table, dragged it over to the figure where she could easily reach it, and arranged the paints and rags and brushes on its chipped, dusty white surface.

Her heart was beating fast now, painful, but also excited, catching the scent and chasing the thrill of creation.

She glanced at the figure, then shut her eyes and took a breath. She needed to remember the scene in the painting, the colors of the room, the evening light, the placement of the window and the chair, the way the shadows fell.

There it was. Kala held the image in her mind's eye and stepped into the pose she used for painting: right foot forward and straight, left foot back and stabilizing.

Facing the figure, she opened her eyes, contemplated its gray-brown color and ambiguous form. Devoid of details...unfinished.

"What am I?" it had asked.

What...what...

Kala held the memory of the painting and imagined the figure as a living human entering that room.

What...what...

But *"what"* was the wrong question.

She needed to ask *who.*

That gave her a shock. She had tried to paint the essence of humanity, but that essence—or the thing she had painted—had ended up a what not a who, a sub-being rather than a human being.

How was that possible? How had she failed so completely?

But those weren't the questions to ask now. Now she needed to ask, *Who was the person sitting in that room by the window?*

Kala reached out and touched the figure's hand.

It stayed still, but she felt its attention on her.

Its hand wasn't cold anymore; its touch was warm, electric, alive with expectation.

Kala held its hand, pressed her palm to its palm, shut her eyes again and listened with the senses of her human spirit.

Who are you? her senses asked.

She held the room of the painting in her mind's eye.

Who would live in a room like that?

She listened.

"It's not your room, is it?" she whispered. "You're visiting a friend. You came to tell them something, but they stepped out, so you're waiting, thinking about what you're going to say, and about..."

She opened her eyes.

The figure watched her. It—no, he. He agreed with her words, resonated.

A quiet thrill.

He understood her. She understood him. And together in a flash, they understood the painting, without knowing clearly what it would look like in the end.

Potential lightning raced up Kala's arm.

She let go of the figure's hand and, in a rush, squeezed paint onto her palette and started mixing colors. The skin tone first, a middle brown with warm red-orange under-tones. It was close to the color of chai-steeped water held to the light.

Kala smiled, smelling paint but imagining the smell of spices.

The brush sounded a wet parting as its bristles lifted from the palette.

When Kala touched the color to the figure's arm, he exhaled a deep-voiced sigh and his shoulders relaxed.

Kala's heartbeat skipped to the tips of her fingers. She applied the base skin tone in quick, lively strokes. Twice, she had to stop and mix more of the color. Working in three dimensions took a lot more paint, and the figure was bigger than the canvas of the painting he had come from, a little under an inch taller than Kala. But soon enough she had the base down. The paint was drying far quicker than usual.

What next?

She glanced at the faceless head. Normally, she would work on the face last, but the figure had been faceless for so long...

Kala blocked out the general features of a human face, then paused to catch her breath.

What did he look like?

She closed her eyes and again took his hand. Listened. Yes, she could see it, in sketch skips of dream lines, in aura hums, not nearly every detail, but enough to start.

Eye shape first, straight on the tops, teardrop curves on the bottoms, medium length, a faint scatter of wrinkles radiating from the outside corners. Brows dark but thin, they would look ready and decisive in any expression. Nose a straight bridge and nostrils that angled back slightly. Mouth–he closed the ragged tear, and Kala mixed a touch of mahogany into the skin tone and healed the tear with painted lips that made the mouth full and wry. Back to the eyes, the whites, the black pupils, deep brown irises, threads of a lighter, luminous brown for texture, dark, short lashes.

Kala brought the memory of the painting back to the front of her consciousness and mixed the color of the light coming in from the window. She touched a clean little stroke of the color to each of the figure's eyes for reflection.

The eyes came alive.

A soul-light from within.

The figure blinked, smiled, looked at Kala.

"My name is Anand," he said. His voice was light and earthy.

"Anand," Kala said, tasting the sound. She had never heard that name before. "I'm Kala."

Anand nodded like he knew her name already.

Kala took his hand. The paint there had completely dried, but it didn't feel like dry paint. It felt like a warm, living, human hand.

"Anand, I'm sorry," Kala said softly. "I tried to...I failed."

Anand shook his head. "You're trying. Keep trying." Then he went completely still again. But his smile stayed and his eyes kept shining with life and he blinked every few seconds.

Kala kept trying. She painted. Small round ears with pierced lobes but no earrings. Very short black hair on his head—it had been shaved a month ago, but it was growing back. Details in his hands, creases and calluses and bits of dirt under the short fingernails.

Did he garden, then?

Kala paused, took a step back. What would he wear? She considered his face. "Anand, what's your favorite color?"

His eyes flashed. "Hmmm." He looked slowly all over the studio. "All of them, but my favorite..." He met Kala's eyes. "Yellow."

A surprised laugh jumped from Kala's lips. "That's not most people's answer, you know."

Anand shrugged, then again went completely still.

Kala opened a new tube of paint and squeezed a generous glob of cadmium yellow onto her palette. A smidge at a time, she mixed in drops of titanium white and burnt umber and crimson red, trying to get a perfect harmony to Anand's skin.

"You were supposed to be the essence of humanity," she said as she mixed. "Blue is statistically the most common favorite color. Why isn't it yours?"

Anand glanced at her, but didn't answer.

"For that matter," Kala went on. "Why are you a man? The essence of humanity should be intersex, or neither sex, or something...more..."

Anand caught her gaze and looked at her steadily. "I'm not," he said.

"Not what?"

"The essence of humanity."

Kala breathed a deep sigh. "I know."

She shut her eyes for a moment. She hadn't painted *Unnamed Essence* solely for fame; a part of her truly wanted to find and depict that mysterious, elusive essence of humanity.

"Maybe it isn't possible," she murmured.

Anand's voice broke into her reverie. "I'm Anand," he said.

Kala made a short laugh. "Yes. Anand." She stopped stirring the yellow paint. "Here, I think I've got the color right."

Anand smiled, gazed forward, and went still.

She gave him a breezy, sleeveless yellow shirt with a texture like linen. For the pants, she used raw umber to make a dark brown to match the yellow, and she worked the yellow in with bits of embroidery in the shapes of little suns and swirls and a climbing gecko.

The pants stopped at the middle of the calves.

Kala had to kneel and stoop to keep working.

Anand had bare feet, calluses on his heels and toes, and high arches where a pinker skin tone met the brown. When Kala finished the details there, Anand curled his toes and laughed.

Kala stood and went over everything, a blending color here, a defining line there, highlights and shadows for folds in the cloth, in the creases of the elbows, along the jaw, behind the ears…feeling the familiar daze of getting too deep in the details of a painting and losing sense of the whole, Kala stepped back to assess.

Anand grinned back at her. He raised his arms over his head, stretched like waking up from a long sleep, then shook it out, jumping on the balls of his feet.

Kala watched him with her face sort of stunned and could only think that he was beautiful and good.

All of a sudden, Anand hopped forward and wrapped his arms around Kala and hugged her. Her brain felt stunned, but her body relaxed. She hugged him back.

He smelled like cardamom and mountain air.

"Thank you," Anand breathed over her ear.

Kala choked up. Before she could find words, he was already letting go, stepping back.

Anand put his palms to the sides of Kala's face, touched his forehead to hers, and spoke-sang something in a language she couldn't understand.

It sounded like a blessing.

Something shifted, settled. The feeling of his hands and forehead faded from her. The sight of him dissipated, vanished like mist, like a sigh of wind.

Kala looked around in a half daze.

She realized she had left the door open. It hung wide, swinging slightly on its hinges, doorknob thumping a shelf every few seconds, letting a bright rectangle of afternoon light strike boldly into the studio shade.

There was someone standing to the side of that bright rectangle, partly leaning against the doorframe.

Kala squinted, then recognized the person. It was Taiwo, the museum curator.

"Forgive me," Taiwo said. "The door was open." He gave her the disarming smile she had particularly noticed the other day when she had first met him. "I could not help watching. It was a beautiful thing to see."

Kala swallowed. What was there to say? It was deeper than words and yet within words, and…she didn't know.

Kala shook her head, nodded, said, "Yes. The door was open."

Kala and Taiwo drove back to the museum together in Taiwo's little red Subaru.

"The police have been at the museum," Taiwo explained on the way. "There was some damage. I spoke to them over the phone and let them know what was happening and that there was no more danger. They will likely want a statement from you later, though."

"Oh," Kala said. She still felt rung out and stunned. "Well, I guess I'll have to, as unbelievable as it is…"

The drive took less than five minutes; the rush hour traffic had already flooded out.

They parked in the street and walked to the museum's side entrance. It was after closing. Taiwo pulled a key from his pocket, unlocked the glass door, and pushed it open.

They walked in silence to the gallery, to the painting.

There, Anand sat in the chair gazing out the window at the painted city and the horizon beyond. He angled his head to show his face. He wore a complicated expression, light and peaceful, but complicated.

"I need to change the title," Kala said as she studied that expression. "It's not *Unnamed Essence*…I guess it never was."

Taiwo nodded. "I'll have a new card made. What will

you call it?"

Kala stared at Anand's face. It was a look of peace that held sorrow and joy together, hope with pain in it…"It's called *Anand Contemplates the Future*." She stopped, shook her head. "No, that's not it…"

It was about the future, but that wasn't all.

And what was in the future? What was he doing?

Kala kept trying.

"It's called *Anand Waits for a Friend*."

That didn't say all of it, she knew, but it was a better hint, and the painting said what the words couldn't. And what the painting couldn't say, Kala would hold in her heart forever.

"Anand," Taiwo mused. "It means a kind of joy, doesn't it?"

Kala turned from the painting and looked up at him. "It does? I'd never heard the name, he just told it to me."

"Perhaps I am remembering wrong," Taiwo said. "But I believe it means a kind of joy. A foundational joy."

"Huh." Kala ran her hand through the tangled mess of her red-brown wavy hair. "That sounds right. I wish I could take credit for—" She stopped herself, shook her head. "No, I don't wish that. I'm just grateful. And I don't know what to say."

"Ha!" Taiwo said. "There will soon be many inter-views—good ones, after the police—and they will be wanting you to have something to say. You are the first artist to have her painting come to life."

"Oh, no!" Kala said. "My dream's coming true, and now I don't want it."

"You will simply tell your story," Taiwo said.

"Yes, and you'll tell yours, and Anand will tell his." Kala glanced at the painting, at the window there and the glimpse of an imagined future for the city, at Anand's face, his complex smile. There was hope in the future. Pain too.

And joy.

Kala took in a strong breath and nodded. "I don't want to think about interviews right now," she said. "I just want to live. And I'm starving."

Taiwo called that short laugh of his. "Would you like to join me for dinner? I believe we both skipped lunch. And I feel, this thing I want so much to talk about, there is no one else who will understand."

"Yes, let's." Kala turned briskly from the painting, strode toward the door, pulled the black metal handle in front of the glass, and stepped into the red-gold light and warmth of the Dallas evening. She and Taiwo walked out onto the rounded square-bricks of the courtyard entry-way, between the crepe myrtles and the live oaks, past the short geyser fountain, and on along the sap-sticky side-walk beneath the feather-leaved boughs of the cypresses lining the street.

DIG, DIG.

Matthew Nordby

ix days' walk. Six days' walk to Fort March.

The army always had one or two old or skittish horses they were content to part with. Gordon Dig, who everybody just called 'Skip,' could make do with either old or skittish, but the six days' walk to get 'em; well, he was none too keen on that.

Oh, he'd walked farther before. Much farther. But it was hot this summer. Real hot. It was the heat that baked Skip's own horse for at least a month.

The last five miles, he had to dismount and walk lest he risk laying up the nag for good.

Either way, Skip couldn't wait a month for her to recover. Had to get a move on.

The trek to Fort March took him two days in the wrong direction, plus the six spent getting there.

Couldn't be helped now. There weren't a better town or fort closer, and not one horse in all of Ludlow City was fit for the ride. When Skip arrived to corral his ol' girl, the available horses overheated just standing there.

"Walkin' it is, then. Nothin' for it."

Now, nobody really knew Skip.

Nobody really knew why he was called Skip, either.

Even he didn't know why people called him Skip. Leastways, he never told.

You ask him, 'Hey Skip! Why do people call you Skip?' Skip would just shrug his shoulders and say...well, he would usually say nothing at all, but if he did say something, it was likely the most unpleasant way of saying "I don't know" you ever did hear.

At the Ludlow City General Store, Skip bought a small rucksack to carry his bedroll, canvas, shovel, food, change of johns, and two big canteens. The canteens weighed heavy when they were filled.

Even so, Skip knew, by the end of the trek, he'd wish he could've carried more.

Hot as it was, there weren't clouds day or night. Skip

thought he might beat the heat a bit by walking under star and moonlight for most of the trek. When it was time to stop, he'd dig into the earth deep enough to where the sun don't heat the dirt.

He could wait out the worst of it like that.

Skip got as close to smiling as he ever did when, on his way to the general store, he saw a family preparing a wagon and a mule-cart.

He heard the children skipping rope and chanting:

> Dig, dig, they hate the dirt,
> Hide down there or you'll get hurt.
> Dig, dig, can't be true,
> Down there, they can't get to you.
> Dig, dig…

Skip didn't stick around for the rest—he needed to start directly.

He knew there wouldn't be brush nor tree for fire or cover. It was too dry for making sparks and that kind of business. So Skip pawned off his coffee pot, his remaining coffee, and a rusty pan to buy some dried meat and bread. He traded his camp ax, some leather, and a few bits of silver to round off his ammunition belt and pouch and had his guns cleaned.

The store clerk took a gander at the arms. Probably weren't used to seeing firing irons this good.

He wrinkled his brow at Skip, but didn't ask questions. Most folk these days knew better than to ask "Which side?" or some such foolishness. After all was said and done, Skip had enough tin for a bath, a haircut, and a shave. He even had enough for washin' his clothes before making tracks.

Skip celebrated his good fortune with his usual, "How 'bout that."

If he had any friends in town, they might say he "Looked like a million bucks!" coming out of the Ludlow

City Barber and Surgery.

Skip thought he and his friends were ugly as a pile of burned boots.

If he replied at all, like as not, he'd say: "You or I ain't ever seen a million bucks to know how it would look on a man."

If he were feeling friendly he'd add: "But I ain't it."

The barber asked him before he left, "Ain't you gonna go with someone? I'm sure there's a stiff around who'd go it with you. Lot of strange talk about the ground between here and the Fort. 'Nother pair of eyes might do you good. It's so dry, the bushes have begun to follow the dogs. 'Nother pair of eyes would surely do you good."

Skip pretended the barber was talking to someone else. He left the barber without a word. Weren't the barber's business where Skip was goin', or who he was a'goin' with. Weren't nobody's business.

Skip set off for Fort March as the daylight dwindled without so much as a goodbye.

He never said goodbye, even in the places he did have friends.

He just left.

Skip's guess was right. As soon as the sun went down, the air cooled off, and the stars began to poke holes in the sky.

Skip gnawed on some of the meat so he didn't have to stop for dinner. By his guess, he'd walked nearly twelve miles before deciding to lay up for the night.

He dug his ditch, laid out his bedroll, and slept peacefully until first light.

n the morning, Skip broke camp, surprised at how much ground he'd covered. He saw the ribs of a broke-down shack close by and was glad he didn't camp any closer to it.

"Full to the rafters with snakes, like as not."

Otherwise, Skip saw nothing of note.

Ludlow City was out of sight. No mountains, hills, or trees were visible in any direction. Only the shadows in the grass told him which way he was going.

The clear blue sky opened above him; brown plains spread out all around him.

Skip drank some water, chewed some meat, and set off again, hoping to put a few more miles behind him before the sun got too hot.

It weren't long before he'd sweat clean through his johns and shirt. He looked back and no longer saw the shack.

"That's good enough."

He set down his pack and began to dig.

Each shovel felt heavier than it should in the heat. The thirst set in, but Skip kept digging. His shovel hit a rock and blasted a ringing pain through his hand and forearm. He cursed, throwing the shovel down and turned his back to the hole, hands on his belt. When the ringing in his hand stopped, he turned to look where his strike ran foul.

Instead of a great sandy rock, Skip saw a pale, blank face with cloudy eyes. He recognized the face. It usually waited until he slept to show up. By Skip's recollection, there weren't much more than a face left to bury.

He closed his eyes and breathed deep.

"In. Hold. Out."

Skip opened his eyes. The face was gone.

Careful breathing helped sometimes. Sometimes it didn't.

A lime boulder the size of an oil lamp looked back at him with a small chip in it. Skip mopped his brow, took a drink, levered the rock to the side, and kept digging. At about a foot deep, the earth was cool to the touch, and Skip pitched his canvas before the sun could dry the slightly damp spot up. He reckoned it was no later than eleven in the morning, and it would be a mistake to travel before five—at the earliest.

"Best git comfortable."

He left one canteen in the sun, knowing he'd need water later and that he'd drink less of it if it were hot. Then he took his boots and shirt off and unbuttoned his johns to his chest. He didn't have anything to pass the time, but he prided himself on not needing much.

On a drive or wagon train, Skip didn't camp near the story spinners and their tall tales, and he especially avoided anyone with a harmonica or a banjo. Sometimes he'd start off unkind with those sorts so they'd leave him alone on the trip. It weren't that he preferred to be alone, but aside from his gun hand, keen eyes, and grit for the road, what did he have to offer them? No, out here, by his lonesome, in the land between forts and little towns that have 'City' in their name, Skip was at his best.

Leastways, he weren't at his worst.

Though the night march left him tired, he still intended to walk all the upcoming night. Skip set his mind to catching some sleep. He bunched up his shirt and propped it on his rucksack for a pillow. As he lay his head down, he thought he saw something shift in the dry buffalo grass.

A small white blur darted past on his other side.

He glimpsed it again around his canteen, catching sight of white fur and a long ear.

"Little varmint."

Skip could tell the visitor was too small to be dangerous, but it pricked his nerves and made the hair on his neck stand on end. Small things with fuzzy white fur usually didn't last long in this part of the world. They'd draw foxes, coyotes, hawks, owls, and wolves like flies to manure. Not willing to spend any more waking thought on the creature's fate, Skip pulled the brim of his hat over his eyes and tried to sleep away the hot part of the day.

A rending shriek ripped him from his sleep.

Skip sat bolt upright, upset his canvass, and squashed his hat down on his face. He climbed from the chaos and reached for his repeater.

The scream sounded again. Recognizing the sound of a rabbit being slain, Skip sighed heavy and tried to calm the thunder in his chest.

"Knew that poor little cuss weren't gonna make it."

Another face rose unbidden in his head.

The bugle boy.

Knew that poor little cuss weren't gonna make it.

Skip shook the face from his head and realized the sun was sinking fast.

Instead of the few hours he intended to sleep, he'd nearly missed his start for the night. He broke camp in a hurry and tore off a piece of bread. He took a long pull from his cool canteen and set to chewing on another piece of dry meat and got on the move.

The stars were bright. The moon was just shy of half full, waxing fuller every night. The prairie, brown by day, spread out in gentle blues under the pale celestial lights. An easy breeze picked up, driving the last bit of the day's heat away with the fading traces of sunlight on the horizon.

Skip didn't know why, but his thoughts dwelt on the white rabbit.

"Not it's fault it. Just unlucky."

Skip sympathized. Skip felt he knew a thing or two about being unlucky. His trip to Fort March, on foot, in the dead of summer, was only the latest entry in a long list.

Another scream split the calm night air. Then another a few minutes later. Then another. Some seemed far off, but Skip guessed most cries were within a mile.

"The rabbits are having a bad night."

He stopped to check his surroundings. Skip figured the carnage was a result of a small pack of coyotes on the hunt. There were too many cries for this to be the work of solitary hawks and owls, and no telltale howling had kicked off, so probably not wolves. He chambered a round in the rifle and made sure to leave his draw chute unclasped.

"Just in case."

The cries stopped, and Skip walked on. He tore off another bit of bread and pulled a mouthful of water from the canteen. He shook the canteen after he drank.

"Need to slow down on that."

As he spoke, something changed in the air. The temperature was mild, and the dazzling night sky lit up the world around him, but Skip started to feel uneasy. He couldn't put his finger on it, though. Then it came to him. Skip heard the rabbit cries coming from downwind. The wind. He could hear the wind and feel it cooling his skin, but it weren't moving the grass or his clothes, and it weren't muddying his hearing. Skip grabbed a handful of dry, almost dead grass and threw it in the air. The parched blades fell to the ground like stones, but the dust Skip clapped off his hands carried fast and free on the breeze.

"Well. I don't like that."

Another scream ripped across the plains, this time from very close by. Skip unclasped his holster and shouldered the rifle. A lumbering gallop approached from the direction of the scream, and Skip wheeled toward it, barrel raised and ready. He saw nothing in the glowing acres in front of him. The scattered thudding came close, faded off, and the screams fell silent. Beads of sweat chilled Skip's forehead, but as the galloping receded, the wind began to disturb the grass again.

Skip let fly taunts and curses in such volume and of such sharpness that would have debarked a tree, if any grew out here. Of all the trips to think he wouldn't need a fire.

He didn't stay for long.

He looked at the stars and regained his heading. He walked a bit faster than was comfortable, and he didn't refasten his holster.

"Ain't stayin' here."

Mile after mile, he trudged until the cold night air and revived breeze pierced his lungs with each ragged breath.

It was hours since whatever it was antagonized him.

He dropped his pack and leaned up against it.

"Just to catch my breath."

Skip woke, feeling the sun biting the skin on his face. Another mistimed sleep, and now it was too hot to go on. Skip shrugged and began digging. The damp, cool earth was deeper here, so Skip dug for longer.

He saw more faces and kept digging anyway. He sweat through his clothes by the time his canvas was pitched, but he was too tired to do more than throw them in a heap. He was thirsty, but hesitated, not knowing how much progress he made in the night. He poured a cap-full at first, then drank deep. When satisfied, he put the now almost empty canteen back in his pack.

That's when he saw them. Yellow eyes situated on the sides of a fuzzy white face perched atop a fuzzy white body. It stared blankly, its long stiff ears twitching this way and that. Its lanky front legs and powerful hind legs seemed comically long for its sleek, underfed body. Skip had seen thousands of jackrabbits in his time on the move, but this one was...a bit different. Black, shiny horns, too big for its head, curled about like ram's horns from its skull around its attentive ears.

"Well, gosh all Friday."

It was unusual enough to see a white jackrabbit, but

one with horns? Skip had heard the tall tales from men who said they'd seen a jackalope, so he knew no one would believe him if he told anyone he'd seen one. He didn't know who he'd tell anyway. But the unlucky critter might just make the trip a bit easier if it meant fresh meat. Skip reached for his holster and slowly drew his revolver. At this range, a rifle slug would burst a rabbit into a paste. But a well-placed revolver bullet might just leave him enough for a day's ration.

Before he could raise the barrel, the rabbit screeched.

The sound startled Skip, and he misfired a single round. The rabbit seemed unbothered, but it loped off all the same. Skip thought about sending another, better aimed round after it until he saw the dirt around his pack growing dark and wet.

The slug had sped straight through the full canteen and obliterated his remaining bread.

Skip sighed heavy, "I hope whatever got your friends last night comes after you tonight."

Now he was in real trouble.

The bullet hit the canteen just a hair above the three-quarter full mark, but on its side, more than half leaked out. Skip combined the water into the undamaged canteen and flung the damaged one into the wilderness.

He crawled back into his diggings and tried to rest, though he expected sleep would remain elusive today.

The daytime heat gnawed at the plains. The cool dirt dried up, and Skip chewed on dry meat. Thirsty again. But Skip held off. He still didn't know exactly how far he'd come in the night or how much further he had to walk. Even if he was off, the Fort would have roads coming and going to it, so once he hit one of them, he'd have a better idea of how close or far he was.

The sweltering sun chipped at his resolve. Rippling heat rose from the scorched grass and played familiar tricks on Skip's eyes, showing him pools of water he knew weren't there.

The white jackrabbit returned to taunt Skip.

The gangly creature sat defiantly, just close enough to annoy him. Maybe it weren't the same one as before. This one looked a bit healthier than the first. But the odds of seeing two Jackalopes with white fur and black ram's horns? Skip shook the extra thoughts out of his head. They wouldn't help now anyway.

"Not this time. You done me in moren'nuff for one trip."

The jackalope blinked dumbly at him.

"Git! Shoo!"

Skip shouted more and threw sand at the rabbit.

The rabbit's blank stare never changed.

As the sun finally began to fall, Skip emerged to get his bearings as the stars came out.

The rabbit loped off as Skip packed the canvas.

"See you 'round."

Skip noticed quickly that tonight was going to be hard. The evening sun left no cool air in its absence. Still thirsty. Skip caught his bearings and guessed he'd traveled a good fifteen miles in the night.

"Two or three more like that, and I'll have it done with."

The missing weight of the shot-up canteen was a relief.

But three more treks would still be a mighty task with so little water remaining. Skip fought the urge to drink by putting a capful in his mouth and chewing it into the dry meat. He caught one more glimpse of the lolloping, horned jackrabbit before he was on his way.

The nighttime heat weighed on him worse than if the sun were out.

He took his shirt off and rolled his johns down to his waist. Still, sweat ran freely down his face, neck, back, and chest. He reached into his pack for more meat and found he'd only one piece left.

"Well, turkey lips."

Just then, he caught a glimpse of sparkling yellow eyes peering at him from a tangle of dead grass.

Seeing the need for food revived, he drew the revolver and fired into the grass.

Missed.

How?

He should have hit the thing square between those goofy yellow eyes.

Blue eyes.

Brown eyes.

Dozens of eyes.

Skip didn't miss, not up close like that.

Should have hit the thing square between the eyes.

He sighed and wandered on.

He paused around what he guessed to be midnight. His throat was dusty, and his stomach began to twist, complaining of its abuse from the last couple days. Skip just closed his eyes and tried to ease his breathing. He sighed as he put the last piece of meat in his mouth. "I can make a day without food, I reckon."

He remembered a time when the resupply didn't come. For more than a month, it didn't come. The taste of grasshoppers filled his mouth. Skip grimaced and tried to spit the taste out. He didn't realize while he was pawing through the pack for his last meat, he upset his canteen, and the rest of his water silently poured out the bottom of his pack. By the time he noticed, it was too late to save any. He only discovered the leak when he began to feel a slightly cooler than sweat feeling running down his back. Upon discovering the empty canteen, he launched into another almighty expulsion of curses and, like its shot twin, flung the vessel into the wilderness. His tantrum cost him all his remaining energy.

Skip slumped against his pack and bowed his head. He might have fallen asleep, but the familiar racket of the lumbering gallop crushed all signs of fatigue.

He leveled his rifle and scanned the darkness. He caught the gleam of yellow eyes.

Skip breathed easy. Slowly he reached for the revolver. If he had to shoot, he'd make it count.

"In. Hold. Out."

A loud, shrill shriek arrived just in time to wreck any nerve Skip had fortified.

He re-shouldered the rifle.

The scream came straight from those unblinking yellow eyes. Skip gritted his teeth and forgot the heat, the loneliness, the hunger, and the thirst.

"Well, c'mon then!"

Skip's shout didn't deter the eyes, but something did happen to them. They jerked and swayed, lurching and swooping in great arches and evasive scurry. They eased a bit closer. Skip exhaled, sights right between those yellow eyes. He tried to push the feeling of his dry tongue sticking to his teeth out. He tried to push the untimely gurgle in his stomach out. He tried to push the salt sting of sweat on his cheeks out. The moon's gentle silver light caught the edge of over-large black horns and white fur.

Skip's barrel dipped.

He watched the white jackalope hop just into view. It was fat and healthy, more like a farm rabbit than a wild jackalope. Skip's stomach groaned loudly. He was again suddenly aware of his tongue sticking to the roof of his mouth.

As he thought of how hungry he was, Skip saw the rabbit swell beyond the boundaries of health and nature. He nearly dropped the repeater. The creature's bloated body nearly made its legs disappear. Another face passed through Skip's mind. The battalion scout. The enemy had caught him and left him on display in a tree. He was bloated and waterlogged by the time he was discovered.

Skip shook the image out. At the memory, the creature changed again. Its fur stretched and tore. Its face elongated, pushing its muzzle and teeth past the ripping fur. Skip watched as the powerful legs lengthened and shredded, and the rabbit decayed into something else altogether. It stood taller than a bison on hind legs; patches of white fur clung to exposed bones and muscles. Its skin stretched so much over its body, that thin tears split across the beast's chest and stomach.

"Oh, save me."

Skip heard the shake in his voice and felt it shudder in his chest. His failing nerves broke familiar in Skip's mind and body. Real familiar. The strength of his back and the sturdiness of his legs threatened to collapse him to the prairie floor.

The memories flowed through his mind unhindered. He remembered lining up to the drums and the fife. Remembered the stink of sulfur powder and scorched grass. Remembered feeling the earth around him roar and shake. He remembered the bodies of his friends flying to pieces under a barrage of cannon fire. Remembered the bits left of men, friend and foe alike, after a doomed charge.

This weren't worse than trying to keep a steady aim under a cannon barrage.

This weren't worse than cleaning up friends with a bucket after a bad day.

Time's up for easy breathing.

Skip recalled a different breath; a soldier's breath.

He squared his back and pressed the rifle stock into his shoulder, eyes down range. Yellow eyes leered back. His steady finger took the slack out of the trigger.

"Square between the eyes."

In, out.
Hold.
"Fire at will."

Corporal William Mooney, who everybody called Jack, thought he was losing his head to the heat when heard the children's voices singing a song. Something about digging. Made the hairs on his neck and arms stand on end.

That was before the heat ripples shaking the horizon revealed an inbound covered wagon and mule-cart. Even a mile off, he knew it weren't no threat. He wished they'd just go on so he wouldn't have to leave the shade of his makeshift canopy. Take their spooky song with 'em.

Still, Jack had his duty.

"Identify yourself!"

The wagon driver waved his hat.

"Name's Wayne Sawyer, and this is my wife, Naomi, my son Will and his wife Margaret, and my other children Thomas, Ellen, Marcy and our baby girl Daphne."

"What's your business at Fort March, Wayne Sawyer?"

"We ain't got no business here, except to get this man some help."

Thomas Sawyer, who drove the mule-cart, pulled back a sheet from the cart bed.

"Found 'im alone on the prairie. The little ones think they recognized him from Ludlow City, but ain't certain."

Corporal Jack surveyed a well-weathered man. He looked like he recently got a shave though his kit and cloth was poor. Even from the gate, Jack could see the signs of a hard man. Aside from a few neat cuts on his arms, face, and chest, the stiff looked to be in good health. Long, lean muscles, a few good scars. He carried a sharpshooter styled repeater in excellent condition, and a Navy model

Colt smoke-wagon that would make even the finest gun hand blush. More'n that, he kept it in a good belt with no lead left in it, and a polished pouch holster. Yep. Ol' boy knew his business.

Cattle guard probably, maybe even law. Maybe both.

Either way, he was well past the age where he ought not be traveling alone. Especially across them plains between Ludlow City and the Fort.

Something was wrong with that spit of dead grass and big sky. Tales popped up as far as Carson City telling of people going it alone and not being seen after or of creatures that weren't right for this part of the world. Even the nearby tribes-folk wouldn't go that way except in a group.

Corporal Jack sighed.

"He alive?"

"He's breathing, sure enough. Hasn't waked or spoken much though."

"Where'd you find 'im?"

Thomas spoke up.

"Two days Southeast. Heard gunshots and screamin' something terrible in the night. Think he was headed this way. Military marks on his arms and chest."

Jack frowned. He knew better than to ask "which side," but he wondered all the same.

"Must have been quite the fight," Margaret added. "He was layin' stripped to the waist in a ditch full of spent shell casings. His eyes were closed tight, and he was mumblin' somethin' about 'dig, dig.'"

Wayne shook his head and fanned himself with his hat.

"He was plumb out of food and water, too."

Jack didn't lift his frown. "What was he shooting at?"

"Buzzards if I know. Whatever it was, looks like our man here got the better of it. All's we could find besides was blood spray, a few patches of white fuzz and a bit of black horn like a goat's."

Corporal Jack sighed and signaled the sentry to open the gate.

"Bring 'im in. We'll see what we can do."

GUARDIAN

James T. Grissom

The Eldest told unbelievable stories of when people lived below the fog, but Adrig didn't know why anyone would bother. The Valley was the only world he knew.

Maybe the Spire was the work of ancient folk who could form metal into something so tall. Adrig helped his father, Bruhan, melt stone at the smithy, forming it into knives and tools. Perhaps if thousands of smiths combined their efforts and built a mould that spanned the entire valley, such a thing would be possible. If there were ever that many people alive at once. Maybe the People had lost the art of making more of the hard, yet brittle white stuff the Eldest called "plastic." But metal birds that people sat inside of...impossible. By his own admission, the Eldest had only heard these stories from the Eldest before him, and he from the Eldest before him. It seemed obvious they were tales to entertain the young. Adrig had seen animals disappear—he hadn't seen a groundhog in ages—so tales of bears and horses were easier to digest.

Adrig walked away from the circle of children too young to work, and the fantasies the Eldest was telling them, carrying his load of collected lumber toward the fires of the smithy beyond his village, Ruhm. That was another reason Adrig doubted the Eldest: it was impossible to burn a fire large enough to make so much metal. There weren't enough trees or dung. He shook his head, looking back briefly at the happy children learning the Histories and Sciences.

Adrig's mother told him the current group of seven Named was the largest in living memory in any of the Five Villages. If the Young One on her hip made it one more Sun Day, the Named would grow to eight. If these eight made it to True Name Day, as Adrig had three Sun Days prior, that would bring the total to over three hundred Souls in the Five. Adrig tried not to wonder what they would name the baby boy. He'd made that mistake with the little girl his mother had lost on the Long Day two turnings ago.

Best to follow the advice of those older than him and not grow too attached to such fragile life. Better to think of them like the lambs so easily lost to cruel winters or, Skies forbid, a lost harvest. Those who survived three Turnings were much more likely to live long enough to grow old.

The smithy's forge stood a few hundred paces from the sheep pens and those only a hundred paces from the last homes of the village. Each was made of stone and was longer than it was wide. Each had the same sharp pointed roof of slate on the short windward side, and clay tile on the long leeward side that almost touched the ground, and all had clever runners to divert rain and snowmelt into the family water barrel. Each had its smoke pipe jutting out at a right angle near the apex. Each had its own garden on the leeward side, protected by the stone house. The sheep were protected by an earthen ramp, twice taller than a man, on the windward side. As always, as with everyone, Adrig kept a lookout for signs of mountain wolves, rabbits, or wild berries, his sling ready for protection or hunting, the pouch at his waist for foraging. He gave the sling a test whirl, making sure the bundle of wood on his back would not interfere. He liked the weight of the hard grey-white stone bits he'd found in the old iron mine best for his sling. The young man walked the path, keeping a close watch until the acrid scent of melting stone and iron announced the smithy around a low ridge of granite as he pushed against the ever-present wind.

"You look thoughtful, boy," Bruhan said as Adrig approached. The melodious tenor never seemed to match the burly, weathered smith. With his brown hair tied at the nape of his neck and lying in a long fan down his back and those huge muscled arms, he resembled one of the bears of legend. But his face was always merry, his blue eyes twinkling between bushy brows and ruddy cheeks. Some said the son would dwarf the father one day. He could almost look him in the eye now and was stronger than many men in Ruhm. Adrig supposed he'd be a black bear, whatever that looked like. His raven hair and green eyes came from his mother.

"Hello, Father," Adrig said, removing his shoulder straps in tandem. He'd once made the mistake of taking out one arm first, and the resulting wrench of his then over-loaded shoulder had left him unable to carry more than any other boy for ten twilights. He squatted to finish removing the burden. The stack stayed upright as he moved away.

"Why so glum, my son?" Bruhan picked up the bundled wood with one hand, showing how far Adrig had to grow.

"Not glum, Father," Adrig assured him. "Just thinking."

"About Stories again?" The smith asked, good-naturedly.

Adrig nodded. His father understood, and there was no reason to speak of it further.

Bruhan patted his back with his free hand, gently pushing him in the direction of the burning ground where they would feed the permanent fire. Any trees that had grown here on the edge of the Valley surrounded by abrupt mountain peaks had long since succumbed to those flames. The fire was far too dangerous to be anywhere else. Coals banked with care were delivered to the villagers to be used in the stone stoves in the great room of each home.

The Five used to be Seven, before that lesson was learned, or so the Stories said. As the pair rounded the smithy, they pulled their face covers up and the wind died. Smoke enveloped them in the enclosure formed by the massive smithy wall and the granite ridge that jutted up ever higher before them as it marched up to join Olwin's Peak. Adrig's brother Patrick sat atop this ridge, waiting to make the day's batch of charcoal. He pulled up his smoke mask and clambered down the cliff wall as Adrig approached.

Bruhan dropped the load, and the brothers carefully untied the bindings so as not to damage any of the precious ropes. No one could remember where it came from, or how to make more. It was stronger than any twine and stretched a bit. Cutting it would be a disaster, and it would melt into uselessness if burned. Adrig's family was considered wealthy to have several yards of the stuff, which they had fashioned into a harness and lashings.

Though Patrick was several Turnings older, he and Adrig were of a similar size and were often confused for one another until they removed their tunics and Adrig's muscles told them apart. Or if they spoke. Patrick had never quite recovered from the shaking sickness that stole twelve souls between his Namings. His speech slurred, and he tended to drool and often laughed at the wrong time. But he could carry out simple tasks when he wasn't staring down the valley wall into the perpetual fog.

"I saw it again, Brandyn!" Patrick exclaimed. He often forgot Adrig had his True Name. He laughed his awkward guffaw.

"In the fog?" Adrig asked, trying to mask his doubt. Bruhan shook his head, raking the charcoal about.

"Yep! It has green, black, and brown skin in patches, like a tree after Harvest Day, and a rock instead of a head! It's almost as big as papa!"

"That's interesting," Adrig said, turning his head so his brother couldn't see his face, see his pity. "Are you sure it's the same thing?"

"Oh, I think there's lots of him." Patrick wheezed another laugh and began stacking sticks over the exposed red coals. Adrig did the same.

"Maybe someone else will see one soon," Adrig managed to say without changing his voice.

"Oh, no!" Patrick exclaimed. "They don't like being seen." The older boy, only physically a man, moved in front of Adrig. His voice lost all of its typical lightness and lowered conspiratorially. "They can hide better than any wolf, but I see 'em."

"That's enough, sons," Bruhan sighed. "Get about it. The coal runners will be here before we know it, and I have to make that spade for Charla."

The boys got the rest of the wood placed and took up the smaller rakes to separate neat piles of smoldering charcoal to be shoveled into sand-filled pails that the runners would bring. They would be delivered to each home, a vital addition to the dried dung each family used to do their cooking and heat their homes. Bruhan was right, and they soon arrived: every young one who had not yet received their True Name and who could carry such a burden. Coal running was one of their many chores interspersed with lessons from the Eldest. The work was hot and tedious, but necessary.

When that task was finished, Patrick climbed atop his ridge, and Adrig helped his father bash iron ore into small pieces with a lead press or hammer. Bruhan had already begun charging the smelter before Adrig's arrival and it was crackling hot. Under his father's direction, Adrig helped adjust the temperature by moving logs nearer or further from the smelter with a long rake or positioning the air covers just so. Soon, father and son were soaked with sweat. Patrick rallied from his eternal watch at intervals to deliver hastily gulped water. Adrig helped separate and move the slag to the forge where Bruhan beat out the remaining impurities, making several rods of crude pig iron. After the smith was satisfied, he chose a smaller length of the pig iron and placed it in the crucible with a bit of coke he thought suitable.

"How much pig to coal, boy?" Bruhan asked his son.

"Three quarters to one." Adrig answered.

Bruhan smiled and sprinkled fine sand over the mixture and moved the crucible into the furnace with long, heavy tongs. Then father and son joined Patrick in front of the smithy, enjoying the wind and lack of smoke, to eat a bit of lunch the elder son had fetched while they worked.

"Who do you think taught me my craft?" Bruhan asked as they lounged after eating.

Patrick started.

"I suppose your father," Adrig guessed. He'd never thought of it before.

Bruhan laughed. "No, my son. Alvish knew many things, but his work was sheep. He was rather small."

Adrig blinked, stunned. Patrick laughed his strange bray.

"Master Darmon taught me all I know about smithing," Bruhan answered.

Both boys scrunched their faces. They could think of no one of that name.

"We call him Eldest now, though he was not always so." His merry eyes glittered at Adrig's dropped jaw. "That old man is wise beyond the stories he made you memorize. He has done nearly every bit of work the Five has to do, and made them better because of those Stories he remembers so well."

Adrig opened his mouth, then closed it again, brows drawing down in furious thought. Bruhan clapped his back, took one more drink of water, wiped his face with the back of his hand, and said, "The furnace should be cool by now." Adrig looked at the sun, surprised that two hours had passed.

Was this his father's way of telling him all of those impossible stories were true? He pondered as they removed the crucible and separated the steel from the slag with hammers. The steel then was added to the other furnace, and Adrig worked the bellows to make it glow reddish white. Adrig watched as Bruhan hammered it out, working the bellows whenever reheating was needed. Once Bruhan finished shaping the metal, Adrig was allowed to quelch it and fit it to the wooden handle Master Thane had fashioned, applying the pin to secure it. Bruhan nodded with approval at the finished spade.

"There are stories, and there are *Stories*, lad," Bruhan said when they were done. "Take that to Mistress Charla before you head home. Patrick will help me tidy up today."

Adrig heard the emphasis on the second speaking of the word stories. But he struggled trying to decipher how one was supposed to separate the two. He thought about this all the way to Charla's home, so lost in thought he didn't notice the importance of a crunch on stone he would not otherwise have missed. He'd remember that footfall in the weeks to come. He even missed the smiles and batted eyelashes of Juni, Charla's daughter, even though those eyes had recently begun to make his blood rush to his checks and caused the adults to chuckle.

That twilight, Adrig dreamed an impossible dream. Monstrous metal creatures that spit fire and objects that devastated the earth. Buildings made of steel, wood, and transparent materials melted. The earth heaved and smoked. People too numerous to count either evaporated or died after boiling in the flesh days or years later. Mountains collapsed or heaved up as the earth echoed the nightmare humanity had caused. Ever toward the north or south, the People moved. Ever higher they pressed into new mountains, until all that existed was the Valley in Olwin's Shelter above the fog. It was not a new dream. It was an old Story. Adrig awoke in the darkness of his home, sweating as if at the forge, and moved outside to catch his breath. It was the light season, and never pitch dark outside. He liked this much better than the dark season with its endless days of dusk. It was Rest Day, and he could think without neglecting duties.

Could it be true?

drig was still sitting outside his home, lost in his thoughts, when a pair of slender legs in soft grey tights blocked his view of the boulder he was examining. If he squinted right, he could make himself believe it was a melted piece of one of his dream buildings. His mind moving at a snail's pace, Adrig followed those shapely legs to green skirts just below the knees, up over the white blouse that pressed outward in a pleasant way, and into verdant eyes framed by a tan and freckled face that had made his breath catch so many times over the last year. Tidy auburn hair flowed freely and danced around her soft and strong shoulders. Her full lips, prone to smiling, were somewhat pouty, which caused his cheeks to flush even worse than usual. An auburn eyebrow cocked, counterbalanced with her lopsided smile.

"Oh, hello, Juni." Adrig managed to get out through the lump in his throat. For some reason, she frowned, looking offended.

"There used to be a child in this village with that name," she said with annoyance.

Adrig tried to speed up his thoughts, but only succeeded in staring blankly at her. The girl sighed, and muttered under her breath, "If you paid more attention, you'd already know."

Adrig frowned, and then his eyes shot up a hair faster than he did to his feet. His mouth hung open as his thoughts caught up with the situation.

He'd missed her True Name Day.

He'd been right in front of her when he delivered the spade to her mother and hadn't seen the difference in her appearance. Even today, he hadn't paid attention to the fact that she was not in the simple loose dress girls wore, or that her hair was not in braids. The girl, no, the woman, before him laughed at his realization.

"Now, I won't blame you for missing my Naming while attending to your duties. The ceremony is only for women anyhow. But I do need to know why you paid me no mind at all when I tried to show you. Thelisa made sure you were the one to deliver our spade for a purpose!"

"What do you mean my mother 'made sure' I—"

She stood stricken, and a hand covered her mouth. "Maybe…" she said in embarrassed tones that Adrig didn't understand. "You'll forget I said that, and I'll let this one pass."

"Yeah, sure," Adrig said, bewildered. "Umm…"

"Gwendelyn," the new-made woman laughed. "I'm Gwendelyn now. You really are hopeless about some things." She laughed all the harder as Adrig gaped. She started to sit, smiled her wry smile, and moved back to lean against the bolder Adrig had been contemplating so intently. She looked at him with measuring eyes.

Adrig took a deep breath and tried to make the chaos of his mind come to some order. Juni was a woman now. *Gwendelyn!* He wouldn't make that mistake again. He hated the month after his True Name Day when most people forgot. No one ever told him why boys always received their True Name at twelve, but for girls it varied. He could probably ask Gwendelyn someday, but not while he was digging his foot out of his mouth today. Adrig had now seen fifteen Sun Days, and Gwendelyn was only a year younger.

Thinking of something so logical helped unclog his mind, and his manners. He bowed quite properly and said, "It is a pleasure to speak your Name, Gwendelyn." Freckles disappeared as the young woman flushed scarlet and ducked her head, but she still smiled brilliantly.

A long moment later she cleared her throat and raised her head, and then stepped away from the boulder with a curtsy. "It brings me joy to hear you Name me," she said formally. Adrig himself flushed deep red at how high she raised her skirts. She'd need to get used to them being so short. They'd run and played together for years and he'd seen her legs more times than he could count, but somehow it was different now. She blushed and dropped her skirt. Yes, things were different now.

"So. What has your mind so occupied?" she asked, a touch breathily as she leaned against the boulder again.

"Well..." Adrig hesitated. "I guess I have to start by saying there are some things I have not said aloud to you since my True Name."

Gwendelyn frowned at this, looking a trifle hurt.

"Not because I didn't want to," he added, "but because you were still in the middle of it."

The young woman's frown turned from hurt to confusion.

"Ugg...I know I'm talking out of order! It's just..." Adrig took another breath. "How much of what you learned as a child do you think is true?"

Gwendelyn's eyes became round as the moon. She opened her mouth to retort, then stopped; her frown faded, and her face became thoughtful. "I suppose some of the Stories are a bit difficult to believe."

Adrig's heart melted in relief. And then he recounted his previous day, the conversations he'd had with his father over the last year, asking if it was all true and being told, "No one is lying, but no one was there, either."

Adrig told her his dream. Before he reached the end, Gwendelyn had forgotten her new station and new clothing and sat on the ground, back against the boulder. Adrig sat next to her and continued to unburden his heart and mind. The stone was too small for them to sit facing the same direction, but this helped him get it all out.

After several minutes of silence, Adrig was afraid he'd said too much. Gwendelyn reached out and took his hand. "Is it better to never doubt and be wrong...or to doubt and have the Stories proven true?" she whispered.

Adrig loved her then. Loved her more than anyone. She understood.

At that moment, Thelisa came around the corner. Adrig started to move away, but Gwendelyn's grip tightened. Thelisa beamed at them and dropped off a basket with some breakfast before walking away. Adrig did not understand. Thelisa was never satisfied with idleness, even on Rest Day. But his stomach rumbled, and he stopped wondering at this as they moved to face each other across the basket. Thelisa had even brought a blanket to sit on. They ate and made small talk. Adrig missed holding his friend's hand.

"Gwendelyn," Adrig said, halfway to a question. "The last Gwendelyn was your great aunt, right? Did you choose this name because you'll follow into herbalism?" The young woman smiled deeply. "And why do women get to choose their Name?" Adrig added before Gwendelyn could respond.

"Which question should I answer first?" She laughed. "Well, you don't get to know the second answer until you're married. So, to answer your first question, yes, I will start apprenticing Mara tomorrow."

Adrig frowned, then shrugged. Some things just were. "You've always loved flowers, so I guess that makes sense. And you've always been quick to help anyone with injury or sickness.I suppose your mother has plenty of help from Leister. I'm glad you can do what you love instead of spinning wool."

The smile slipped slightly from her face. "Do you wish you could do something else?" Gwendelyn asked, a bit surprised.

"Not exactly," Adrig replied. "At least, not anything specific. I enjoy helping Father with the forging, but could do without the coal work. I know it's important, and Patrick and Kendle can't do it alone, but I don't particularly love smelling like a fireplace all the time. Still, I don't mind. I just wish…I don't know. I just feel like I'm missing something. I could be doing something more…valuable.

For the Five."

Gwendelyn leaned across the basket and kissed Adrig's forehead, shocking him into silence. She sat back down and looked at her hands. "You smell fine, and you are valuable by being you. But I think I understand. That's why I'm going to be an herbalist instead of a weaver. We all need clothes, but I can learn to fight shaking sickness, or the long cough, or a dozen other things. I hope that's not prideful."

"Not at all," Adrig said. "That's what I mean." He stood and helped her do the same. "Would you like to go to the stream and find some honeysuckle?" All the previous smiles faded from the radiance on Gwendelyn's face.

"I'd love that! But unfortunately I have to help sort out my apprentice payment. We've been working on a year's worth of bandages for Mara." She was excited and sad at the same time as she helped gather the remnants of breakfast and fold the blanket. "Maybe I can answer your second question in a couple of years," she blurted. Then she pecked his cheek with a kiss and trotted away.

"Second question?" Adrig asked himself aloud when she was gone. Then he stopped as if struck by lightning, remembering what Gwendelyn had said.

You don't get to know the second answer until you're married.

"I could use your help with the garden." Adrig jumped as if a wolf had appeared from nowhere. Thelisa laughed, coming back around the corner, and grinned an all-too-knowing smile.

"Of course, Mother," Adrig said, his voice weak. Somehow, the smile on Thelisa's face made him feel like one of the pebbles being pushed around on a board for a Game of Nine. But he didn't know who the players were, who was winning, or where he fit.

The next day, after the coal had been delivered, Bruhan allowed Adrig to tinker in the forge. A bit of limewater was sometimes used in the moulds to make pig iron instead of the more typical and arduous process of making a huge bed of coal and iron ore, cracking stones and then using masses of sand to create the pig iron that would be turned into steel.

Adrig wanted to quickly make some steel, so he chose the limewater. Father said it was a useful trick when you needed a smaller amount of crude iron to work with, but not very practical when working on bigger projects. But Adrig loved trying new things. He grabbed a mould and put in far too much limewater, but Bruhan didn't say anything.

Without thinking, Adrig grabbed a rock from his sling pouch instead of the bucket of iron ore. The stone began to bubble. Adrig stared in wonder while Bruhan stood up straight to watch, still saying nothing.

Adrig used a pair of tongs to remove the rock. Where the bubbles died down, a green ooze remained behind. Adrig knew that some rock ores could be crushed and mixed with other agents to create a liquid that, when heated, became metals. He prepared the lead press and crushed a few of his sling pellets. As he'd hoped, when he added the remaining hard pellets to the lime, it came to a rapid bubbling boil, but the transition was not as complete as he hoped.

"Let it sit overnight," Bruhan said, breaking his silence. The father was as intrigued as the son.

The next day at the smithy proved Adrig and Bruhan had good intuition. The proofed solution was now a green liquid. "What do you think, Father? Charcoal?" Adrig asked. Bruhan nodded.

Father and son tried endless combinations and treatments over the next week until they were able to perfect a process involving much waiting, mixing, coating, and milling to produce a ball that the lead press could not squash. Indeed, the tiny ball dented the lead!

"Lad, this is impressive, and I believe it could be useful, but it takes too long, and it's impossible to shape after the mould has set. I'm not telling you to stop making them, but it must come after all other duties."

Adrig nodded in agreement, but he discovered over the next few days that these new pellets were perfect for rabbit hunting, so he made as many as he could to use in his sling.

Adrig's days began as light grew from the gloaming into true sunrise. He would strap on his collecting apparatus in order to gather the deadfall and cut wood for the first hour or two with help from the coal runners. Then he would leave them on the village green, and Adrig would haul the collection to the forge while they attended the Histories and Sciences. His friends Kywin and Shain helped him keep the group in a tight knot while gathering their bundles. They also helped keep an eye out for wolves. Both were apprentice carpenters with the skill necessary to sort the healthy fallen branches from the rotten, or cut down selected branches, always careful not to strip the forest bare. Wolves hid there, but fire was life. There was not enough dung to warm the homes or cook meals. His friends were also learning the art of crafting larger trees into useful things and would return with their masters after this chore to find the best trees to fell.

Adrig would stay at the forge after delivering the last of the lumber. He always started by helping Bruhan and Patrick prepare and pass out charcoal to the runners. Kendle, a fellow villager close to Adrig's age, worked as Bruhan's junior apprentice. After the coal work, Adrig assisted with the forge and was allowed to make his new pellets once all other work was caught up.

His time away from the forge was consumed by Gwendelyn. Life in the valley never stopped while the sun was up, but it was customary to enjoy a lengthy lunch after morning routines, and to finish most work two hours before sunset. These two hours were free unless a goodwife caught an unsuspecting youth or man who looked bored and roped them into some task.

Adrig, to the dismay of his friends, would spend every bit of his free time with Gwendelyn if she was not otherwise occupied. For some reason, free time came often for them, and he caught sullen glances from those less fortunate as they weeded gardens, hauled water, or assisted with supper preparations. At first, Adrig had trouble trying to fill their time together. Gwendelyn's new clothing made their old hobbies inconvenient, if not impossible. No more climbing trees or splashing in streams. But they still searched for flowers by the meandering waters or lounged near the Great Water, looking out across the valley at the other villages around it. Mostly, they talked. Adrig had never talked so much in his life and was surprised not to grow weary of it. He didn't consider himself especially witty, but Gwendelyn laughed often and returned sarcasm in kind in delightful ways. She coloured in a way that made his heart race when he used her Name and beamed in a way that made him weak when he shortened it to Gwen.

On one such day Gwen asked him to help her find some mushrooms in the forest. Adrig found he didn't care what they did. So, he agreed without argument. He spotted one with crimson veins that he thought was pretty and stooped to pick it up for her.

"No, not that one!" Gwen exclaimed. "That will turn your bowels to water for days," she laughed. Adrig jerked back, and she giggled. "Only if you eat it," she amended.

"Oh, What colors are good?" he asked.

"It's not always the color, but solid colors are best. Sometimes you have to look underneath or pay attention to what direction they point or grow. Ah, there's a trumpet! Not medicinal, but tasty!" Gwen used her foraging knife to carve off a bit, rubbed it off, and took a nibble. "Mmm. Here, you try."

Adrig popped it into his mouth. "I like that."

"How can you tell? You barely chewed!" she said with mock severity.

"I have a fast tongue!" Adrig quipped.

Gwen raised an eyebrow and quirked her new secret smile. "Is that so?"

Adrig had no idea how to respond to that, so he shrugged while she laughed at him. Gwen turned to gather the rest of the mushrooms and placed them in a small belt pouch. Adrig glanced around looking for more and saw that the light was getting very dim. He didn't want to end their time together, but he also didn't want her to be in danger.

"The light is fading," he said with a sigh. Gwen looked around and nodded with sadness in her eyes. She walked to him slowly, looking up at him from under her lashes. Adrig's body vibrated as she grabbed his hand.

"Thanks for helping me look," Gwen breathed. Her face was expectant, but her eyes became doubtful. Exasperated, she growled, "This is the part where you kiss me."

Instinct took over. He put one hand on her face, turned it up to his, and kissed her. First, it was chaste; just a peck on the lips. Then it was a deep kiss that made blood rush to embarrassing places. She clung to him and either did not notice or did not care, so he lost himself in it for what seemed like eternity. Eventually, regretfully, she sighed in content and pulled away, still holding his hand. Adrig's mind was still reeling, his blood still raging through him.

And then he heard it.

It started with a deep rumble at the edge of perception.

Adrig swung around, his sling whirling in his hand. Gwen screamed as the rumble turned into a growl and they saw two massive black shapes approaching.

Everyone in the valley understood that the mountain wolves were deadly, but they were mostly interested in the sheep, and a stone to the ribs usually sent them fleeing. But this was not the path between the pen and the forge or the village and the pen. This was wolf territory, and it was approaching twilight. Fear turned Adrig's belly to ice.

"Gwen, I want you to slowly back away until they can't see you, and then you have to run. Climb if one chases you." Adrig was proud that his voice held steady.

"I can't leave you!" she cried.

"Do it now, Gwen!" Thankful to the Skies, he heard her shuffling away. The wolves didn't move toward her, but hunched, ready to launch in any direction.

Adrig yelled in his deepest voice. He let loose a pellet in his sling and grabbed another from his pouch before it was fully away from him. The stones could wound one if he was lucky, then he'd climb the closest tree.

The wolf squealed in pain and terror and then fell over. Adrig saw that its skull was a bloody ruin. The new pellet had killed a wolf in a single hit. Impossible!

He loaded the sling and began the whirl again. The remaining wolf looked at its companion, growled, and flashed away into the dark. Adrig let the sling slow and gazed at the downed wolf, feeling numb.

"Come ON!" Gwen grabbed Adrig's hand and pulled him into a run.

They ran all the way to the village, where they attracted a crowd. The first onlookers shouted questions, and those shouts brought others asking after the commotion. Adrig dropped to his knees, shaking, and Gwen burst into tears.

"He saved me! He killed a monstrous wolf!" she shouted.

Chaos broke loose. It took some time for everyone to

understand what had happened. Adrig was grateful that nothing was mentioned about the kissing, the excitement seemed to cloud the minds of the adults, and no one seemed to doubt they were just collecting mushrooms and had lost track of time. The few that Gwen pulled from her pouch quelled any further questions on the subject.

Charla started to pull Gwen toward her home, but she brazenly kissed Adrig in front of the crowd. Not as intense as before, it was a kiss any goodwife would give her husband in public. Children ewwed or laughed, older boys snickered, older girls stared with dreamy expressions, and most adults hid their smiles and turned away. Charla hugged them both before Gwen was quite finished. And then firmly led her daughter away.

Thelisa patted Adrig on the shoulder, beaming. "You did well, son."

Most of the men and older boys crowded around Adrig as the women shooed the young ones toward their suppers. Bruhan stood by his son, his back straight with pride. "Tell us, Son; tell us everything," the huge smith said. "How did you kill it?"

Gwen's father, Zachary, did not look as if he knew whether to be upset or proud, but everyone else was riveted. Adrig recounted the encounter with as much detail as his nerves allowed, showing the pellets he had made to the group.

"I'll trade you a cask of my mead for two pouches of those things!" Davish shouted above the chatter.

"I'll give you a full sack of threshed wheat!"

"I'll build you a new table!"

"QUIET!" Everyone was shocked into silence. Bruhan never raised his voice. The melodious tenor was quite terrifying when raised to a baritone roar. "Please, gentlemen. My boy is shaken. We will make the pellets, but Adrig needs a meal, a cup, and some rest."

The mild tenor returned, and any ire at the shout was

soothed by the reasonable words. Bruhan led his son home, and Adrig had his first cup of mead.

Adrig awoke, surprised by sunlight streaming through his small window. Panic gripped him and he jumped up. Patrick's bed was empty, of course. He'd gone to the forge hours ago. Adrig donned his trousers in a hurry and stuffed his shirt tails into them in a haphazard fashion as he stomped into his boots. *Father's going to be furious!*

He rushed out of the small room and, to no surprise, the great room was empty, the dung fire beginning to cool. That mead must have addled his wits to make him sleep in so late. He didn't feel the same silly rush of relief and hilarity he had while repeating the story to his family the night before. His heart sank as he recalled telling the juiciest details.

"I never knew it could feel like that to kiss a girl. She was becoming a part of me, and not just because I could taste her tongue in my mouth!"

Patrick had laughed like a horse. Bruhan chuckled. Thelisa's eyebrows threatened to move permanently into her hairline. She looked shocked, and a trifle angry, but then she shook her head and laughed ruefully.

Reality slammed back into Adrig as he opened the door to see Thelisa, Mistress Charla, and Mistress Mara—not to mention Gwen—sitting in a circle sipping tea. All of them turned to look at him with varying expressions of amusement and expectation. Gwen, however, maintained a blank expression he'd never seen on her.

Adrig bowed, "May the Sky kiss your Souls, mistresses." He felt phony talking with such formality, but smiles deepened on them all, including Gwen. "And forgive me for being abrupt, but for the first time ever I've slept past my duties and must hurry to the forge to assist Baba." He blushed for using such a childish wordwomen nodded their approval.

"No need to worry about that, my son," Thelisa said. "Your services are needed here today."

Adrig frowned in confusion.

"How can I help?"

Mara stood. For some reason, Charla appeared to be struggling not to frown at her. Gwen blanked her face again, and Adrig's hands began to sweat.

"What is the meaning of life?" Mara asked.

Adrig's jaw dropped before he could stop it. None of the women were smiling now, they wore matching, blank expressions. After a few torturous seconds, Adrig remembered that this was the first question of the Recitations. He, like everyone in the Valley, learned these from the time they could speak, but he was only ever asked by the Eldest, either during the Histories and Sciences, or on Sun Day.

"To live at peace, and as one." He rushed it out to cover his lapse in memory.

Charla stood and asked, "Who are the People?"

"Those who have overcome the violence of our past and strive only against the elements, and never against another Soul." Adrig couldn't grasp what was happening. This wasn't a childhood lesson or the annual worship service.

"Why are the People in this Valley?" Thelisa asked as she stood.

Adrig took a breath. "To escape the final outcome of hate and live a life of love, blessed by the Sky, which was obscured by our violence until we climbed Olwin's shoulders and rested in his Shelter."

Gwen stood. "Who do you love?" Her face was blank, but her voice shook.

"You," Adrig blurted out. "I mean...every Soul who lives under the Sky." Adrig blushed again, but Gwen beamed. For that matter, so did everyone else.

"Who is beyond the Sky?" they asked as one.

"The Maker of all, who weeps for what we have done to our entrustment. The Love of all, who raised Olwin from the earth to protect those who sought peace. The Protector of all, who helps us remember so that we will never repeat the violence of our fathers." Adrig still had no clue what was going on, but the smiles made it easier to continue.

"What does the Maker hate?" they all asked.

"Only hate itself. This is the reason we live at peace, love all Souls, and protect all Souls from violence and hate."

Gwen stepped forward. "Will you guard me, while I guard you?" she whispered the question.

This wasn't in the Recitations, but Adrig didn't hesitate. "Of course I will!" he exclaimed with a passion he didn't know he had. "For as long as I live."

The sun had never shone so bright as her smile.

"It is done," Mara said with a wide grin.

"It has begun," Charla said, almost crying.

"May it never end." Thelisa *was* crying.

Gwen walked up to Adrig and kissed him chastely on the lips. The women let out an undulating cry of joy like they did on Sun Day.

"In one year, I can tell you that secret," Gwen told him, joy filling her voice.

Adrig was confused, but his heart began to warm with a strange intensity. Something vastly important was happening, and he had a small inkling of what it might be. Then the Eldest walked into view, smiling. Behind him came Bruhan, Patrick, and Gwen's father, Zachary.

All but the Eldest stopped to form a line with the women. The Eldest continued on and stood behind Gwen and Adrig, facing the others. He took one hand from each of them, then placed one into the other, cupping his hands, one above and one below, in a four-handed gathering.

"Love rules us all, and love grows here today. Gwendelyn, will you accept the love of Adrig and use the next year to master your craft to serve the People?" the Eldest asked.

Full realization sunk into Adrig as his hunch was proven. His head grew light.

"I will," she said, unshed tears making her eyes sparkle.

"Adrig, will you spend one year proving your love for Gwendelyn and the People by mastering your craft and proving your loyalty to this woman?" Adrig's mouth went dry. He was getting betrothed! Dry mouth or not, light head or not, he had no doubts.

"I WILL!" he yelled with joy. Everyone laughed, including Gwen and the Eldest.

"Then let it be known to all Souls, Gwendelyn and Adrig have increased our capacity for love and will spend the next year preparing for the rest of their lives. They are joined today in a way only the Maker can undo. May the Skies bless us all, and these two."

The crowd began the triumphal yell again, and soon the entire village was gathering, joining in the joy.

Adrig had been on the fringes of these celebrations before but had never seen the ceremony, which was always a private affair. In all practical terms, he was married. His knees gave way and he fell to his rear. Gwen laughed and helped him to his feet and kissed him once more and the crowd cheered. The morning was a whirlwind of congratulations, and a lunch feast of pre-baked bread and uncooked fruits and vegetables was enjoyed by all.

Finally, it occurred to him that it was Rest Day. He wasn't supposed to work at the forge today. He hadn't neglected his duties. He'd fulfilled them.

The next few days were depressingly similar to those before the engagement ceremony, and it became ever more difficult for Adrig to spend time apart from Gwen. But a marriage was as much for the community as it was for the couple. Every Soul had an obligation to support the Five. Adrig had been taught this from his first breath, but he'd never experienced the burden of putting the villages ahead of his own joy. Bruhan nodded in understanding when he confided this to him and encouraged him that a year may seem like an eternity when you are young, but it passed ever faster the older one became. Bruhan also explained, in embarrassing detail, why waiting a year was important to protect Gwen's health.

So, father and son continued much the same as they had before. The coal still had to be made, and the pellets were in high demand. Shears and barrel bindings, plow blades and hinges, the simple business had to be done. And, somehow, he began to take simple joy in a job well done. Bruhan inspected a wheel rim Adrig had made from start to finish one day.

"This is fine work, son," the smith said. "Fine indeed." He sounded sad saying it.

"Thank you, Father. Would you like me to deliver it to Master Jarl?" Adrig didn't understand the sad tone. Was the wheel rim acceptable, or not?

"No, we'll have Patrick deliver it. How about you help me with a scythe?" Adrig was surprised. Bruhan hadn't let him help with anything that sharp yet. He guessed that his father was melancholy because Adrig was getting older and better every day. Suddenly it hit him.

"Master Bruhan," he began, addressing him as an apprentice to his master. "We have one wheelwright. We have one herbalist. We have one carpenter, and right now, we have one smith…" He let the words linger, the question unspoken.

Bruhan sighed heavily. "Carpenters have plenty of work, and two may be needed. Same with herbs. I could see the need to have someone focus on the coaling business while one smithed. But I know that would leech your joy. Kendle and Patrick can manage both when Kendle gains a bit more strength. The fact is...Ruhm doesn't need two master smiths. But Carson in Belfri is nearing sixty; I'm not sure how long he can keep going, and there haven't been any likely lads in that village to apprentice him." He also let the words hang. Adrig empathized with the sadness. He'd wondered about this very subject before. Bruhan had a good twenty years left in him, and Kendle showed aptitude as a junior apprentice.

"Mistress Alice lost her apprentice, too," Adrig remembered. Katrin was a sweet young lady who had succumbed to fever last winter.

Bruhan nodded. So. In all likelihood, when Adrig and Gwen finished their apprenticeships they'd have to relocate to Belfri. The weight of it lodged in Adrig's throat. One had to serve the good of all Souls, not just one village. Adrig grew up hearing this, but it wasn't easy to reconcile.

Bruhan cleared his own throat. "That's still a year away," he said, trying to sound like his cheerful self. "Let's make the scythe, and tomorrow we'll do some pellets. What should we name them?"

The change in subject served its purpose. "You want me to name them?" Adrig asked, amazed.

"Lad, I gave some guidance, but the invention is yours and I've made that known." The pride in his voice was blatant. So obvious that Adrig couldn't speak for long moments.

"Wolfsbane."

Bruhan beamed. "That sounds perfect. Now, about that scythe."

The rest of the afternoon was spent on the fine, sharp blade that would be attached to a pole stave that Adrig's friend Kywin had produced under the direction of Master Thane. Adrig had never completed the sharp edge of anything before. He'd helped with shears, but Bruhan had always applied the edge, and Bruhan made all of the razors. This time, the master smith talked his apprentice through the work. As Adrig hammered the ring onto the stave, Bruhan beamed. It was perfect. And Adrig still had a year to learn.

"I'll deliver this one, Father," Adrig volunteered when it was finished. Master Thane's workshop was right next door to Mara's. Bruhan smiled and nodded. He knew just as well as Adrig why he wanted to go.

A short time later, Adrig stood outside the door to Mara's workshop, which was near the Great Water. He watched through the open awning as Gwen followed Mistress Mara's instructions to mix some concoction. This workshop had the second largest fire in the village, and the place was made of stone with nothing but sand for 30 paces in any direction. There were small bellows and vents and levers to heat the alembics and pots to the right temperature. Adrig loved watching the rapture on Gwen's face as she got it right. She excelled at what she did, and she loved her craft.

"No dear, that's too much heat, tamp that vent a bit," Mara said, a bit sharply. Adrig frowned and stepped away from the window, not wanting Gwen to see him catching her misstep. But there was no need. Gwen took it in stride.

"Sorry Mistress, I was watching the still and it's bubbling," she said.

There was silence for several seconds.

"Well, I guess we are both running a bit hot today," Mara said with embarrassed grace. Then she laughed and Gwen did too. "Now, both are steeped. What's next?"

"Pour out the lilac dilute into a bottle, stopper it, submerge it to cool, then mix with the warm green lead mixture and pure water," Gwen answered without hesitation.

"Good! And what is this used to treat?" Mara asked.

"Sweet urine and blacktoe." Again, Gwen did not stop to consider her answer.

"I swear, girl, you'll replace me in less than a year." Mara didn't seem to know if this was positive news or bad. Another silence lingered. "Now, now, I'm just teasing. The Valley needs as many of us as it can get; you'll be one of the best, and I can say you were my 'prentice!" They both giggled. "You can stop snooping and come in now, boy, we're done."

Adrig jumped and walked in, chagrined. Gwen wrapped him in a warm embrace. "I'm getting it!" Her face beamed with excitement.

"Yes, she is. You had better make sure you match her, boy," Mara said with her typical severity.

"He already does," Gwen retorted.

Mara sniffed. "Away with you. I'll see you at daylight. And bring me some fennel."

"Yes, Mistress Mara," Gwen promised. "Why are you holding a Scythe?"

Adrig jumped again, and his jaw dropped once again for what seemed the hundredth time in the last few weeks.

"I have to run to Master Thane, be right back!" Adrig took off like a rabbit and Gwen laughed like it was a mid-summer jape.

Mater Thane's shop was only a few hundred paces away. He stayed near the Great Water to bundle trees together and pole them to or from the other villages so that no one took too much of the precious wind break from the forest around most of the lake's edge. He handed off the scythe to Shaine who would deliver it to Master Blount in Eldberg. The carpenters doubled as messengers, hauling lumber to each of the villages. The farmers in Eldberg traded lumber for wheat. When he turned, prepared to run back to Gwen, she was right behind him, and he jumped again.

Gwen laughed her magical trill. "I swear, you're half frog these days!"

"I'll show you frog!" Adrig jumped to her and swept

her up into a whirling dervish of a hug and dance.

"Oh, barf!" Shain yelled.

Gwen and Adrig laughed and walked away, hand in hand. After a wonderful afternoon, like all evenings of the next year, both were mildly depressed when they had to retire to their separate homes.

The scythe received so much praise that all of the area farmers commissioned more. Bruhan began to train Kendle in some of the forging after the coals were finished, and Adrig was no longer required to collect timber; his skills were too valuable. He acted more in the role of his father with the coaling process, directing Patrick and Kendle in the even distribution of the precious commodity. Bruhan and Adrig divided the mundane tasks and the forging of the new Wolfsbane pellets, which everyone across the valley now wanted. Smiths from the other villages came to learn the new craft, but Adrig's were always better.

One morning, Bruhan made a visit to Belfri to assist old Master Carson. After directing the lads in the coaling, Adrig settled in to make Wolfsbane pellets as there were no other outstanding commissions.

On a whim, he decided to make a scythe out of the Wolfsbane metal. He was unsure if the stone mould would work with the new material, but he thought Bruhan would forgive his tinkering if it failed. So, he prayed. He wasn't much for the spiritual, most in the Valley were very pragmatic about their faith. It was so much a part of their culture that it didn't require overt expression. Adrig poured the molten metal into the mould and began to ask for assistance, feeling awkward.

"Skies above, and Maker of all, I'm not sure how this works. I wasn't taught how to talk to you, apart from the

Recitations or a simple 'help me' or 'thank you,' but we're told you want us to be protectors of peace. I'm strong, but a lot of Souls aren't. Can you please help me be strong for them? Can you please help this work to make life more peaceful for them? More peaceful for Gwen?" Adrig felt silly.

Take it out of the mould. NOW.

Adrig didn't think about the voice. Didn't quite know if it was his own, or someone else's. He took it out, even though it was too early. Sure enough, the metal hadn't set. When they made the pellets, they cooled to completion in the mould and were then harder than any rock, stone, or gem. It was still white hot.

Finish like it's steel.

Again, Adrig followed the command. They'd tried this early on, but it had failed to work. The metal was too hard for the hammer when set. When heated to this temperature, the hammer pounded the metal into useless shapes that were impossible to break when cooled. But he raised his hammer anyhow. Something stirred in Adrig as he struck. Strength seemed to radiate all through his body and into the hammer. He struck, and blinding light sparked.

Keep going!

Adrig shut his eyes to slits just large enough to see where his strokes landed. The flashing continued, but the metal stayed whole. After long minutes, it was thinned out on the edges, forming a blade.

"Okay, Maker, now what?" Adrig asked, feeling ten kinds of a fool.

Fire!

Adrig lurched. That was a direct answer. Choosing not to think of the implications, Adrig stuck the blade into the flames again and pumped the bellows. This had never worked before, but he was compelled. He continued praying under his breath. "Skies, Maker...do your thing, I guess..."

The fire roared to life, almost too hot to stand. Sweating buckets, Adrig let the work take him. He retrieved the blade from the flames and took it to the wheel, sharpening it the way he would with normal steel. Again, blinding white sparks accompanied his work. His head was as light as if he'd had ten cups of mead, but strength still pulsed through him. He removed the blade from the wheel and quenched it, causing the barrel to hiss and steam to fill the workshop.

Suddenly, it was over. He crashed back to reality and surveyed the finished blade. It was perfect. He tested the edge and cried out, sticking his cut thumb in his mouth. He'd never experienced an edge that sharp, not even a razor. Then his heart sank. It was too straight. This wouldn't work in the sweeping circles the wheat farmers were used to, and he'd forgotten to make a circle for attaching it to a stave. He knew that he'd be unable to add that after the fact.

"By the Skies, Son. What have you made?"

Adrig was shocked to hear his father, and more shocked by how low the sun was. He'd worked clear through lunch. Patrick and Kendle stood staring, and Adrig recalled them asking if he wanted to stop for lunch, asking if all of the bright lights were normal. The young man began to shake. "It just...felt right," he said weakly. He offered the blade to his father.

Wonder filled Bruhan's face as he inspected the new marvel. "Darmon told me about this. The ancients before the ancients used these." He looked at Adrig with sadness and fear. "To do violence. This is a sword."

Adrig paled. Peace was everything to the People, and he'd made a device of violence. A pellet could be used to feed Souls. A knife was used for a hundred common things. But a sword.... Looking at it, Adrig feared that its sole purpose was to kill. He wretched in the corner.

"Why, son?" It was all that Bruhan could manage to say.

Adrig had no words, so he told him everything he'd done that morning. Every prayer he'd made. He remembered it all. Patrick and Kendle gaped as Adrig repeated the Maker's words but were able to corroborate what they had seen with what Adrig was saying. Relief and amazement filled Bruhan's face.

"We must consult the Eldest," Bruhan said when Adrig finished speaking. "Kendle, be a good lad and fetch him. Tell no one about this. No one. Tell the Eldest we have a question about the Sciences that is urgent." Kendle ran to obey.

Patrick shrugged and returned to his cliff while Bruhan and Adrig took turns appraising the blade, emotions shifting between fear and admiration.

"Leave us, please, Kendle, and speak naught of this," the Eldest said when he walked in. He'd ascertained the situation immediately. "What have you done?" The question was as close to anger as Adrig had ever heard in the old man's voice.

"Tell him everything," Bruhan said in a neutral tone.

Something Adrig could have never guessed happened next. The Eldest's demeanor changed from the stern visage of a judge to rapture, and he began to cry. Streams of silent tears poured down his face. He took the blade in his hands and dropped to his knees. He raised his wet face to the ceiling and began to speak in gibberish. Once, twice, three times, the blade flashed as it had during forging. Bruhan and Adrig were stricken with terror.

"The Maker has answered your prayers, Master Adrig," the Eldest intoned.

Adrig dropped to his bottom, smacking hard against the stone floor. Bruhan grabbed a table to steady himself.

The Eldest continued. "A time is coming when you will need this blade to be our Guardian. You must make a hilt for it. I'll help you. I see the questions in your eyes. Let us finish the work first."

All three men crafted a hilt for a sword. Something none of the People had ever done. The Eldest insisted that only Adrig swing the hammer, telling him to pray as he had before. Adrig felt even more foolish doing so in front of the two men, but the strange strength invaded him again, and a beautiful hilt with the symbols of the Sky, Olwin's peak, and the Maker were etched into the sweeping crossbars and fitted to the blade. With a flash, more blinding than any before, the two pieces were joined. The pommel was wrapped in leather like they did for butchering knives. Adrig cried out and dropped the sword. The symbols were now repeated from hilt to the point of the blade.

"Pick up your scimitar, Guardian," the Eldest commanded.

Adrig did so, and peace and strength filled him. Bruhan swelled with pride, looking at his son. "What was that word? *Simtar*?"

The Eldest sighed. "I do not have the years to teach every detail the Maker has revealed to me. Scimitar. It was a weapon of a people lost to the ages. You say you set out to make a scythe. The scimitar is curved, flat, and single edged. The Maker guided your hands."

"Darmon…" Bruhan began, then stopped. "Apologies, Eldest. What is happening?"

"The Maker's will is being made apparent. It's time for you to learn of the Mysteries." Father and son heard the distinction in an otherwise simple word. "These words have been reserved for the Eldest and his apprentice, but it seems that times are changing."

"The Stories are true, Master Adrig. Today, I hope, proves that to you. Now, listen and remember; I'll only say this once. A sword was the beginning of the Cataclysm, and a Sword will be its end. Men of violence created the first objects of destruction driven by power and greed. The Guardian will forge one compelled by the desire for peace and protection. Before the Guardian, violence begot violence until objects of great power destroyed that which the Maker entrusted to the Souls. Yet, in an act of Mercy, Olwin's Shelter was raised from the floor of the earth and Olwin, the first Eldest, led a remnant to safety to start a new life of peace. But the spirit of violence lives on. The spawn of violence survived. A time will come, perhaps has come, when the spawn of violence will devour all that remains below the fog and assault the last bastion of peace. The spawn live only to consume and prolong their miserable existence. The People and their sustenance will, in the fullness of time, be all that is left to consume. They will come. They will ravage. Unless a Soul of Peace stands guard. Weep for the time to come. It will be the final test of the Maker to see if all Souls are damned or if the Remnant will reclaim what was lost. These are the Mysteries. Speak of them to no one except an Eldest or their apprentice unless a sign is given, so that greed will not malign the one who might become Guardian."

A long silence filled the room. Adrig and Bruhan could not speak, or even think.

"I wasn't trying to do anything wrong or selfish, Eldest, I swear," Adrig breathed.

"And that is why you are the Guardian," Darmon answered. "We should make something to keep that hidden while allowing you to carry it. And you have to learn how to use it. I fear the time is fast approaching when you will need it. Tell no one. Bruhan, as your father and master, had the right to know, and it may be that Kendle and Patrick will let it slip that the blade exists, but discretion is paramount until another sign is given."

Tell him what the watcher has seen.

Is that you, Maker, or my conscience? Adrig thought. There was no answer. But it made no difference, so Adrig told the Eldest about the fantasies Patrick had told them of creatures exploring the valley. He also recalled the steps he'd heard so long ago on his way to deliver the spade to Charla.

"I wish you had told me sooner, Bruhan," the Eldest admonished. "But perhaps I would have dismissed it as you did…before today. I fear the time has surely come. I want every forge in the valley producing your Wolfsbane pellets from dawn to dusk. Bruhan, I'm afraid I'll need Adrig for many of those hours. I've only memorized the Histories and Sciences, but I may be able to work out how to train you to use that thing. We might as well begin now."

And so, for several weeks, Adrig was taken to a clearing for a few hours per day in which he and the Eldest used sticks the same shape and weight of the scimitar to learn how to use it in defense of the People. The People were told that the Eldest had predicted danger from the forests and to arm themselves with Wolfsbane pellets. The natural assumption, which was not corrected, was that the wolf attack made him fearful that more would come. The hardest part of those weeks for Adrig was not telling Gwen, and the hurt on her face when he told her nothing was wrong, when clearly something was. He longed to tell her everything, but he was compelled to obey the Eldest.

Three weeks later, on another Rest Day, Gwen and Adrig were lounging and chatting by the Great Water. The conversation was pleasant, as most were, until Adrig became morose and felt forced to lie, saying nothing was wrong, nothing was clouding his mind. Most times she could distract him from his new reality and he could pretend nothing had changed.

"Then, Mara said that I was coming along in my studies and let me prepare the tincture for poor Aldeen's gout. She's never let me do one alone before, so I guess that means she thinks I'm getting good! But I still have a long way to go. Nina does everything by herself, but she's almost done with her apprenticeship."

She was so sweet. Obviously, she was good, but she stayed humble. Adrig loved that about her. "Do you think Ruhm needs three herbalists?" Adrig silently berated himself for being so blunt. Gwen's face clouded. She hadn't thought of this yet.

"I guess Nina might go to Belfri. Mistress Alice still hasn't gotten a new apprentice." Gwen was confident. Her smile returned.

Adrig took a deep breath. "What if it's us who need to go to Belfri?"

Gwen blanched. "But...our families..." She was even pretty when she was upset. "Master Carson doesn't have an apprentice either...is this why you've been so melancholy? Oh, Adrig, you could have told me! I'll go anywhere with you. I'm so relieved! I thought maybe you were having second thoughts..." Her voice trembled.

"Never!" Adrig exclaimed. He grabbed her into a hug and kissed her with all his might. He loved her for her bravery and hated himself for not saying there was more to be melancholy about. But he let it pass.

"Well," she said breathily, "well...that's fine. I'll miss my family, and I know you'll miss yours, but it's not like we can't see them whenever we need to. It won't be so bad. I think that's a great idea. Mara actually took me to help Alice with a huge batch of mange wash for their sheep and she's so sweet!"

Adrig couldn't take it anymore. He couldn't lie to her.

"I'm glad you're fine with that, and that you get on well with Alice. But..." He swallowed hard. "There's more."

"You can tell me anything, Adrig."

"I..." Adrig had a hard time continuing. How could he keep the confidence of the Eldest and stop hiding things from Gwen? It seemed impossible.

Prayer.

Just that. That one word.

If that's really you, Maker, I could use a bit more help, Adrig thought.

Gwen began looking scared again as he delayed.

Teach her, Adrig.

Adrig reeled. It was only the second time he'd received a direct reply, and the first time he was addressed by name.

"What is it, Adrig?" Gwen's voice shook again, and tears welled in her eyes.

"I'm so sorry, Gwen. I'm not trying to unnerve you. I don't know how to explain everything. Something happened to me. Something strange, and it's got me all mixed up. But I promise you, it has absolutely nothing to do with how I feel about you, or us, or wanting to spend the rest of my life with you."

"Oh, okay. Well, that's comforting!" The tears fell. "Don't worry! The tears are relief! But please. Just tell me if you can," she finished shyly.

"I started praying." It was a lame start. The confusion in Gwen's face told him it was far from enough. "Not the normal, 'Skies above preserve us,' but more like just talking to the Maker."

"Okay…"

Adrig could tell she still had no clue what he meant. "Do you remember from the Histories and Sciences how the Eldest taught us that there used to be things called churches with priests who were supposed to be the only ones who could tell us how to live?"

"Yeah. They used their authority to get rich and control people. The Eldest said that if we all shared the truth, no one could disguise it to manipulate us. Right?"

"Right! But, what if…what if part of what they did was right, but done for the wrong reason? Part of what those priests did was teach Souls all sorts of prayers, and not just our quick cries for help or Sun Day Recitations. We only do that when we're learning, once a year on Sun Day, or apparently at betrothal ceremonies. I think...I know... there's Power in praying more. It doesn't have to be some memorized Recitation. It only has to have...heart? Heart! Heart behind it. You just have to talk to the Maker like you would talk to your mother or father, asking for help or guidance or the ability to help the People in a new way." Adrig ran out of steam. This wasn't going well.

Gwen looked at him in silence, searching his face for a time. He worried that he sounded like a fool. But then she smiled and asked, "Why is that so strange? The Eldest said that everything good comes from the Maker. Why not pray for more good things?"

Relief flooded Adrig. He felt like he'd dropped a gigantic weight of timber off for the coal fires. It made him brave and gave him a spark of inspiration.

"Could you...try this? The next time you're mixing one of your cures, ask the Maker to make it more effective. To make it work better. To make it heal faster. Can you do that?" Adrig flushed as he asked. None of the People talked this way.

"Teach me how?"

Beautiful, selfless, trusting Gwen. Adrig's heart was trying to escape his chest, being so filled with love for her.

"It's simple. Just...talk to the Maker like you'd talk to me and have...hope...that it will be heard and answered." It seemed so paltry laid out that way. "Like this." Adrig took Gwen's hand and looked at the sky the way the Eldest had looked at the ceiling of the smithy.

"Maker, I don't have fancy words. But with all my heart, I need Gwen to understand me in this. Please, help us share this with each other."

Gwen gasped. Their hands were growing warm. Not warm, hot. Her eyes went out of focus for a moment, and she gasped even louder. "Did you say that?"

"No. What did it say?"

"I swear a voice said 'granted.' I know it wasn't just me thinking." Her eyes grew wide. "The Maker answers you?" she asked with wonder.

Adrig shrugged. "Sometimes."

"That's wonderful!" She sat looking at him, dazed. Then her forehead wrinkled in thought. "What did you pray for? Something at the forge? You told me to do it with my cures."

Maker, help me do this right.

"At the forge, yes. But…I'm sorry, Gwen, I don't think I'm allowed to say what…not yet." Adrig waited with agony as she explored his face again.

"'Trust him.' I heard that in my head." She took a deep breath. "I do trust you. I don't want you to betray what you shouldn't." She finished with a beautiful smile. "Thank you, Adrig. This is a great gift."

The next day, the Eldest came to collect Adrig from the forge for their fencing lesson. Adrig still didn't understand the name. There was no fence involved. They went to their clearing and continued working on swatting each other with their stick-swords and trying new ways to stop each other and get around those blocks. The Eldest was surprisingly agile still, so it was no easy task, but Adrig had a much longer reach, and was far stronger, so he had the advantage when trying to strike. When the Eldest made him do nothing but block, and not try to slash back, it was much harder, but he seemed to be catching on.

"Eldest, is there anything else in the Mysteries I don't know?" Adrig asked as they paused to catch their breath.

The old man looked at him shrewdly. "There is much I know that I haven't had the time to tell you, boy."

"Boy" again, not Adrig, or Master Adrig. Then again, everyone was a boy, or girl, to the Eldest. He tried not to let it bother him.

The Eldest sighed. "It is not mine to tell. The signs aren't laid out in detail. For instance, the sign of the Guardian was: 'When what is forbidden is undertaken with a pure heart, the Guardian has come.' Not much to go on until the situation arises."

"So, I'm guessing there's a sign for when someone should be trained to be the next Eldest?" Adrig wondered aloud.

"Yes," the Eldest answered. "But that's not you."

"Oh…no…that's not what I meant!" Adrig assured him.

The Eldest explored his face, much like Gwen had. Then he barked a quick laugh. "I was much like you when I was your age. I didn't believe half of what Master Ekrid told me as a boy, but I wanted to know everything. I drove the man mad by questioning him. But then I displayed the sign and he laughed for days, saying the Maker had a fine sense of humor. I trained under him for twenty years before his Soul made its journey. No one has displayed the sign yet, and I don't know if I have twenty years left in me. I wish it were you, truth be told."

Adrig flushed with embarrassment.

Ask him about the Healer.

"What about the Healer?" Adrig spoke the silent words.

The Eldest was shocked. "How…did you just *hear* that?"

Adrig nodded.

"Well, I guess I have to make some visits today. No, ask me no more. Thank you for the prompting, but, like the Guardian had to remain secret until it was time, so too with the Healer. Please, do not repeat those words." The Eldest glared at him until he nodded. "Good. Well, back to the forge with you; we've both got work to do." The Eldest set out in the opposite direction, and Adrig obeyed.

That night, tragedy struck the Valley, and the next day, the People were in mourning.

Adrig awoke to the keening cry of the people an-
nouncing a Soul's Journey. That chanting was always
heart-rending. He hoped with all his heart it wasn't the
nameless Young One Thelisa was weening.

He dressed in a hurry and went outside under the
gloaming. Many of the village folks were gathering on the
green. Kywin was sobbing, trying to tell them something.
As Adrig approached, his heart was torn in half.

What remained of the Eldest lay a makeshift litter that
Kywin had dragged in from the forest.

"I just found him like this!" he yelled through his sobs.
"It had to be wolves!"

Adrig gazed in horror at the body of the Eldest. This
was no wolf attack. The wounds were all wrong. One leg
was missing from below the knee, but it didn't end in a
ragged mess like every other wolf attack injury he'd seen
before. The leg was cut clean, and the puncture to his
stomach was too small to be from the maw of a beast. He
looked for his father and saw him approaching the body
of his hero with tears streaming down his face.

"Who will sing the rites?" someone wailed. The Eldest
did that, or his apprentice. Only the Eldest was now dead,
and he had no apprentice. The undulation screeched to
a crescendo. The People were without leadership for the
first time since Olwin led them to the Valley.

A sick worry stabbed Adrig in the gut; those wounds
could have been made by a sword. He ran to his room.
The Scimitar was still in the case that was made to look
like a portable tool set for his trade. Adrig opened it to
be sure, and it was there—and not covered in gore. The
thought of this thing being covered in any gore, and the
memory of the torn body of the Eldest, created images in
his head that made him expel last night's supper in his
chamber pot. But Adrig knew that no wolf had caused
those wounds.

IT IS TIME!

Never had the voice been so loud. Adrig covered his ears to no avail. The voice was from inside but it was not his own. He gazed at the dangerous beauty.

"How?" he asked aloud.

"Not a wolf," Bruhan said behind him. "But you already know that. What now, son?"

Adrig stared at his father, horrified. Why was Bruhan asking him?

"What now, Guardian?" Bruhan asked again.

They come with the sun.

Adrig swayed under the weight of it all. He was too young; he'd only seen fifteen Sun Days. But he obeyed. He took the sword, which he called Reckoning, and held it in a strong grip. A tenuous peace filled him, and the blade shone with a yellow light the color of the noonday sun. Bruhan's eyes fixed on the glowing blade.

"By the Skies!" he yelped.

"For the Skies and the Maker," Adrig said. His father didn't mock him, so perhaps it was the right thing to say. Reckoning shone brighter. "Father, assemble everyone, please. Tell them all that everyone who can swing a sling needs to get them and the Wolfsbane pellets and meet on the green. Everyone else should hide in their homes." It was strange to order his father. Stranger still for his father to run to carry out the command.

Adrig dropped to his knees. "Maker...I'm not strong enough, give me the strength to help my people. GWEN!" He started to jerk to his feet, to run to find her.

She will be well. I am with you all.

Adrig stayed on his knees. He tried to trust that this was truly the Maker; that he wasn't dreaming or going insane. "Help me...please."

The glow of Reckoning softened. Shades of red and orange joined the yellow. It was like the fire of the forge. This hue gave Adrig comfort. In order to create pure steel, you had to destroy the dross with fire and strength. The thought calmed him, but they weren't the words of the Maker. It was the first lesson his father had given him at the beginning of his apprenticeship. Resolve claimed him.

The fire of Reckoning grew as bright as the furnace fires.

Adrig walked outside to lead his People.

As he approached the green, he saw that Bruhan had been obeyed. Stark silence greeted him. Every eye fixed upon the flaming something in his hands. He was surprised by how many boys and women were in the crowd, but Bruhan was right. No one with strength could be spared. Patrick was the only one who did not look awestruck. He was staring at the blade too, but not in fear and awe, but in...recognition. Adrig's bowels almost turned to water when he saw Gwen and Mara holding slings. Gwen slowly approached him; everyone else was silent.

"Is this what you couldn't tell me?" she asked.

Adrig nodded. "I'm sorry, my Love. It wasn't time. I'll need you, Mara, and Nina to set up a station for healing the wounded."

"What wounded? What's happening!" That was Master Thane. Many echoed the call.

Adrig held Reckoning aloft and it glowed brighter still, silencing the People.

"I didn't ask for this," Adrig began. "I prayed to the Maker to help me make something that would help our people live at peace. I was trying to make a new form of scythe. But the Maker had something else in mind. I know...I sound crazy. My only evidence is this." He waved the sword. "I'm not the Eldest." He choked back a sob, looking at the man. Someone had blessedly covered the wrecked body. "But he gave me a name. Guardian. I don't deserve it, but...I'll die to live up to the name." A few whispers began at that. "Something is coming. The Eldest warned me and Father, but he didn't know when it would happen."

"What something?" That was Mara. She wasn't combative. She was terrified.

"'The Spawn of Violence,' he called them. I don't know what they look like, but they've consumed everything below the fog. We're the last things on earth for them to consume. And they started with him." Adrig pointed Reckoning at the Eldest's body. It changed color to the black of mourning, but somehow still glowed.

Wails erupted from the People. Adrig raised the sword again, and Reckoning glowed like the noon sun once more, too bright to look at directly. The people stared in awe and their wails were cut short.

"I know what they look like," Patrick said in the silence. Everyone, including Adrig, stared at him.

Of course.Why didn't I think of that? Adrig chided himself.

"They have green, black, and brown skin in patches, like a tree after Harvest Day, and a rock instead of a head! They're almost as big as papa!" Patrick explained.

"Where do they enter the Valley, Patrick?" Adrig asked.

The simple boy in a man's body looked excited. "Follow me, I'll show you!" He set off.

"Ten men stay with the herbalists and guard the forest edge, everyone else follow me. Gwen, send runners, the fastest children we have left, to the other villages to warn them of extreme danger coming from the mountains or forest." Adrig was both surprised and happy when no one argued and, instead, moved to obey. It was strange. He didn't like it.

That is why you are the Guardian, the Maker assured him.

Adrig was not surprised when Patrick led them to his ridge near the smithy. He pointed to a pass. "That's where they come in," he said. Adrig climbed down the wall to address the crowd.

"As many as can fit on that ledge and swing a sling while sitting, take positions there. Patrick, point them out when they come. As many as can get on the roof of the shop, take positions there. Everyone else, stay ready to relieve them." Adrig started to clamber back up the ridge, but Bruhan stopped him.

"I think it would be best if you stayed here and kept leading. I don't think that sword will be of much use on the wall, and those folks are just as good with a sling." Bruhan explained.

Adrig nodded at the wisdom in that but hoped he wasn't letting people down. He climbed the roof of the smithy instead, and Bruhan smiled with encouragement and acceptance and followed him up. Father stood by son, waiting.

A wet squelch and solid thump preceded a short gurgling scream behind Adrig. At the same moment, Patrick yelled "There!"

Adrig looked behind him and saw young Andrew lying on the roof, a long piece of steel and wood sticking out of his chest with more wood out of his back. Dismay rolled over him. I've already failed!

"Half of you, look behind!" And there were some of the creatures approaching from the path toward town. "Sling! Now!"

Several pellets hit the first one in line, dropping it. They looked like Patrick had described them. The flesh was mottled and swollen, oozing puss. The faces were human-like, but wrong. The skin was half melted with bone showing in some places. Their heads did look like a rock, but when the first went down, it appeared to be some hat that fell off, revealing a patchy-haired skull with angry fissures of red and green over burnt flesh. They were hideous.

Adrig glanced back and saw another group struggling to take the pass, but the pellets from above were causing them to duck back. For a harrowing moment, Adrig was wracked with indecision. Then he leaped down from the shop roof right as a spear passed through the space he had vacated. Several of the demons rushed toward Adrig with shocking speed. Wolfsbane pellets felled one, but then Adrig was in the fray, too close for the slingers to avoid, so the townspeople focused on creatures trying to find cover or throw their spears.

With a roar, Adrig rushed the three closest to him. All of the lessons he'd gone through with the Eldest lay forgotten as he swung Reckoning again and again. Everywhere he struck, not only did the blade score true, the corruptions turned black and began to harden and solidify. The blade cleaved through arm and chest, leg and head. The first two dropped, but the third was faster, more vicious. He danced with his spear and stabbed into Adrig's leg. Adrig yelled in agony and knew his life was at an end. Bruhan's hammer took the monster in the head, and it fell instantly.

"Easy, lad, easy." Bruhan ripped his shirt and tied it over the wound. Adrig found he could still limp along if he didn't put too much weight on the injured leg. The group of creatures in front of them was dwindling, and hope soared in Adrig's chest.

"Adrig!" A voice shouted.

Adrig and Bruhan stumbled around the shop into horror. Dozens of the not-men were in the yard slaughtering his friends, his people. Righteous rage flowed through him.

"For the Skies and the Maker!" Adrig bellowed.

He and Bruhan rushed into the battle, swinging with hammer and blade. Reckoning changed to a pure white light, and strength coursed through Adrig's body. He forgot the pain in his leg and destroyed the dross. Master Thane had found a stave in his shop and was knocking creatures down that Adrig or Bruhan finished off. Other men and women had also grabbed implements from the shop. A scythe, a plough shear, hammers, staves, those on their feet used what they could grab, but too many of the People were going down. The group of about sixty had dwindled to twenty, including ten still on the roof who had all switched their attention to the yard, picking off targets that were fleeing from Adrig and Bruhan to find easier prey.

Suddenly, all went still. Every creature in sight was down. Only the cries of the injured and the gasping breaths of those on their feet disturbed the sudden peace. It was over.

NOT YET.

Adrig straightened just as the monster leaped over the ridge and pounded to the earth. It was like the others, but massive, three times their size.

"RUN!" Adrig screamed as he rushed the beast.

But no one obeyed. Every slinger hit it with pellets. The Wolfsbane sunk deep into its flesh but did not slow it much. Master Thane swung with his stave, but the beast ignored the splintering wood, wrapped a mighty hand around the carpenter, and threw him against the smithy wall with a sickening wet crunch. Everyone ran except Adrig and Bruhan.

"Father, no!" Adrig yelled as the smith swung his heaviest hammer at the monster. Adrig's yell attracted the attention of the beast, and Bruhan's hammer shattered its knee. The beast bellowed so loudly that Adrig almost dropped his sword to cover his ears. The monster turned its molten eyes upon Bruhan, and fearful rage strengthened Adrig's focus. It grabbed Bruhan, and Adrig was terrified that he'd never talk to his father again.

"MAKER!" He yelled and slashed with all his might. The beast bellowed again, louder, as its arm separated from its body. The creature began to convulse. Smoke poured out of blackened holes where the Wolfsbane pellets had entered its flesh before.

DON'T STOP!

Adrig hammered the beast with Reckoning. Everywhere the blade struck, flesh or limbs were petrified or sheared off. The smoke intensified and the convulsions repeated. The monster dropped to its knees, but its already wrecked knee could not support its weight, and the creature fell with an almighty crash to the ground. With a final wild roar and in retribution for all who had died, Adrig swung wildly and cleaved the skull in two. The beast shuddered, then blackened and died, looking like petrified wood.

Adrig rushed to his father and pulled him from beneath the dismembered arm. He was breathing, but with obvious pain. The monster had surely cracked his ribs.

"Father!" Not knowing why, he laid the blade on Bruhan's chest. "MAKER!" he shouted.

Bruhan's eyes fluttered open, then closed. Adrig dropped to the ground in despair. All around him, so many of his People lay dead among dozens of blackened rocks that used to be monsters. Here and there, the beasts retained their original form. Adrig shook off his despair to serve the Remnant. He took the sword from Bruhan's chest and stabbed it through the remaining corpses of the monsters. As he did, they also blackened.

Around him, the survivors looked lost. They surveyed their dead and the blackened monsters. As Adrig finished the last beast, the People shouted their defiance. They were alive, and angry at death.

Adrig returned to Bruhan to say goodbye. The survivors did the same with their kin.

Their Kin!

Adrig shouted, "To the village!" Shame at forgetting made them move faster as they all raced to the green. Halfway there, they stopped in dread. Some thirty people were walking towards them. Most of them had some injury. It took a moment to realize that among the crowd were people from all of The Five, not just Ruhm.

"Gwen! Mother!" Adrig shouted. Others with him called out for their loved ones.

A miracle of beauty stepped out from the crowd and ran to Adrig.

"I'm here," Gwen cried. "I'm sorry...Thelisa...Momma, Pappa...it was so horrible, Adrig."

She cried in his arms. He felt close to empty, but he knew he was blessed beyond so many others.

"How did they get here so fast?" he asked, pointing at a group of folks from other villages.

"They're the only reason we are still alive. They got here an hour after you left. The runners found that all of The Five Villages had been hit, but your Wolfsbane helped most survive. There are about a hundred on the green too injured to move. We were coming to help since you'd been gone for so long. Right after they got to us, a dozen monsters attacked. They said only five or six had been to the other villages. We got them down, but it was close." She was shaking in his arms, and Adrig noticed the makeshift brace on her arm.

"We? You fought!" Adrig was frightened out of his mind.

"I had to. All of Mara's supplies were at the shop and what was in our pockets ran out fast. It was help or hide, and I couldn't just hide. Please don't be angry with me." She hugged him tighter.

"Angry? No, my Love, no, just scared." He realized everyone was looking at him, waiting.

I'm no leader, he lamented.

Adrig sighed and released Gwen, but still held on to her unbandaged hand. He addressed the crowd.

"Thank you for coming. So many didn't survive..." He choked back a sob at the pain of loss. "We've all lost someone we love today. The Maker sent us Wolfsbane and Reckoning to save a Remnant." He raised the sword now pulsing with the soothing forge-like flame. Those who had not seen it before gasped. "I wish I had never had to swing this thing, but it saved us. I hope we never need another. The Spawn of Violence are gone. Let's help gather the injured and assist the herbalists as much as we can. Let's bury our dead. We must prepare our kin for the Soul Journey. For the largest funeral the People have had. I'm not much of a leader, but I will try my best to help us rebuild if you'll have me."

"Guardian!" The crowd cheered. Adrig felt sick.

I'm glad I could help, but I wish this were a scythe... Adrig thought.

Granted.

Cries of wonder arose from the People as the sword changed shape before their eyes. It elongated, curved, and settled into the form of a scythe, but still bore the holy symbols engraved on blade and metal shaft.

Carrying the dead and injured back to town took three trips for those who were healthy or whose injuries were not severe. Adrig was bone weary as he sat trying to catch his breath. His heart told him that his time of leadership was over, but how could he make them believe it?

"Adrig!" Gwen's cry shocked him to his feet, and he ran to her. She was standing over his mother and father. Thelisa had given her life to guard the door of one of the homes that contained the young. She stood long enough for help to arrive, but fell before they could come to her aid. He ached for them both. He looked at his father's body, stripped for cleaning, and dropped to his knees, amazed. The holy symbols were branded onto his flesh. Flesh that was rising and falling once more. The ribs were healed. Bruhan was alive.

"How!" Adrig asked Gwen.

"I saw this in his chest, right where those brands are, and I took it out." She held up a piece of blackened rock. A finger from the monster, or a bit of it anyhow. "When I took it out, Bruhan gasped, opened his eyes, then fell asleep. The brands came from nowhere."

No, not nowhere, Adrig thought. He grabbed his scythe, Reckoning, and told the mourners to search the bodies for any of the black bits. Everywhere they found them, he touched the blade to the injury and, after removing the bit of stone, that Soul revived. Twenty-three who were dead lived again. But one hundred and three did not, and dozens were seriously injured.

He touched everyone with the blade, just to be sure. It only healed those who were infected with the Spawn's touch. Strangely, the holy symbols only appeared on Bruhan.

While he performed this work, shouts of awe tried to distract him. He assumed it was the work of the Maker in healing the Spawn Touched. But when he was finished, he noticed far more people working than before. In a daze, he walked to Gwen who was pouring a tincture into Patrick's mouth. The young man had struck his head falling off the wall in the assault.

Patrick's eyes shot open.

"Hello, Guardian," he said with more lucidity than Adrig could ever remember hearing in Patrick's voice. "Father will be Eldest now, and I'll be his apprentice."

Adrig could only stare. Patrick showed him that the three holy symbols were now on his arm, though Adrig had not touched him with Reckoning.

Patrick laughed a joyous, clear laugh. "Your prayers are getting stronger, Healer," he said to Gwen. "The Maker hears them and answers. Always answers if we use the right ears."

Adrig broke down and cried. They were tears of loss and joy, and of gratitude above all.

SEAHORSES

R. T. Swindoll

The pet store clerk flashed an award-winning smile at the family approaching the checkout counter. He would have liked to help the young mother juggling the aquarium, stroller, and kids, but The Pet Exchange was family owned and operated, and the owners set strict policies. All sales final! No substitutions, exchanges, or refunds! And the clerk had to wear the sea green uniform and stay behind the counter—those were rules, too. The last thing he wanted was to break a rule and get assigned to tank duty.

"Did you find everything, Miss?"

The mother plopped the aquarium on the counter and turned to her eldest who was hanging all of his five-year-old weight on her other arm. "Stop it. We are not getting iguanas."

The clerk scanned the barcode and peeked at the baby in the stroller. A chubby boy munched on his fingers, slobber everywhere.

"That it? Any fish to go with it?"

The mother reached around the stroller and tapped a toddler who stood extremely close to the counter, so close the clerk hadn't even seen him there.

"Bubwee, give the nice man the fish."

Bubwee? What a *weird* thing to call a child.

The clerk leaned over. Bubwee stood in little navy blue sneakers gazing at a navy blue seahorse swimming in a plastic case. The owners must have left it out for him. The clerk shivered and would have liked to help the boy lift the case to the counter, but he didn't want to contaminate the imprinting process. Rules were rules. And he hated tank duty.

"Put it right here. You can take it right back."

Bubwee set the plastic case with the seahorse on the counter.

"Turns out this is a pot-bellied seahorse and lives about five years in captivity. And it's *special*," the clerk followed the script, "because it comes with a few promotional items for the little tykes. If you're interested."

He pulled out the seahorse crib mobile and the seahorse board book, both products made by the owners themselves. They had self-published products like these all over the world, little tie-ins to their business that kept the customers in their orbit.

For the mother, it was just more to carry. "Fine."

The clerk handled payment, then let little Bubwee handle the case. "Take good care of him."

Bubwee looked up. "It's a him?"

Hell if he knew. They all looked alike. Sometimes he couldn't even tell the owners apart.

"Sure is."

The mother plopped the board book into the stroller where it soon entered the mouth of the baby. The eldest was forced to carry the small box with the crib mobile, which he claimed was heavy enough to break his arms. When she wouldn't relent to carry it for him, the child narrated how he would cut the mobile apart when they got home and enlist the dangling seahorses into his soldier armies. The mother took the aquarium and, balancing it on the back of the stroller, issued a weary, "Come on." Little Bubwee shuffled out last.

The clerk watched them go.

He knew the owners made products that, in time, would give the mother back far more than she had paid for this little excursion. They would make her deliriously happy. But more than anything, he wanted to tell the little toddler, Bubwee, that everything would be all right—the seahorse usually imprinted on the most active child, and nine times out of ten that was the eldest in a family of three boys. Except he'd seen how they'd looked at each other.

It was against store policy to speculate. So the clerk consoled himself with a glance at his employee-of-the-month portrait and tried to forget he'd ever met little Bubwee, lest the owners decide to peek at his thoughts.

He was mortally afraid of tank duty.

B ubba stayed away from that little seahorse for five years. It was *weird*. And hanging around weird things could infect you.

Like his nickname, Bubwee. They called him Bubwee because it sounded like his birth name, Bubba—Bubwee was just how he'd said it as a baby. Then it infected him. Now every day in second grade, Bubba's classmates circled him, teasing, "Bub-wee, Bub-wee," because he couldn't run five minutes at recess without his allergies flaring up and leaving him sucking air like a fish.

He tried to change his name to Bud or Bob, except that just turned the bub-wees into bud-wees and bob-wees. And the constant medications didn't help much either.

But he was turning seven today. Bubba had big plans for his birthday—special plans. He was skipping school—that part his mother had planned, since she'd scheduled an appointment for Bubba at the eye doctor that same morning. He didn't care. He was going to go home afterward and enjoy a little solitary play time. Sloth-hang from the bunk beds and let his eyes glaze. Make paper crafts. Maybe cash in some tablet time for video games. No bub-wee today. Not on his birthday.

Then the eye doctor said Bubba needed glasses.

"You don't have to wear them now," Mom said in her super sweet voice. "Just at school."

Just at school. Just at the most devastating hour of his social life.

So Bubba felt like a limp party balloon when he got home with a pair of wobbly glasses "his face would grow into." The moment he tried to sloth-hang, they fell right off.

He liked the world the way it used to be: a soft, blobby blur. Glasses put angles on everything. He hated it. He wanted to cry.

Mom picked up the glasses. "Bubwee, if you put them on and look around—"

"Shut it, Mom," Bubba said and turned away in the bunk bed.

Mom looked on the verge of clapping, that thing she'd learned from his classmate Jolie's family. Even the teachers clapped now when someone wasn't paying attention to the rules. But Bubba couldn't hear in one ear and had tinnitus in the other, so it never worked on him like it did on everyone else. Mom took a collecting breath, left the glasses in the case on Bubba's desk, and left for her book and hammock in the backyard.

Bubba hunched in bed. He hated being the weird one: the middle kid, the only one in his family with allergies and hearing loss, the only one who didn't like brussel sprouts, the only one in the whole neighborhood who ate all his candy on Halloween night—not just one piece!—the only one who got in trouble at school for running in the halls or talking during class. He just wanted to feel *special* on his special day. But the big, dumb world had given him a birthday present, and it was glasses. Capital-W *weird*, stuck on his face.

He slunk down the ladder and put on the glasses. The pictures on the wall popped in vivid color and clarity. If this was his life now, he might as well get used to it.

He looked across the room at the old aquarium, and through his glasses he caught all the light dancing in the water. The aquarium stood where Eli's crib used to be; Mom had moved the aquarium here after the youngest, Eli, graduated from the crib to the lower bunk in Bubba's room. But the crib mobile still hung from the ceiling over the aquarium, still caught the breeze from the AC that spun the little paper seahorses ever so slowly in revolving circles. It marked Beastmaster's domain, the pot-bellied seahorse that the eldest had named. That navy blue blob had outlived all its fish friends, maybe even ate some of them. Bubba remembered how Beastmaster used to be tiny and fast—used to dart around when Bubba banged the glass, swimming zig-zags in every direction like its life depended on it. Now it hid all the time in the fake seaweeds, bloated, and wouldn't hardly come out except at breakfast, lunch, and dinner.

Mom had said it was "behavior consistent with an intelligent aquatic lifeform."

Bubba just thought it was what *weird* looked like on a fish alien.

He drew near to inspect the fishtank with his super-powered sight. Every bitty bubble appeared perfectly clear in the recessed lighting of the tank. Bubba bent his head to peek behind the sunken pirate ship and find Beastmaster. There it was, floating perfectly still. Bubba saw every detail: ribs, tail, and snout.

It shouldn't have surprised him, but Beastmaster had eyes. Little bitty black ones—all pupils, no lids. They seemed...lonely.

He felt drawn to comfort Beastmaster—to reach into the water, give it a gentle pet, tell it everything was going to be OK. But Bubba knew better. Mom said germs could make Beastmaster sick, and he didn't want Beastmaster to turn out like those other zombie fish it had once shared a tank with.

Before school got out and his brothers came home, Bubba slaved at his desk to trace seahorses on paper and used his favorite colored pencils to make them real. Fungus green. Orange-utan. Sky blue. Through his glasses, the lines were sharp and the colors popped. He cut them out with care. It was easily the work of someone twice his age.

He taped the cutouts to the aquarium glass so that Beastmaster could see them and know he wasn't alone. He could come out and play without fear. He had lots of fishy friends.

Bubba stepped back from the tank, flush with joy. He soon noticed how empty his room felt. How forgotten. The pictures on the wall were of Bubwee, the two-year-old. There were old board books still sitting on the open shelves. He peered through the window at the neighborhood street, wishing for someone he knew to pass by, worrying, growing angry that he didn't have any friends at school, furious that the whole wide world was perfect except him. He wanted to scream!

He stopped himself. Screaming indoors was definitely off-limits. If Mom caught him, he would lose tablet privileges and video games were practically his only friend. Except, maybe Beastmaster, his old pet.

So Bubba zig-zagged around the room and laid his frustrations on the board books, sweeping them off the open shelves with a careless hand. He jerked open his closet and wrenched down the mountain-stack of model sets, action figures, and hand-me-downs that had collected here like garbage, and threw them all on the heap. He got behind the aquarium, tripped on the cord, but managed not to fall. He rose on his toes to grab the embarrassing Bubwee pictures and toss them, too, on the pile.

He cinched up the glasses on his sweaty nose. It felt amazing, making a huge mess. "Welp," he told himself with a crooked smile at the lower bunk, "Eli's present to me can be cleaning up our room."

Every delicious smell wafted from the kitchen where Mom made Bubba's birthday dinner. The king Bubba himself slouched on his upper bunk, sipping a boxed lemonade that he'd sneaked from the fridge while order-ing Eli to sort out the mess on the floor. "I mean, most of it's trash. So you figure out what you want to keep."

The cheerful kindergartener smiled. He was oblivious to the injustice being asked of him. Like most kids in town, Eli just loved the work of making things neat, whether it be straightening the sheets on his bed or scouring the sea of trash that Bubba had spewed from corner to corner in their room. Eli had already separated the books from the toys and arranged the pictures on the floor as they had once hung on the wall.

"I like silly Bubwee pictures," he commented. "They're so funny."

Bubba tried hard to sound like Mom. "Those are going in the garbage. Sorry—not sorry."

He bent and massaged his ear where the new glasses were rubbing the skin raw, pouting over Mom not letting him get the cool sunglasses instead of these bottle-bottom frames. He sipped the lemonade, hearing the straw slurp up its last drops and, groaning, tossed the box into the room where Eli pleasantly collected and disposed of it.

Only seven hours left of his birthday. Three hours, if he counted till bedtime. Already he could feel the *special-ness* slipping away.

"Eli, what is with you and the other kids? Why do you love rules so much?"

The boy shrugged. "I just do."

Bubba slinked out of bed and swam around Eli's piles. "Yeah, but they're like being trapped in a little fish tank. Don't you ever want to get out...act a little *weird* some-times?" He stopped at the window and peeked out at the darkening evening. Through his glasses, the streetlamps were beady sharp.

Eli hummed as if merely thinking about the question put his mind in danger. "No way. If there were no rules, the kidnappers would get us."

Bubba scoffed, but he couldn't disagree. Kidnappers hid in weird places…maybe the king of weird himself was a kidnapper! He spun around and creeped up toward the aquarium like a kidnapper, remembering how his toddler self had picked Beastmaster over all the other seahorses just because it matched his navy blue sneakers. Bubba wanted to see the color now through his new glasses, but the water was dark—darker than normal, but that was probably because it was getting dark outside.

He looked down to check on Eli's progress. Eli had sorted everything; even the old board books were stacked on the ground, their corners limp and frayed with the soggy stains of teething. Bubba made a moldy face; he didn't even want to touch them. On top of the stack sat a book with a bright seahorse on the cover, titled, *Your Amazing Brain!* Bubba lit up, remembering more of that yucky smelling pet store where Mom had taken them as kids, remembering this weird book cover, which he'd stared at for hours as a child, but no one'd ever read aloud to him.

He decided to be brave and pick it up. "Do you remember this?"

Eli wore a puzzled look. "Of course."

Bubba opened it to the first page. A yellow illustrated seahorse narrated the story of an underwater world.

> *The brain is amazing! Look at what it can do.*
> *What number do you see? That's right! The number 2.*

A big number 2 made out of bubbles filled the opposite page.

Bubba groaned, reminding himself this was a baby book and not some buried treasure from childhood. He turned the page. The illustrated seahorse was frowning.

Oh no! Where did the number go?
I can't see it anymore. But do you still know?

The bubbles on the opposite page had scattered; the number 2 had disappeared. Bubba could already see the pattern as he turned for the next page: seahorse, bubbles, seahorse, bubbles. He felt vaguely familiar with the story. Maybe he *had* read it before but had just forgotten it, because it was so boring.

It isn't hard. Your brain to the aid!
Close your eyes and see the bubbles remade!

Bubba noticed how Eli had closed his eyes and was smiling like one of Grandma's Precious Moments. "Knock that off," Bubba snapped, unsure why his own stomach was churning. The AC kicked on and brought a chill to the room. The lazy mobile swung over the dark aquarium. His eyes fell back to the page and the bubbles, which showed a number 2, only faintly, as if it was on the verge of being forgotten.

An old stain wiped across the page. Bubba made a face and turned it quickly.

The cartoony seahorse was now laughing.

That's right! 2. But how can this be?
Your brain must remember everything you see.

The bubbles now clumped in the shape of a brain.

Eli grew excited, reached over, and turned the page. "This is my favorite part."

Bubba frowned at Eli's familiarity with the book. On this page, the cartoon seahorse had congealed into a yellow seahorse-shaped brain chunk. It had no mouth, but was still speaking.

I'm the hippocampus!* I draw pictures for your brain.
Everything you see and hear. Every joy and pain.

The bubbles were greatly magnified and filled the opposite page. Reflected in each bubble was the face of a little boy, the same face experiencing every possible emotion—smiling, shrieking, storming, sobbing. Below, there was a note that read,

*Hippocampus means seahorse and it looks like one, too!

Bubba didn't feel well. He caught an unpleasant whiff of lemonade on his breath as he asked Eli, "When did you read this?" Eli had only been a baby when he'd munched the corners of this book. Far too little to read it.

Eli only shrugged.

From far downstairs, Mom called to say it was time to come down. The birthday dinner was ready. Bubba wasn't ready, though. He had one more page to turn. He felt his allergies constricting his throat. The room seemed stuffy. Or *infected*.

He couldn't help himself. He turned the page and stared at it. His mouth gasped for air.

The friendly yellow seahorse blurred and shredded into four pieces before his eyes. Bubba fumbled with his glasses, unsure if what he was seeing was real or if his lenses had somehow stopped working.

Without me, you wouldn't know who you are.
So care for your little seahorse, and we'll go far!

The bubbles shrank and showed the wider scene. All along, the underwater world on the page had been an aquarium inside the little boy's head.

When Bubba snapped the book shut, Eli began clapping for the story—loud and off-beat, like a zombie might clap. He'd been doing this since he was a baby.

Bubba backed away from Eli. The boy's smile was too thin and wide—but maybe that's how smiles were supposed to look with glasses on. Or maybe it was the glasses making everything suddenly *weird*. Bubba threw off the glasses. He wanted to see normally again—his *special* way of viewing the world. He backed into the aquarium and realized a disquieting absence of sound. The tank was not humming.

Bubba turned sharply and looked again into the dark water, around the seahorse cutouts, and behind the pirate ship. He couldn't find Beastmaster anywhere.

He needed light. Bubba tagged the light switch, and the room lit up. That's when he saw the aquarium power cord knocked out of the wall.

"No!"

Eli kept clapping. Mom called again for them to come down.

Bubba panicked, recalling how his foot had snagged the cord earlier today when he'd gone behind the aquarium to knock down those pictures. He quickly shoved the plug back in.

The tank filter lurched back to life, spurting a mist of bubbles and algae across the surface of the tank, where Beastmaster bobbed belly up and did not move.

Dead.

His oldest friend, Beastmaster, was dead. He'd killed him.

Bubba threw up on the carpet.

The birthday was canceled. Bubba had a fever of a hundred and two and had to go straight to bed. Mom made him drink a tall glass of water. Her last words to Bubba were, "Make sure you stay in bed all night."

But he woke in the middle of it. Bubba sat up. The room was a dark blur. The red numbers of his alarm clock below his bunk told the time; he had to squint through the sleepies in his eyes to pick out the numbers. 1:23 exactly. His birthday was over. The aquarium and its comforting hum and nightlight were gone. Dad must have taken it out after Beastmaster...

He clutched his stomach. His throat felt parched. He reached for the glasses on his face, but they were missing. He wanted to fall back asleep, but his body was sweltering in an old pair of fleece-footed jammies Mom didn't mind him throwing up in. He felt his head—hot, but the air outside the covers felt icy cold, and now Bubba realized, as his feet began to twitch, that he had to go potty.

He groaned loudly. Did he really have to go THAT bad?

His legs twitched back and forth, dancing for relief, until finally, he forced himself to climb off the bunk. Eli was not in the lower bunk. They'd probably moved his little brother to a different room because he was sick.

Bubba trudged for the door; it opened with a creak. The AC rumbled the house, but all else was quiet. The door to Mom and Dad's bedroom was closed. The door to his older brother's room, too. Only he was awake. Ugh. Dumb bladders. He crossed the hall, passed the blobby family photos that Mom made them take for the internet, to the bathroom and its soft white glow.

He went potty. A long shiver ran down Bubba's back and made him squeak. The house was so much colder than usual. The AC must be on turbo.

He didn't want Mom and Dad to know he was out of bed, so he didn't flush and crept quietly back. All he wanted was to cuddle his pillow and to go back to sleep.

But when he reached the doorway to his room, he stopped, frozen before a dance of lights on the far wall beside the bunk bed. The clock still read 1:23; above the red numbers Bubba saw fuzzy, blue, shimmering waves cast through the wide gap in his curtains. Probably that porch light from the neighbor across the street again, passing through the bad haircut tree in the front yard. This wasn't the first time the light had made a creepy shadow on Bubba's wall.

But there was another shadow blocking the light that didn't move. A *weird* shadow. As if a pointy suit of armor were hovering in the nearby tree.

Bubba pulled back. He couldn't go in his room now. He almost darted into Mom and Dad's room, but didn't want to get clapped at. If someone was hiding in the bad haircut tree, he would have to sneak downstairs and try to spy it from the family room window. He could do this!— calm his own fears, prove he was a normal kid that could sleep through the night, not some freak who freaked out about tree shadows.

Down the stairs he crept, keeping his eyes on his footies so that he made no sound or slip. There were blue dancing lights on all the walls downstairs, too, being cast through the house's many windows. It was foggy outside, or so it seemed to Bubba without his glasses. He took in a breath at the landing of the stairs and glanced across the hall, toward the front door.

Framed in the large window of the front door was a human shape.

Bubba screamed—and caught his mouth with his hand. He wasn't supposed to be out of bed! He was breaking the rules! He listened in the dark for steps in the upstairs bedrooms.

Nothing. He'd escaped.

His fright at the shape in the window soon gave way to concern. It looked like a little boy standing outside. He was short and skinny. His face pressed to the glass like he was looking in, but a vague outline of bushy hair gave away his identity.

Eli.

"What are you doing?" Bubba whispered hoarsely into the air, as much to himself as to his little brother who would not be able to hear him across the hall and on the other side of the front door.

Bubba waited for Eli to move, but when Eli persisted to stand there looking in, like an idiot, he wondered if his brother had actually locked himself out.

What was Eli thinking, going out of the house in the middle of the night? He knew there were *kidnappers* out there—criminals that would offer you food, steal you away, and make you live with a family you didn't like. Bubba had to rescue him!

He shivered and ran for the door. He could see his breath panting in the cold house as he silently scurried closer to the image of Eli in the window.

Bubba halted suddenly, blinking at something that wasn't right. Eli's straight white teeth grinned in the dark like he was throwing a birthday surprise, and the joke was on the middle child in baby jammies who'd embarrassed himself in front of the neighbors. Bubba ducked to the wall to make himself invisible. His hand reached for the porch light switches, so he could get a better look at the face Eli was making, but he found only blank wall.

The switches were missing.

Bubba froze, confused. Eli in the window didn't seem to move. Or see him. Or breathe.

Creeping closer to the glass, Bubba observed the truth about his brother's frozen form and saw a ripple in the paper of his clothes and skin. Eli was flat; the edges of him, jagged. His eyes were large black beads drawn without pupils or eyelids.

Bubba startled backward and slipped in the fleece footies, screaming now for the stairs, lunging three steps at a time to reach the safety of Mom and Dad's bedroom. Forget the rules and the clapping; he needed to be safe!—

to wake up from this nightmare!

Flinging wide the door, Bubba jumped between the blanket mounds where his parents slept and buried his face in the bed pillow. Only then did he realize the bed was unmade. The sheets cold.

Light flooded the room. Bubba looked up.

Pasted against the headboard above him were horrifying cartoon cutouts of Mom and Dad, their expressions painted on their faces, looks of care and concern meant to say everything would be all right. Bubba screamed at the empty eyes and clawed himself out of the entangling sheets, off the edge of the bed, and into a trembling lump on the floor.

A voice spoke from across the room. "I've never seen them make drawings. He probably thought you'd like it… at least I think it's a 'he'."

Bubba hid between the bed and the wall and gave one wide-eyed glance at the intruder in the bright room who had spoken. A guy in a sea green uniform stood beside the open bedroom door, blocking Bubba's only escape. Bubba ducked low, scrunching into the crawl space beneath the bed, and listened to the guy's strangely familiar voice.

"They keep the air clean. No germs or infection. The pantry's stocked, so help yourself." The ends of the guy's sentences dropped to a mumble, which Bubba could barely hear. "Plenty of books…paper…but he'll like it more if you jump around and stuff. Give him a show. Or—I hate to say it—try to escape."

Bubba watched the guy's blurry shoes beneath the crack of the bed. The feet shuffled, but never came any nearer. Only the blowing AC made any sound, and Bubba noticed, despite sprinting up the stairs and panting incredibly fast, he could take long, deep breaths.

His breath eventually slowed just enough for him to speak. "W—where's my f—family?"

"They haven't been *them* for a long time, just like the

rest. Maybe you're too young to see it. That's what the owners do: play tricks with the hippocampus—I don't know, *hypnotize* it. Eventually, everyone forgets you ever existed. That's rough, I know, but The Pet Exchange couldn't work any other way. If it makes you feel any better, you're the *special* one. He picked you—he likes you! That's a big deal. He wouldn't want you to think you didn't have any friends."

"H—he?"

The guy got quiet. When he spoke next, it wasn't to answer Bubba's question.

"I only came to give you these." He placed something angular on the floor at his own feet. Bubba squinted and figured it was his glasses. "Whether you wear them is up to you. You might not want to. Some don't last the night when they find out what happens when a seahorse dies. Hell, being blind might make tank duty a breeze."

As soon as the guy said that, he walked out. Then the room's bright lights vanished, plunging Bubba into blackness.

It took Bubba several minutes to work up the courage to peek his head beyond the edge of the bed. Shimmering waves danced on the walls again. He crawled across the floor to the glasses and put them on. Every detail sharpened, but the photos on the walls were still just blobs. The walls and furniture, only a crude imitation of his house—not the real thing. Bubba cast his gaze upward, past the AC filter, to the lofted ceilings. There was no roof, only glass, and he could find no words to name what floated there. Only bub-wee. It filled the oceanic sky like a gnarled thundercloud: a navy blue seahorse head, staring right at him.

THE WELLSPRING

Michael Hustead

Legend tells of the Wellspring, a river that cascades into a pool, the waters of which erase a person's memory if they drink from it. Grieving people have been searching for it for centuries; Dorian found it in five years.

Rain fell in a steady drizzle as he rode his horse down from the Skullridge Mountains and stopped on a ridge overlooking a valley. Dorian shivered. It had rained for three days straight, and there'd been no shelter in the mountains. His tattered cloak was waterlogged, and his clothes were plastered to his skin. Water dripped from his hood in a constant stream.

Is that a light?

Dorian mopped his face and squinted, struggling to pierce the veil of rain and mist. There it was again. A flicker of light not far down the valley. A fire, perhaps.

Who would build a fire out here in this god-forsaken place?

Dorian snorted at his own naivete. As if there were any place that *wasn't* god-forsaken. He sat for several minutes brooding as he stared with unseeing eyes.

We sacrificed so much, and for what?

His horse stamped and shivered in the cold, bringing Dorian back to himself.

"Right," he patted the horse's neck. "I'm tired too, Torgen. Let's find somewhere dry to spend the night."

He turned his horse and rode down from the ridge, picking his way carefully in the dim light. When he reached the treeline, Dorian stopped and dismounted. He pushed his sodden hood back from his head, revealing a face deeply lined by care and pain and browned by long exposure to the sun. His blond hair mixed with gray and made him look older than he was. Dorian stretched his tired muscles and breathed deeply, listening to the rain patter on the leaves above.

"What do you think, Torgen? Should we camp here and continue on in the morning?"

The horse shivered slightly and pressed close against

Dorian's side. Dorian scratched absently behind Torgen's ear and considered his options. The logical thing would be to find a dry patch here under the trees. He might even be able to get a fire going if the wood was dry enough.

Dorian yawned and stretched, groaning as his left shoulder popped. A brief spasm of pain flickered across his shoulder into his chest. He closed his eyes and breathed through the pain; the cold always aggravated his wound.

"Time heals all," he muttered. "Biggest lie ever told."

Dorian's mind drifted to the brief flicker of light he'd seen in the valley. Where'd the fire come from? It couldn't be a campfire, not in the open in this weather. Could there be a homestead all the way out here?

An image arose in his mind of a warm cabin inhabited by a family of young pioneers. They'd be hardy people to make a home out here, but brave and kind to travelers. Perhaps, they'd invite him in and give him food. For the space of an evening he would be warm and dry. Maybe he could even make a home for himself with them. No doubt a homestead could use another set of strong arms to do the work. He'd have a second chance at life.

A ghost of a smile flit across his face. A passerby might have wondered to see the lines smooth away and reveal the face of a much younger man. But there were no passersby. He was alone, and second chances were for children's stories.

Dorian's shoulder spasmed again, and he grimaced as he opened his eyes. The moment had passed; he was once more a weary traveler marred by grief and war.

Torgen nuzzled at his hand, and Dorian returned to stroking the horse.

"Come on," Dorian said. "Let's keep going. I want to see if we can find that fire I saw."

Torgen snorted and nipped at his hand. Dorian snatched his fingers away with an oath and cuffed the horse across the nose.

"Don't give me that. I'm tired too, it's just..." Dorian sighed. Why was he so insistent on venturing back out into the rain?

He supposed he was just lonely. They hadn't encountered another human being in weeks, it would be good to speak to someone. Besides, it would be wise to get news about the country; he might learn something useful. Dorian took a firm grip on Torgen's reins, careful to keep his fingers away from the horse's mouth. "We're going on."

Dorian didn't try to ride. The trees were too low here, and he had no wish to pick his teeth on a low hanging branch. Better to walk. Besides, he had a hunch Torgen might throw him off out of sheer pique if he tried to mount. He took a moment to adjust the packs on Torgen's back. The rain had soaked into the bundles, and they hung in a lopsided knot from the horse's side. Dorian worked slowly, his half frozen fingers struggling with the straps. It was time he didn't want to lose, but it gave them both a chance to have a breather before going on.

When the packs were securely strapped down, he took hold of Torgen's reins again and led the way down through the trees to the valley floor. As the ground leveled out, the forest gave way to plowed fields.

Dorian knelt down and examined the ground. This was cultivated land. He thought of the flicker of light he'd seen from the ridge. Not fellow travelers, then. Did someone actually live here?

The fog had lifted. There was no moon and the night was dark, yet Dorian thought he saw a flicker of light again off to his right. If this field was any indication, there might well be a farmhouse ahead.

Encouraged, Dorian pressed on. There was no road, and the plowed ground was muddy and uneven. Dorian stumbled repeatedly in the darkness, but he gritted his teeth and continued, ignoring Torgen's rumbling snorts of irritation.

After an interminable period, and one nasty turned ankle, Dorian emerged, limping from the field. A small cabin stood before him, firelight shining through gaps in the shuttered windows. He heard laughter inside and then the sound of a fiddle playing.

Dorian's mouth fell open as he listened, spellbound. When had he last heard music?

He hurried to the door and raised his hand to knock. He hesitated.

How would these people react to a stranger pounding on their door after dark? This was no village or walled city. Dorian looked down at himself. His clothes clung to him like a second skin. He was plastered with mud, twigs, and leaves. Hardly a respectable image.

He lowered his hand. What could he possibly say to these people, anyway? What was the point of talking to them at all? He'd finished with humanity the day he set out to find the Wellspring.

Dorian sighed and turned away from the door. He spotted a small barn not far from the cabin. It would be dry there at least, and he could get a few hours of sleep. Maybe in the morning the rain would let it up.

"Come on," he muttered to Torgen. "Let's go."

He trudged away from the cabin, the music drifting after him, its soft notes hanging tauntingly on the wind.

The barn was small and cramped. Two pigs and a sturdy plow horse were already sheltering within it, but it was dry and shielded from the wind, and the floor was strewn liberally with straw that was also still mostly dry. Dorian tied his horse loosely to one of the beams where it could reach straw and water. His blanket and cloak were both soaked, so he hung them from a rafter to drip dry and rolled himself in the straw for warmth.

Sleep was a long time coming, and when he finally slept, he dreamed.

He stood in a council chamber, crystal goblet raised in salute to the fiery young king standing at the head of the table.

"Think of it, friends," the king said. "When we have taken the worship of the true God to the whole world, then there will be peace. A new kingdom. A kingdom of light, laughter, and love where there will never again be sorrow, or hunger, or death. An eternal kingdom."

Dorian's heart soared at the king's words. There was so much suffering in the world. To think that they could end it all. He'd give anything to be a part of that grand adventure.

The dream changed, and Dorian saw himself riding into battle beside his king, carrying the worship of the true God to the heathen nations. Kingdom after kingdom fell before them. Dorian himself led the raids on the temples, smashing idols with his hammer and shattering the power of the pagan gods. With each victory, their power grew and their enemies were driven before them like cattle.

In his dream, Dorian soared like a bird above the conquered lands, surveying the fire and famine that followed in his king's wake. He heard the wailing of widows, and his heart cringed. But it was necessary. Before paradise could come, the evil in the world must be rooted out. There could be no mercy for those who opposed peace.

Besides, this was not his doing. If there was war, it was the fault of the pagan nations who clung to their idols and held their people in bondage to false gods.

Finally, he stood on the battlements of the ancient city of Tal'Radesh, staring up at the turret where the flag of his king fluttered triumphantly in the breeze.

"Did we do it?" he asked, turning to look at the king.

"It is finished," the king said, clapping him on the shoulder. "Welcome to paradise, my friend."

The dream changed again. Civil war ravaged the countryside. Crops burned. Cities collapsed in ruin. Dorian knelt in the midst of a battlefield—carnage raged around him as armies strove against each other, but he noticed none of it. Dorian held the shattered body of his king in his arms. Blood and dirt caked his

lord's beautiful face, the broken shaft of a spear twitching with
every labored breath.

Then the king went still, the spark fading from his eyes, and
Dorian wept as his dreams faded into oblivion.

Something prodded him in the side, and Dorian woke with a scream, thrashing his way clear of the hay as he reached for a sword that wasn't there.

"Hold on, stranger. Don't move or I'll split your head."

Dorian froze, his chest heaving. A lantern sat on the ground, casting a small circle of yellow light in the stable. An elderly man stood next to the lantern, hefting an ax in his hands. A younger man, barely out of boyhood, stood at the old man's side and held a pitchfork leveled at Dorian's chest.

"What are you doing here?" the old man asked.

Dorian blinked, still half in his dream. The younger man prodded him with the pitchfork. "We're talking to you," he spat.

Dorian winced and shifted away from the pitchfork. "I'm just passing through. I didn't mean any harm."

The man grunted and exchanged a look with the younger man who scowled. "Not too many people pass through here."

"I'm searching for something," Dorian replied.

"Searching?" the old man asked. "Or running away?"

"Sometimes there's not much difference between the two."

The old man sighed. "True enough." He squinted down at Dorian a moment longer, then stepped back and lowered his ax. "Are you hurt?"

"Heard you cry out," the man said, seeing Dorian's confusion. "That's how I knew you were here."

Dorian frowned. "Bad dreams." He kept his eyes on the younger man who continued to shift nervously across from him, the pitchfork still aimed at Dorian's chest. Dorian waited. His muscles tensed. He didn't have many options. There was no way he could get to his feet before the man could thrust with the pitchfork.

"Come on," the old man said. "You might as well come inside and get warm." He picked up the lantern and walked out of the stable without a backward glance. The younger man remained where he was a moment longer, glaring down at Dorian; then he followed the old man out of the barn, though he never turned his back on Dorian or loosened his grip on the pitchfork.

Dorian hesitated a moment, and then climbed to his feet, grunting as his stiff muscles protested the sudden movement. He brushed hay from his clothes and followed the receding light of the lantern. The rain had stopped, and a cold mist hung in the air. Dorian shivered and followed closely after the men, who led him toward the cabin. An elderly woman stood in the open doorway, a frown creasing her face.

"Who is it?" she asked.

The old man shrugged. "Traveler sleeping in the barn. Seems he was having a nightmare."

The woman eyed him uncertainly. Dorian winced, conscious again of his muddy and bedraggled appearance. He doubted his nap in the straw had improved his look.

"Bring him inside," she said, disappearing into the cabin.

They followed her, and Dorian sighed as the heat from a fire washed over him. He stopped just inside the doorway and closed his eyes, breathing deeply.

"Don't just stand there," the old man said. "It's cold enough as it is, best close the door."

Dorian shut the door behind him and stepped toward the fireplace, his hands outstretched to the heat. Behind him, the young man picked up a heavy wooden beam and placed it into latches so that it settled across the door. Dorian watched, noticing that the door was unusually thick and the cross bar even more so. The old man saw him examining the door and grimaced.

"Dangerous times," was all he said.

"Bandits?" Dorian asked.

"No," the man said, shaking his head. "Not this far out. But the satyrs have multiplied in the wild since the empire fell. Their raiding parties pass through the valley sometimes."

Dorian had encountered satyrs before. They were vicious and deadly, taller than any man and filled with a wild, brute strength, but they were no match for mounted knights and had been driven nearly to extinction in the days of the king. He wasn't surprised to learn that the beasts were flourishing again at the edges of the wild.

"Why don't you leave?"

"And go where?"

"Somewhere where there aren't monsters, somewhere with civilization."

The old man barked a wry laugh. "We moved out here to escape the warlords and the bandits. Nothing but murder and rape left back in *civilization*. The satyrs may be monsters, but at least they don't pretend to be anything different."

Dorian opened his mouth to protest, but there was nothing to say. The king was dead. The empire was in ruins. The eternal kingdom was nothing but vanity and chasing after the wind. The man was right. At least the monsters were honest.

The old woman stood up from where she knelt beside the fire. "Enough of this talk. Come. Eat." She set a bowl on a table by the fire.

Dorian stared at the food. His stomach ached with hunger. It was a small kindness, but it seemed an eternity since he'd had even that. Tears welled up in his eyes. He blinked them away.

"Here," the old man said, watching him. "It's not that big a deal. Just a bite of food."

Dorian nodded and sat down. He ate in silence while the old couple looked on from chairs by the fire. The younger man leaned against the wall by the door, his pitchfork still held loosely in his hand. Dorian could feel the man's eyes on his back, but he ignored him. The food was hot, and it warmed him from the inside out.

"I'm San," the man said. "This is Nel, and the young man there is my grandson Alb."

"Dorian," he replied around a mouthful of stew.

"What brings you here?" San asked.

"I'm looking for a river."

Alb sneered. "They don't have rivers where you came from?"

Dorian ignored the comment and addressed San instead. "This is a special river. It's supposed to make anyone who drinks from it forget the past."

San leaned forward, staring hard at him. "The Well?"

"The Wellspring? You've heard of it?"

San and Nel exchanged a long look, neither of them answering. Dorian clenched his hands; his nails bit into the wood of the table.

"Please," he said. "I have to know."

"We shouldn't tell him anything," Alb said, stepping forward. "We don't know anything about this man."

"Alb," San said, shooting the young man a warning glance. Alb muttered to himself and strode out of the room.

"Forgive him," Nel said, a sad smile flitting across her face. "He lost his parents in the war when he was a child. We brought him out here with us, but it's been hard on the boy."

"The war was hard on many people," Dorian said. He stared down at his hands. In the flickering firelight, he could almost see them still stained with blood. "I don't hold it against him."

With effort, he tore his gaze away from his hands and looked at the couple. They were watching him as if they guessed some of his thoughts. Nel's eyes were kind, though she said nothing.

"What can you tell me about the Wellspring?" he asked. "Have you heard rumors of it?"

"More than rumors," San said. "I've seen it."

"You've seen it," Dorian repeated, his voice catching. He leaned forward, nearly coming out of his chair in his eagerness. "Where is it? How'd you find it?"

San shrugged. "Stumbled across it, really. Not too long after we came here. I was exploring down at the far end of the valley with the boy. Must be a couple of years ago now. The Well—what you call the Wellspring and others call the Fountain of Forgetfulness—runs out of a fissure in the cliff wall there and pools beneath. A small waterfall really, but it makes no sound. In fact, sound of any sort seems to vanish in that clearing."

"How do you know it's the Wellspring?" Dorian asked. "Did you drink from it?"

San huffed. "Do I seem like someone who's had his memories erased? No, I didn't drink, but I could tell. The air is strange there. Even the scent of the water makes you start to forget. Alb and I lost half a day standing there day-dreaming." He stopped and shook his head. "We almost didn't make it out of there. Couldn't remember who we were or what we were doing. The Well's a dangerous place even if you don't drink, son."

Dorian stared into the fire without speaking. He'd been searching for five years, and the Wellspring was only a few miles away. His hands shook, and he squeezed them together in his lap.

"Why are you looking for the Wellspring?" Nel asked.

Dorian's eyes flicked to the woman, then back to the fire, unable to bear the intensity of her gaze. "I want to forget."

"Obviously," San snorted. "You're still young yet. What could you have to forget that's worth seeking that Spring?"

Dorian didn't answer immediately. What did he have to forget? A decade of war, destruction, and death. The blood of his king staining his hands. A life wasted. A dream denied. A new creation, no different than the old.

"A lie," he said, simply.

"Must have been a whopper," San said.

A bitter laugh welled up inside him, and Dorian threw back his head and cackled at the ceiling. Across from him, San and Nel exchanged alarmed looks but said nothing.

"You have no idea," Dorian said, wiping tears from his eyes.

Nel reached across the table and took Dorian's hand. She met Dorian's eyes, holding his gaze.

"Son, I don't know what's happened in your life," Nel said. "But trust me. Don't go to the Well."

"She's right," San said. "That river doesn't have any answers for you."

"I don't need answers," Dorian replied, taking his hand away. "I gave up on answers a long time ago. I just want to forget."

"Do you want to forget everything?" San challenged. "You don't get to pick and choose, you know. The Spring will take it all, the good and the bad. You'll have nothing left."

Dorian was silent for a long moment, then he shook his head. "I already have nothing left. Maybe the Wellspring can give me a new beginning."

"Well, you know your own mind," San replied. He rose from the table and helped Nel to her feet. "You can sleep in here by the fire. I expect it's more comfortable than my barn."

The old couple went into the next room, closing the door behind them, leaving Dorian alone. He sat by the fire far into the night, staring into the flames, remembering dreams of glory and a new world that never came.

He left shortly after sunrise. The rain had stopped and

San and Nel stood in the doorway of the cabin to see him off.

"Don't go," San said, watching Dorian saddle his horse.

"I have to." Dorian gripped the saddlehorn and hauled himself slowly up into the saddle, wincing as he settled into place.

San shook his head. "You don't have to. Stay here with us. We could use the help, and you look like a man who could use a quiet life."

Dorian met his gaze and hesitated. Was the old man really offering this to him? Could there be a life for him here? He looked around, trying to imagine what it might be like to stay and be a part of this family. His gaze fell on Alb who leaned against the side of the house with his arms folded, glaring at him. The young man hadn't spoken all morning, but he was clearly furious at the suggestion that Dorian stay.

Dorian shook his head. Who was he fooling? There was no life for him here. All he had to offer these people was a legacy of violence.

"Thank you," he said, and at that moment he'd never meant any words more in his life. "But I can't stay here."

"Life is what you make of it, son," San said. "You can always start fresh."

"A nice sentiment," Dorian replied. "But there's only one way for me to start fresh."

"In that case, take Alb with you," San said. Alb shouted a wordless protest, but San cut him off with a glare. "He can show you the fastest way."

Dorian raised an eyebrow and looked at the red-faced young man. "I don't think he'd care for that."

"He's a good lad," San said. "He doesn't trust strangers much, and these days who can blame him. But he can help if you let him."

Alb glared at his grandfather for a moment and then shrugged his shoulders. "Anything to get you on your way."

Dorian eyed the young man. He doubted Alb would prove good company, but if he knew where the Wellspring was it might be worth it. "Fine," he said, with a short nod.

He waited a few minutes while Alb fetched the old plow horse from the barn. The young man worked efficiently to saddle and ready the horse, then slid smoothly into the saddle.

Dorian nodded at the old couple, turned his horse and rode out at a trot, heading south, with Alb following behind. When he looked back, he could still see San and Nel standing outside their cabin watching them. He hesitated for a moment, then shook his head and kicked his horse into a gallop, eager to put some distance between himself and the settlers.

They rode hard through the morning, only stopping for short breaks to stretch their legs and rest the horses. Torgren was refreshed from the night in the barn and didn't need much rest, but the plow horse wasn't used to being ridden. Toward midday, they entered a stretch of dense forest. The trees pressed in close around them, and they were forced to dismount and make their way on foot.

Dorian heard voices up ahead and stopped, motioning for Alb to be quiet. The young man slipped up beside him, his face tight with anxiety.

"Are there any other settlers at this end of the valley?" Dorian whispered.

Alb shook his head. Dorian handed his horse's reins to Alb. "Stay here."

Alb opened his mouth, shut it again, and gave a short nod. Dorian crept forward through the trees, planting each foot carefully to avoid making a sound. Just ahead, the forest thinned and a small clearing appeared through the trees. He crouched behind a tangled web of briars and peered through the branches.

Tall burly figures covered in coarse, rust-colored fur

stalked through the clearing. Broad, ebony horns ending in razor sharp points curled from their heads. Dorian sucked in his breath through clenched teeth.

Satyrs.

Dorian swore under his breath. He crept backwards, scarcely daring to breathe. If the satyrs discovered him, he was a dead man.

One of the satyrs stepped into view between two trees. The monster tugged on a rope, and a line of people stumbled into the clearing after him.

Dorian froze.

They were human. He saw men, women, and children of all ages tied together by ropes around their necks and hands. Dorian shook his head. Were these prisoners slaves of the satyrs or something worse? He'd heard rumors that the satyrs ate human flesh, but they'd never been confirmed.

He watched as the satyrs kicked and shoved their prisoners into line. *There must be at least a dozen of the beasts,* he thought. *How did the satyrs become so bold?*

Dorian shoved the thought away. It didn't matter now. What mattered was getting away. He crept away from the clearing and hurried back to where Alb waited with the horses.

"Come on," he whispered, taking Torgen's reins. "We have to get out of here." Speaking under his breath, he told Alb what he'd seen in the clearing.

"We have to go back," Alb said as they led their horses out of the woods.

"Why?" Dorian asked, swinging into his saddle.

"To warn my grandparents."

"They already know the satyrs are in the valley," Dorian replied. "There's no point in going back."

"But what if the satyrs attack the cabin?"

Dorian closed his eyes. "Your grandparents are no fools. They can take care of themselves." He opened his eyes again but couldn't quite make himself meet Alb's gaze. "I'm going on. If you want to go back, you can."

"Fine," Alb spat. "Go chase your precious Wellspring." He pointed south. "It's that way. On the far side of this stretch of woods, there's a canyon. Follow it all the way down."

Dorian watched until the young man dwindled into the distance, then turned his horse and rode on.

He made his way slowly along the edge of the forest, searching for a way around the satyrs' camp. Dorian rode in silence, lost in his thoughts. His mind returned endlessly to the sight of the prisoners hobbled together like cattle, and the thought of what would happen if the satyrs raided San's farm.

"Not my fight," Dorian said aloud. He dug his heels into his horse's flanks, urging it on. The sooner he found the Wellspring, the better. He rode without incident, and shortly before midday, he found it.

The land had been falling steadily, the ground becoming muddy and wet as the day wore on, and Dorian rode slowly, wary of stumbling into a sinkhole. Before him, a narrow canyon opened up.

The ground here was rocky and uneven. Dorian was forced to dismount and lead Torgen on foot. Soon he'd drink from the Wellspring, and it would all go away. The wars, the needless slaughter, the lies.

A vague sense of unease settled on him and he frowned. This was what he wanted, wasn't it? Why should he hesitate?

It didn't make sense. There was nothing in his life he wanted to remember. In his mind, he heard the sounds of battle. The clash of weapons, the screams of men and horses, the groan of crumbling stone and burning wood. The cries of children.

Dorian shivered, shaking off the memories. No. He couldn't go on like this. He quickened his pace, stumbling over the uneven ground, but he no longer cared.

Something San had said troubled him, however. Was this his whole life?

He frowned. There'd been good times too, before the war. Friends he'd made as a squire training to be a knight. The day his king called him to serve and knighted him. His family. His wife.

Dorian closed his eyes.

Could he forget her?

He stopped, realizing he'd reached the end of the canyon. A wall of tumbled rock rose before him, creating a slide. Water gushed from between the rocks, bubbling down the cliff into a pool, which spread from wall to wall and blocked the end of the canyon. The water shone clear as glass, and Dorian saw all the way to the bottom. The pool was quite deep.

Despite the waterfall, Dorian noticed the air was heavy and still.

He walked to the edge of the Wellspring with slow, hesitant steps. This was his moment. Dorian inhaled deeply and stopped, blinking slowly.

Why was he here?

Behind him, his horse nickered and he jumped. He'd half forgotten he had a horse. Dorian backed away from the water, struggling to collect his thoughts. He was a knight. He'd come here to erase the memory of his failures. To get a new start, a true new start free of the horrors of his past.

He turned back toward the water, but hesitated again.

Was this truly what he wanted? He frowned. Of course it was, and yet...

He hated what his life had become, but could he part with all of it? Was it worth sacrificing the joy to erase the pain? He took a deep breath, inhaling the scent of the water. Forgetfulness rolled over him, washing away the pain and the doubt.

Dorian had no idea how long he stood like that on the edge of the Wellspring. It was the stench of smoke filling his nostrils that brought him back to himself. Thick plumes of black smoke darkened the horizon to the north.

The north. Dorian blinked, struggling to collect his thoughts. Why should that trouble him?

Then he remembered. San's farm!

Dorian swore loudly as he turned and ran from the Wellspring's banks. He snatched up Torgen's reigns and hurried back through the canyon as quickly as he could. He stopped for a moment and looked back where the tantilizing waters glistened in the afternoon sun.

"I can always come back," he said, shaking his head. Then he turned his back and walked away. As soon as they reached level ground, he climbed into the saddle and urged Torgen into a swift, mile-eating trot.

He rode hard, pushing Torgen as fast as he could, but night had fallen and the moon began to peak over the tops of the mountains before he reached the homestead. He prayed to any gods that might be left that the family would be safe. The smoke could have come from something else after all, but as he drew closer to the homestead, he caught the scent of fire and ash and knew what he would find.

With a shout, he drove his heels into his horse's sides and galloped forward. The smoke thickened as he rode. Soon he was coughing and choking. His eyes stung from the smoke, and he paused to wrap his cloak around his face. A moment later, the cabin appeared before him. Dorian pulled back on the reins; his horse reared to a stop so suddenly it almost sat down.

The cabin and barn were destroyed. Flames flickered fitfully in the ruins though the fire had nearly burned out. Dorian swore and slid down from his horse. He rushed forward, but the heat from the wreckage drove him back.

Dorian coughed and choked on the smoke, tears blinded his eyes. He staggered back and stared wildly around for any sign of life.

Nothing.

He called out, but there was no response. Perhaps the family had fled before the attack. Perhaps they were hiding in the woods. But what about Alb? Had he made it back in time? There was no sign of the plow horse.

Dorian ran around to the back but saw nothing. He called out again; a mocking silence answered. Dorian fell to his knees and stared at the burning cabin.

His eyes trailed over the ground, torn and ravaged by hoofs. Dorian froze. He leaned over and placed his hand next to the hoofprints. They were massive. Each one nearly twice the size of his hand.

"Satyrs," he cursed.

A lump settled in his chest. The raiders he'd seen that morning down the valley. It must have been them.

"This is my fault," he whispered. He should have turned back with Alb. He'd been so focused on finding the Wellspring that he hadn't listened. Another failure in an endless stream failures throughout his miserable life.

He stood up slowly, brushing dirt and ash from his hands. "Enough is enough. I'm going back to the Wellspring. It's time to end this."

Dorian strode back to his horse and moved to remount, but another thought hit him like a lightning bolt. The satyrs were taking prisoners. He'd seen them roped together that morning. The family could still be alive. The thought rallied him briefly, but despair swiftly quenched any hope.

So what if they were alive? He'd counted nearly a dozen satyrs that morning. He couldn't possibly kill them all.

Dorian pulled himself into the saddle and rode slowly away from the ruins. There was nothing he could do for San and his family. Nothing he could do for the other prisoners either. If he followed, he'd only be killed too.

He stopped.

Why did that matter so much? His life was over, what

difference did it make if he died?

But Dorian didn't want to die. Life had been sweet once, and somewhere deep inside he clung to the promise that the Wellspring would provide the solution. If he could wipe away his regrets maybe he could build something again. A life worth living this time.

He stared over his shoulder as the roof of the cabin caved in and collapsed in a shower of sparks. Could he live a new life knowing he'd left all those people to the satyrs? Dorian shuddered. That was the point of the Wellspring, wasn't it? To make him forget his failures? What was one more in the grand scheme of things? He wouldn't even remember it.

Dorian thought of Nel's sad eyes watching him with compassion, of her hand reaching out to him in comfort, of San welcoming a stranger into his home and offering him a place to stay.

Dorian stared down at his hands.

He'd taken countless lives trying to build paradise. What if now he had the opportunity to save some?

Dorian's jaw tightened. He couldn't turn his back on those people, not even for the chance at a fresh start.

"It's time you did something right," he said to himself.

He slid down from his horse and cut loose the straps binding his packs to Torgen's back. They fell to the ground with a clang that rang in the night air. Dorian cut open the ropes that bound the packs shut and unrolled them to reveal his old armor. It was dented in places, and rusty, but still serviceable. Dorian moved with purpose, his fingers remembering the steps as he strapped on each piece. It was difficult without the help of his squire, but he made do. At last, he unwrapped a massive war hammer, its edges inscribed with silver runes that gleamed in the moonlight.

As his hand closed around the war hammer, the runes blazed with silver fire that lit up the night around him.

Dorian blinked and shut his eyes against the blinding light. Power jolted through him and he gasped. New strength coursed through his veins that rolled back his aches and pains. Even the ever-present throbbing in his shoulder seemed to fade away.

After a moment, the runes dimmed to a silvery sheen, and Dorian slid the hammer into a harness attached to Torgen's saddle and climbed heavily onto his horse's back. He'd forgotten how hard it was to move in armor.

"Come on," Dorian yelled and urged Torgen into a gallop. Even in the darkness, the satyrs' trail was clear. Their hoofs had churned up the ground in a wide swath leading east. Dorian followed the trail at full speed, eager to catch the marauders. As the night wore on, the trail led into the woods, and Dorian was forced to slow down. If he rode into a tree or broke his horse's ankle he'd rescue no one.

He rode cautiously, sensing he was close to his quarry. Before long, Dorian caught a glimpse of firelight through the trees. He halted and dismounted, leaving Torgen tied to a nearby tree.

Dorian crept forward as carefully as he could. He moved deliberately to avoid making a sound. Not an easy prospect for a man dressed in full armor, but his training returned to him as though it were yesterday. The camp came into view between the trees, and he stopped to survey the scene.

The satyrs were fast asleep around the fire. They hadn't even set a guard. Dorian grunted. Why should they? They were in the middle of nowhere. Even if someone stumbled onto their camp, only a fool would attack.

He grinned.

If there was one thing Dorian had decided about himself, it was that he was the biggest fool in history.

He crept closer, searching for the prisoners, and spotted them at the edge of the camp. They were still tied together, and the rope itself was tethered tightly between two trees. He could cut it easily enough, but then what? There was little chance he could lead all the prisoners away without waking the satyrs. And even if he did, the beasts would pursue as soon as they awoke. Satyrs could run nearly as fast as a mounted man. They would catch them long before they could reach any kind of safety.

No. If Dorian was going to rescue the prisoners, he'd have to kill the satyrs or drive them off.

"Right," he muttered to himself. "A frontal assault. At least it has the advantage of simplicity."

He crept back to his horse and mounted. He wished he had a lance, but there was neither time nor means to make one.

Dorian chewed on his lip, suddenly aware of how alone he was.

He set his jaw, reached down, and drew his war hammer. The power surged through him again, and he breathed deeply, absorbing the strength and courage it gave him. He'd wielded this weapon in many battles, but never for a cause as good as this. If his tattered life could be exchanged for the lives of those prisoners, it was a price he'd gladly pay.

Dorian set out at a slow walk, careful to make as little noise as possible. The satyrs clearly weren't expecting an attack, and he wanted to get as close as he could before they heard him. When the camp came into sight, he kicked his horse into a gallop and charged, bellowing at the top of his lungs.

The reaction was instant. Satyrs leapt to their feet, baying at each other in alarm. Dorian rode down the first beast he came to, trampling the monster under his horse's hoofs. He swung his war hammer to either side, slaying two of the satyrs on his first pass through the camp. Dorian reined his horse in as he reached the far side of the camp and turned for another pass.

An axe clanged off his hastily raised shield and sent

shivers down his arm. Dorian struck out, smashing the axe aside and crushing the monster's head with the backswing. The satyrs pressed in close trying to pull him down, but Dorian spurred his horse on, Torgen kicking and biting as he charged. Dorian killed three more of the satyrs before they broke and fled to the far side of the clearing to regroup.

Dorian took advantage of the breather and rode over to the tree where the prisoners were tied. He pulled out a short dagger and sawed through the rope that bound them together.

"Run," he bellowed before turning to charge again. But the satyrs were already on top of him. A spear plunged into Torgen's chest. The horse reared, pawing at the air, and then toppled to the side.

Dorian fell with a thunderous crash. The blow knocked the wind from his chest, and he lay gasping on the ground. Before he could rise, the satyrs swarmed.

A hoof stomped on his wrist, and he cried out in pain. The satyrs stomped again and again, and the war hammer skittered out of his gauntleted hand. The warhamer's power vanished, and Dorian gasped, nearly blacking out from the sudden weakness. He grabbed for his weapon, but the satyrs kicked it away.

The monsters crowded around him, raining blows down upon him. Dorian's armor turned most of the strikes, but with every impact, he felt the metal buckling. A satyr's axe bit deep into his side and he cried out. He tried to roll, but one of the monsters kicked him in the head, its hoof denting Dorian's helmet.

Lights exploded across his vision and he lay stunned.

A volley of loud cries carried to his ears, and out of the slit of his visor he saw the freed prisoners charge into the fray wielding weapons they'd snatched up from the fallen satyrs. San himself held the broken haft of a spear, stabbing and jabbing into the monsters' backs.

The attack gave Dorian a brief reprieve, and he fumbled for his war hammer. As his fist closed over the shaft, power surged through him once more. The pain of his wounds faded, and Dorian bounded to his feet. He swung the war hammer over his head and sprang into the satyrs' midst with a roar. The runes flashed in the moonlight, and silver fire flooded the woods.

This new attack proved too much. The satyrs broke and scattered, fleeing into the trees. Dorian rested his hammer on the ground and leaned on the shaft for support as he gasped for air.

San and Alb ran over and helped pry the dented helmet off his head. Dorian blinked when the straps gave way and the helmet slid free. He opened his mouth and sucked in deep lungfuls of fresh air. His side burned and he pressed at it, almost surprised to see his fingers come away stained with blood.

"Here," Nel said, rushing to his side. "Let us help you."

They fumbled with the buckles of his armor in the dark. Dorian tried to help but pain and exhaustion beat upon him in waves. It was all he could do to stand. When the last piece of armor was lifted off, exhaustion overcame him, and Dorian sank to the ground, propping his back up against a tree.

"This isn't too bad," San said, inspecting his wound. "The armor stopped most of it. Alb, get the fire going and let's heat some water."

Nel and San tended to Dorian's wounds, binding and dressing them as best they could with stores taken from the satyrs' camp. Before long, Dorian sat resting by the fire.

"How did you find us?" Nel asked, sitting down beside him. She handed a waterskin to him, and he drank deeply. She took a bucket and a scrap of cloth from Alb and began washing the sweat and grime of battle from Dorian's brow.

"I came back to the cabin and saw what had happened,"

Dorian replied. "I followed."

San looked up from where he and Alb were sorting through the supplies. "What about the Well?"

"I don't know," Dorian said. "I found it, but...I couldn't bring myself to drink. Maybe the past isn't something you can just erase."

"What will you do now?" Nel asked.

Dorian shook his head. "I don't know. I've been searching for those waters for years. My life hasn't had a purpose in a long time."

Nel rose in silence and slipped away toward where the others were sorting through the camp. San watched her for a moment and then gestured.

"It looks to me like there are a lot of people here who would disagree. If you'd drunk from that Well, what would have happened to us?"

"You don't know my story," Dorian replied.

"So tell me."

Dorian sighed, but then he began to talk. He told San everything. Nel came up while he spoke with a little girl at her side. The two stood quietly, listening as Dorian told the story of his life.

"We were supposed to save the world," he said, when he'd finished. "To be honest, I don't think it's going very well."

"You can't save the world by forcing everyone to believe what you believe," Nel said.

Dorian laughed grimly. "So it would seem. But what am I supposed to do?"

"It seems to me you've made a decent start," San said, gesturing at the camp.

"Stopping those satyrs didn't save the world."

"No," San replied. "But you freed a group people from torture, slavery, and death. That matters."

"So what now?"

Nel stepped forward, holding the little girl's hand.

"The satyrs stole this girl from her village." She reached out and placed the girl's hand in Dorian's. "Why don't you take her home?"

Dorian stared at the little hand clasped in his callused, scarred palm. He looked up at her. The girl stared shyly back and gnawed on her lip. She couldn't be more than seven years old. Dorian blinked, surprised at the sudden wetness of his eyes. He'd devoted his life to war and hadn't saved the world. But he could bring one little girl home to her parents, and that was something.

Maybe, just maybe, it was the start of a new life.

THE SHELL GAME

Adam D. Jones

"*November 15. 9 a.m. I'm Norman Teller. Welcome back…to the Cereal podcast. After driving since three in the morning, I'm finally approaching the blink-and-you'll-miss-it town of Attacus, Texas, and, other than this pitiful excuse for a town, it's just tumbleweeds in every direction. I can see the boarded-up factory from here, casting a shadow over empty houses. It's the tallest thing in town except…look at that. Another one of those billboards. I've never seen anything so desperate. Listeners, if there's one thing I'm not going to do in Attacus, it's visit the Monster Smash, whatever that is.*"

Norman turned off his phone's recording app to focus on the road and drummed on the steering wheel in anticipation.

Attacus. His soon-to-be claim to fame. He'd driven sixteen hours the previous day, and then slept four hours in his car before driving the rest of the way. Norman was itching to knock on every door and look under every rock in the forgotten Texas town.

Attacus was the home of the first breakfast mogul, the man who invented floating marshmallows, and Norman was going to be the first person to uncover the true story behind the founder and his now-dying city. The factory had shut down forty years ago amid the disappearance of the cereal baron, Charles William Attacus. Norman sensed a mystery awaited him in Attacus. Something provocative. Something no one else had discovered. Something that would put him on the map when he published his new podcast: Cereal.

ONE MILE TO THE MONSTER SMASH, proclaimed the billboard. He'd counted at least twenty of those on the way, starting when he was only FIFTY MILES TO MONSTER SMASH. Each sign announced the distance to the upcoming tourist trap alongside a cartoonish drawing of a classic monster in a funny situation; his favorite had been the confused vampire trying to make a withdrawal at a blood bank.

Norman had no interest in visiting a sad roadside attraction. He was on a mission—a mission to learn everything he could about the fate of the great Texas cereal tycoon. But as he got closer, he realized his gas tank was empty and his bladder had reached critical mass. His eyes settled on a few small words written on the bottom of the Monster Smash billboard: CLEAN RESTROOMS.

"November 15. 9:05 a.m. I'm happy to tell you that the gas pumps work at this…Monster Smash, but the sad news is that I'm simply standing outside of a glorified convenience store with a few monster decorations in the window. I was expecting to be underwhelmed, but this is worse than I imagined. I'm walking across the parking lot now to the front door, hoping to quickly find the little podcaster's room and escape before the locals try to sell me everything in sight. The real monster in any small town, of course is—"

"Welcome to Attacus!" said a woman.

Norman, startled, shoved his phone into his pocket. He hadn't expected to see anyone under the age of seventy in this town, let alone a young woman with bright blue eyes and a face that could grace the cover of a magazine. The dark clothes, lip ring, and wrist tattoos didn't hurt either. She offered the brightest smile he'd ever seen while she held open the door.

"Did you come to see the monsters?" she asked.

"No." Norman walked past her and looked around the store. "I'm a podcaster."

"Well, I happen to know that some podcasters believe in monsters."

Norman ignored her. His eyes finally settled on a bathroom sign on the far end of the building.

"You'll need the key to get in there." The young woman dashed toward the sales counter. "Don't worry. I can see you're in a hurry."

Norman tried not to perform a pee dance. She returned and held out what appeared to be a femur bone with a few keys dangling from one of the knobby bits.

Norman reached for the bone, but she pulled it away. "My name's Lila."

"Norman." He snatched the bone from her. His bladder was not giving him time to stand on ceremony. "Norman Teller."

He walked as fast as dignity would allow in front of a pretty woman, but froze in place when he saw the bathrooms and stared blankly at the baffling signs on each door. One was labeled *Succubus* and the other *Incubus*. Panic swelled in his belly.

"I'm a succubus, if that helps." Lila shouted from across the store. "But I won't judge if you wanna use the succubus bathroom. We don't discriminate at the Monster Smash!"

Norman rushed through the Incubus door and was thankful to see a row of urinals.

"Are you here to see my monsters?" Lila asked, the moment he emerged. "Everyone loves the tour. I bet that's what your podcast is about."

"Not even close, I host a show called *Cereal*."

"You named your podcast *Serial*?"

"Yeah, but it's about…cereal."

She seemed unimpressed.

Norman realized he should buy something to eat, food he could keep in the car while he canvassed the town, but as he scanned the aisles, he noticed something else: a series of dining booths along one wall.

"Do you think I could set up my recording gear over there to do some interviews? To pay you back, I could mention your store in my episodes."

"That sounds like fun!" Lila clapped her hands. "But who are you gonna interview?"

"Anyone who comes in. Someone ought to know about the collapse of Attacus and the cereal wars of the 1970s. I'm not leaving until I've squeezed a story out of this little town."

"Ohhh, *cereal*. Well, there ain't many people around here." She leaned in, very close. "Some people think my monsters ate 'em all."

"No one thinks that."

Lila shrugged. "Whatever you say…I happen to know what happened to Charles William Attacus, but with your attitude I might not wanna be on your podcast." She turned away, glancing back with wide eyes like a hungry puppy.

Norman sighed. "I'd love to take your tour."

"You're gonna love it, Norman! Ever seen a real monster before?"

"Of course not. Look, I'll pay you for the tour and then we can just skip—"

"Not a chance." She gripped his wrist with a shockingly cold hand and pulled him through the store. "Sorry. Gets chilly in the freezer."

Norman finally noticed large, deformed footprints had been painted onto the floor, all leading to a yellow door in the corner, as if a monster had walked through the aisles. The door itself was decorated with a simple sign: *Here be Monsters! (Please complete purchases before enjoying the monster gallery.)*

"It's five dollars for the tour." She held out her hand and waited. "Or ten, if you wanna guess."

"Guess what?"

"If you wanna guess which one's real!"

"None." He handed her a five-dollar bill. There was another in his wallet just like it, crisp and new, but he had no intention of giving it to her. "None of them are real. But since I only paid you five, you don't have to bother telling me I got it right." Norman knew a shell game when he saw one.

She playfully waved the five-dollar bill in front of his face. "Knock it off, Norman. Monsters usually have a sweet tooth, but they just might eat a sourpuss."

Beyond the yellow door, a wooden staircase led them down to an ordinary basement. Only a few lights were working; some flickered and clicked, but most of the room was shrouded in darkness.

"What's wrong with my lights?" Just inside the doorway, Lila batted a series of light switches off and on, but nothing changed. "Oh, no, those monsters are at it again. We'll just have to be brave in the dark, okay Norman?"

"You don't have to give me the whole act." He followed her to the bottom of the stairwell. "I'm sure it's a good attraction. I'll even give you a star rating."

"I don't do it for the ratings, I do it for the monsters. They get lonely if no one visits. Ever wonder what it's like to be the only one of your kind? Oh, look, here's the mummy!"

She brought him to a long ice cream freezer, but instead of popsicles he saw the shape of a man covered in dusty bandages. Norman caught his breath at the sight of a rotting, skeletal foot emerging through a hole in the worn cloth. Whatever it was, it was a good fake.

"Came from Memphis," Lila whispered, like she didn't want to wake someone from a nap.

"Memphis…Memphis, Egypt? Are you saying your basement has an intact mummy from the great temple of Ptah?"

"What's Ptah? No, honey, the Memphis in *Tennessee*.

They found it when they were making a parking lot for that big fishing store. Oh, come see the Mothman."

Norman dragged himself along. In a dark area blocked by velvet ropes, Norman could *just* make out a silhouette that must have stood ten feet tall and six feet wide. He stepped closer and saw two red circles near the top, catching the light like two large eyes glaring down at him.

"Cute trick," he muttered.

"No one's ever called him cute before." Lila tapped his shoulder. "Step back. You don't wanna get too close to the Mothman."

Norman was sure that if he stood too close he would be able to tell that this creature was just a few trash bags topped with bicycle reflectors.

Lila pushed him further along. "Now, come over here to this cage and be quiet. Look under the blanket and you'll see—"

"Bigfoot? Really?" Norman saw a pair of hairy feet sticking out from under a blanket. It moved up and down, like a creature underneath was breathing in its sleep. Simple animatronics, surely.

"Do you smell something?" she asked.

Norman sniffed. "I do…"

"Does it smell like something spoiled?"

"You know, it does actually—"

She playfully slapped his arm. "Then stop being spoilsport! Now pay attention, mister college, this ain't no Bigfoot. It ain't the Lake Worth Monster or the goatman, neither."

"There's a difference?"

"Oh, you think every big hairy monster in the world is the same? That he just roams around the whole country? His feet ain't that big. For the record, this is a bonafide Boggy Creek Creature. It smells as bad as the Skunk Ape, but it's a lot nicer. A sweet old teacher from Arkansas sent this one to me so people would stop hunting him."

Norman watched the blanket rise and fall in an even pattern. Clever trick, but an obvious fake.

"Now over here we've got a—ooh!" Lila ran into something. "What are you doing here?"

She stopped in her tracks in front of a concrete statue. A winged creature, seven feet tall, holding out a sharp talon, that just happened to be in their way.

A gargoyle. Norman frowned. He was losing valuable time to this silly tour.

Lila waved a finger at the statue. "I've asked you to stay in the corner when I have company, Claude."

"Claude?"

"He's from Notre Dame. Thinks he knows more than everyone."

"You brought a statue of a gargoyle from Indiana?"

"No, the Notre Dame in France, stupid. Just walk around him. Claude doesn't like being ignored—DO YOU CLAUDE?"

Norman let out a sigh as he stepped around the statue. He couldn't help but notice the stone eye closest to him was opened wider than the other. Another of her tricks, leading him around that side so it looked like the creature was watching him.

"Now, this one's kind of hard to see." Lila pulled him close, into the darkest corner of the room where the broken lights flashed madly. "It's one of them shadow things, the kind you always see out of the corner of your eye."

Norman stared. The shadowy corner was filled with paint cans, boxes, and other junk that threw odd shadows when the lights flashed. "He just...stays in this corner?"

"I figured out a trick. You see, if you make a circle of salt he can't get out...oh, no. Norman, what have you done? Your shoes!"

Norman gazed down at the ground and saw he had stepped onto a wide circle of salt. More accurately, Lila had *dragged* him there so he would "accidentally" disturb the salt.

"You let 'im out! Now you're gonna see that shadow man everywhere. Take me a week to catch him again."

"What a shame." Norman spied a metal door held shut by a big, brass padlock. "What's back there? Yeti?"

"Yeti's aren't real. That's just a meat freezer."

"Naturally. Well, is that the whole tour?"

"For you it is. I mean, for another Abe Lincoln you could guess which one is real and I'd tell you if you got it right, but you're not interested in that."

"I'm just here for a story. The rise and fall of Atticus is perfect for my podcast. The way Mister Charles William Attacus brought this town together with his factory and then mysteriously vanished. Did you know he invented floating marshmallows? But the factory moved to a secret location, and then the town slowly died. No one knows why."

"Oh, I can tell you that. Mister Attacus choked on a marshmallow, and his wife sold the brand."

The lights flickered in a cacophony of empty clicks. To Norman, it sounded like Lila's monsters were laughing at him. "That's it?"

"Mrs. Attacus kept the sale a secret so people would think the brand was still wholesome, then she moved to Tahiti."

Norman's knees weakened. "How do you know—"

But a loud *DING* from upstairs interrupted him.

"Oh, a customer. They might need help with the gas pumps. Come on." Lila pulled him back to the stairs. "It's not safe to leave you down here alone."

Norman collapsed into a booth and pulled out his phone. The recording app was ready, his thumb hovered over the record button, but he couldn't find a single word to say. Lila had taken every bit of wind from his sails.

But while he stared at the laminate top of the cheap table and fumed at his bad luck, he realized something was wrong in the Monster Smash. From behind the sales counter, Lila was speaking in a very worried tone of voice. Across from her stood a man and a woman who looked serious enough to land in her exhibit.

"I never seen 'im. Honest." Lila said to the stalwart pair, who only stared back from behind their sunglasses. "What was his name again?"

"Johnny Mayhew." The woman pulled out a small note pad and flipped through a few pages.

"And where did you find his body?" asked Lila. "I thought this was a safe town."

Norman saw a glint of metal at the woman's belt and finally recognized the police badge. *Detectives!* Norman felt his mouth go dry. He'd stumbled onto a story after all. And the name seemed familiar. Johnny Mayhew. He turned his ear to the conversation.

The detectives didn't offer much of an answer to Lila's question, only that Johnny Mayhew's dead body was found that morning by a truck driver who'd stopped in Attacus for a bite.

"Mind if we look around?" said the man.

"I gotta see a warrant first." Lila said it like an apology. "Bad for business having you snoop around. Sorry. I'm really sorry. I hope your case goes well!"

"Don't leave town," said the woman.

Lila watched the detectives leave and then slowly made her way to the booth to sit across from Norman. For the first time, Norman noticed her clothes were unusual. They were old. Vintage. Not something purchased from a cheap store in the mall. Her black lace choker could have come from a museum. An honest-to-goodness Goth girl here in the dead Texas desert.

"Johnny Mayhew...why does that sound familiar?"

Norman began searching on his phone.

"Hard to get a signal this far out." Lila touched his hand with a cold, delicate finger. "Norman, I'm sorry that there's no story here."

"Are you kidding? I just stumbled onto an unsolved murder in a small town!" Norman lowered his tone and put on his announcer voice. "Pure evil rears its angry head against a backdrop of fading American innocence." An idea formed in Norman's mind, something that might make this trip worth it. "Lila, where do you think they're keeping Mayhew's body?"

Lila pulled away from him with a hard stare. "I wouldn't want you to get in trouble...but the mortician works out of St. Clymene's Anglican Church, in the basement. He preps the bodies there for the funerals. You won't be able to get in though. They're having a memorial service right now for a hiker who went missing last month."

"You guys have a missing hiker, too? That's great! How do I get there."

"I've never been, but it's a small town. Just keep going and turn left at the stop sign. Left. It's a little ways."

Norman grabbed his things. "If I hurry, I can sneak in through the funeral and examine the body! The Cereal podcast is back!"

"You're gonna make a murder podcast called *Cereal*?"

"Why not?" He returned to his announcer voice. "Welcome to Cereal, part of your complete podcast!"

Lila shook her head.

He hit the stop sign and turned left, but the road only led him out of town and into an endless desert. Lila, who didn't appear to have left her convenience store since the seventeenth century, had been wrong. He spun the car around and hurried back in the other direction. To him, it was a race. Norman realized he was probably the only podcaster who knew about the murder, but once the story broke, investigators would swarm into Attacus like buzzards.

He made it back to the intersection and continued on. Just outside town he saw a red-bricked bell tower rising over the old church. A marquee out front told of a funeral for someone named Boyd, who Norman gathered was the missing hiker.

Boyd, Boyd, Boyd... he muttered to himself, memorizing the name, as he put on a sad face and walked into the church. A robed man greeted him.

Norman shook his hand. "I'm here to pay my respects to Roy."

"Boyd?"

Oops. "That's the one. Any place I can be alone?"

"You came to a funeral to pay your respects...alone?"

"It was our tradition."

The priest gestured down the hall. "You could try the columbarium."

"Thanks." Norman clapped the priest's shoulder. "Boyd loved columns."

Keeping his face downcast, Norman wandered the hallways until he was certain no one was around. He ignored signs pointing him to the columbarium and instead headed down a poorly lit stairwell toward the mortuary. He had never seen a dead body, and his feet threatened to turn back, but thoughts of podcasting fame kept him moving. He pushed open the unlocked door, reminding himself to write a line about the ignorant trust found in small towns, and crept through the empty mortuary.

Beyond a series of caskets, laying on a metal cart, was a dead body.

It couldn't be the hiker, whose body was never recovered. This had to be the corpse of Johnny Mayhew.

The pale body was mostly uncovered. The sheet was disturbed, revealing wounds and bruises. A disfigured hand dangled under the sheet's hem, and somehow the man's chest looked...collapsed?

He needed a closer look, but Norman paused at the sight of something glistening on the floor. Like pieces of sand, here and there, almost like footsteps...

Salt.

Just as Norman understood what he was looking at, a voice from behind told him to put his hands in the air.

Norman realized very quickly that he was not in trouble. The detectives asked for his whereabouts on different days, dating back ten years, and Norman used social media to show them he had been nowhere near Attacus. It didn't take much convincing, and Norman could see why.

These two weren't looking to solve a murder, they were looking to solve a string of murders going back a decade. He wasn't even a suspect.

The woman had found one part of his story suspicious. "You're here because of your...broadcast?"

"Podcast! Cereal, the story of Attacus. People love stories about murder. The mortuary door was unlocked, so I looked around. That's all. I promise."

"And you don't know anything about anyone else being in here?" asked the man.

Norman thought about the salt on the floor. "No, sir."

The man flipped through his notes. "Podcast...hmm. You told us you never met Johnny Mayhew, never heard of him until today?"

"That's correct." Norman wasn't lying about that, even though the name still rang a bell.

"He was a podcaster, like you."

The bell rang louder. Norman's mind finally opened

the right file and remembered why the name Johnny Mayhew was so familiar.

The man raised his voice. "And you're absolutely certain you've never heard of him?"

Norman looked the detective square in the eye. "Never."

Norman hurried back to the Monster Smash and sat in a booth where he could watch Lila work. She handled the afternoon rush, bagging groceries, handing out the bathroom key, and cleaning up spills, with seemingly endless energy.

All the while, Norman was pulling up the show that had made Johnny Mayhew something of an urban legend amongst podcasters. Mayhew had hosted a bonkers program called *The Abnormal Paranormalist* for over two thousand episodes, and each was more ridiculous than the last. He'd found fame at the start of his career when he uncovered a ring of liger smugglers, but ever since, he'd been obsessed with finding strange creatures that no one else believed in, not even in the darkest corners of the internet.

Norman skipped through the final ten episodes, in which Johnny Mayhew took on a very serious tone.

"No one believes in this kind of thing," came Johnny's voice through Norman's headphones. *"Not in ages. Not even the paranormal community thinks it's real. But these disappearances in Texas are no myth. I'm going to prove that something isn't right out here."*

The podcast played the spooky tones that ended every episode of *The Abnormal Paranormalist*, and then...nothing. Norman realized he had just listened to Johnny Mayhey's last bow, an episode called "Moving to the Light," on a journey that ended with his mangled body laying underneath a church.

Norman didn't notice Lila had left the counter until she was sitting next to him in the booth. Very close.

"What an afternoon, Norman. It's been murder around here."

"I bet."

"You gonna stick around? There's not a lot to do in Attacus, but it's nice having someone to talk to." Lila's deep blue eyes threatened to make him forget his mission. "Oh, great. Now the gas truck is here."

Lila ran outside as a large tanker pulled in. Through the window, Norman watched her wave the driver toward the gas hatch in a corner of the parking lot.

It was the chance Norman had been waiting for. He dashed to the counter and grabbed the femur bone, certain one of the keys would open the metal door in the basement.

The gargoyle waited at the bottom of the stairs, positioned so Norman had to squeeze past it. He looked at its snarling face and couldn't remember which eye had been larger. The big hairy monster was in the same place, sleeping in its cage, but now a furry hand stuck out from under the blanket. Confusing shadows invaded every corner of the room as the lights flashed off and on in hypnotic patterns.

Norman reached the metal door and realized Lila had been lying about it. There was no deep humming from the other side, a clue he should have noticed sooner. This was no freezer.

He tried a few keys before one of them opened the padlock. He threw the lock aside and pulled on the handle.

The first bone that fell was a femur, just like the one he held in his hand.

A few finger bones trickled to the ground, followed by a cracked human skull. Norman stepped back. The bones filled a space behind the door that went further than Norman could see. Hundreds of bodies, easily.

"You weren't supposed to see that."

Lila stood in the center of the basement.

Norman reached for his phone. If he was going to confront her, he was going to record every bit of it. He turned on his camera and put the phone in his pocket so the lens pointed out, and then turned to face Lila. "Where did you get these bones?"

"I sell them. It's just for fun."

Big fat lie. Norman hadn't seen any novelty bones for sale. "That's not what I asked. Lila, where did you *get* these bones?"

She didn't respond.

"Don't want to talk?" Norman strolled to the center of the room, directly in front of her. "Fine. I'll do the talking. I think you gave me the wrong directions to the church on purpose. You got there first so you could look for evidence that would link you to the murder. I think you killed Johnny Mayhew because he found out you've spent ten years killing the citizens of Attacus. He thought *you* were the monster, because Johnny was smart enough to recognize a shell game when he saw one. Smart guy, but not smart enough, was he?"

Lila opened her mouth like she wanted to yell. The sudden movement shocked Norman, but she shut her mouth tight. She was obviously trying to say something, but Norman was on a roll.

"There are no monsters, Lila. Never were. There is only...you. When the authorities test those bones, they'll find out that innocent little Lila has been behind a long string of unsolved murders, and then we'll all know the *real* truth. That we only blame monsters and demons for our problems when we're scared to turn on a light and face the facts!" Norman opened his wallet and threw his other five-dollar bill at her. "I'm ready to make my guess, Lila. I know which monster is real, because the only *real* monster in this world...is ourselves!"

Norman was especially proud of the last part, and was thankful he had said it clearly into his mic.

Lila clapped. "Norman, that was beautiful. It really was. You're so smart."

"Thank you."

"And your podcast would have been so good."

"Maybe you can listen to it...in prison! Wait, what do you mean, it *would have* been good?"

A grunt came from behind him, followed by a shuffling noise. Norman felt warm breath on his neck, and the curved sharp object that now rested on his shoulder could only be described as part of a claw.

Lila looked away. "You should have put your money on the Mothman."

There's plenty more where that came from!

For free books and new releases, go sign up for the newsletter at <u>AuthorAdamJones.com</u>!

Copyright Information